KINDRED SPIRITS

BOOK TWO OF SOLID ROCK SURVIVORS

KINDRED SPIRITS

JOHN F. HARRISON

Kindred Spirits
Copyright © 2023 by John F. Harrison. All Rights Reserved.

For information about this title or to order other books
and/or electronic media, contact the publisher:

Pressing Way Books
www.jharrisonwrites.com

ISBN: 978-0-9980568-2-1 (print) | 978-0-9980568-3-8 (eBook)

Printed in the United States of America

Cover and Interior design by 1106 Design
Edited by Arlene Prunkl of Penultimate Editorial Services

Unless otherwise indicated, all scripture quotations are from the
New King James Version (NKJV), copyright 1982 by Thomas Nelson, Inc.
Used by permission. All rights reserved.

Names: Harrison, John F. (John Frederick), author.
Title: Kindred spirits / John F. Harrison.
Description: Concord, MA : Pressing Way Books, [2023] | Series: Solid Rock survivor series.
Identifiers: ISBN: 978-0-9980568-2-1 (print) | 978-0-9980568-3-8 (eBook)
Subjects: LCSH: Christian fiction. | Vocation--Fiction. | Gifts, Spiritual--Fiction. | Older people--Abuse of--Fiction. | Veterans--Fiction. | Family secrets--Fiction. | Spirits--Fiction. | Friendship-- Fiction. | Kinship--Religious aspects--Christianity--Fiction. | Landlord and tenant--Fiction. | Christianity--Psychology--Fiction. | Spiritual life--Christianity--Fiction. | LCGFT: Christian fiction. | BISAC: FICTION / Christian / Suspense.
Classification: LCC: PS3608.A783474 K56 2023 | DDC: 813/.6--dc23

Dedicated to the memory of Eli and Jim, two casualties of the pandemic who left this world before anyone was ready. At different times of my life, both were friends and kindred spirits to me. We will meet again.

TABLE OF CONTENTS

PART ONE
EVERY ANT
IN THE ANTHILL

CHAPTER 1
DESTROYER

A Friday in June

Someone always cried. And that wasn't even the worst of it. What started in tears might end in real trouble. Rosalyn Pitts closed her eyes and rubbed her temples, but the pounding in her head did not abate. Her stress level had climbed all morning as she contemplated having to leave people disappointed, angry, and maybe even frightened. Roz, as her friends called her, had been through this twice before. For the umpteenth time, she wished she had discovered some helpful technique for softening the blow. Since she had not, she settled for putting a box of tissues on the round table and reminded herself to say something encouraging to each of the chosen.

Phil was first, and it soon became clear that he wouldn't need any tissues. Phil had always been the guy with multiple irons in the fire. The youngest person in the department, he was full of energy and always hatching the Next Big Thing. Roz could almost see his attention drifting to Plan B and Plan C. He took the news of his job loss like someone relieved of an annoying chore. She informed him of his severance package, directed him to Human Resources, and thanked him for his contributions to the team. He left her office with a spring in his step.

Pam was next. An efficient worker, she had always held herself at a chilly distance from the other employees in the department. It was as if she were seething all the time, but under the surface. No one knew who or what caused this anger, but her prickly personality and self-imposed social isolation had made it easy for the decision-makers upstairs to let her go. She glared while Roz delivered the news and did not say a word when Roz thanked her and wished good luck as she left.

Two down, two to go. Best to get it done right away, as prolonging unpleasant tasks gave them more emotional weight. Roz picked up the phone and called Julianna.

"I know why I'm here," Julianna said, before closing the door. "Half the floor is talking about what happened to Phil and Pam. I assume I'm next."

Word traveled fast through the maze of cubicles, though Roz doubted "half the floor" knew yet. "I'm sorry to have to say you're right," she confessed.

"How many are being laid off?"

"Company-wide, they're reducing head count by thirty."

"How many of us are getting the boot in this department?"

Roz had no compunction about revealing the larger figure, as the company was going to issue a press release confirming it. While only four people from her department were being let go, details that granular were not for general consumption, so Roz kept the answer vague. "There are only a few from our group."

Julianna leaned forward, as if keen to know the answer to whatever question was coming next. "And how were the lucky few from our group selected?"

Roz shook her head, her admonishing look making her feel like a parent who had caught a child reaching for the cookie jar before dinner. "You know I can't tell you that. I can only tell you about you. And you already seem to know about Phil and Pam."

"Okay, tell me this about me. Was I selected because of my transition? I know you've never been comfortable with it."

Four months ago, Julianna had been Julian, one of only two men in the department. He had taken a brief medical leave. Upon returning to work, Julian had informed HR that he was to be known thereafter as Julianna, preferred pronouns *she/her*.

Roz studied her soon-to-be-ex-coworker. Julianna's appearance was almost convincing. The floral Bohemian-style outerwear worn over jeans and a dark-blue top looked chic. A stylish haircut featured bangs that couldn't quite hide a heavy brow ridge, and light makeup struggled to soften the angular facial features. The ever-present lace choker was doubtless there to obscure an Adam's apple. Still, someone who had never known Julian might notice nothing amiss . . . until Julianna spoke. The voice was a tell. But that was no business of Rosalyn's.

Yes, Roz had misgivings. From her childhood up, she'd been taught that male and female were distinctions of biology, simple and objective. Adults with two X chromosomes were women, while those with both X and Y chromosomes were men. Science had no way of swapping out the chromosomes from the body's cells, so a person's gender was an immutable characteristic. That had been a universal truth until a few years ago, when someone decided that biological sex and gender were no longer synonymous, and people could be whatever gender or genders they felt like. Despite the novelty of that idea, it was now socially unacceptable to gainsay it or even question it. It was as if a voter referendum had managed to repeal objective reality. At this rate, it wouldn't be long until people sent twiggy anorexic women off to liposuction clinics because they identified as fat. Roz found it all surreal, and more than a little baffling. But regardless of her thoughts on the matter, she was certain that she had never discriminated against this person.

Julianna's question still hung between them, so Roz replied, "My comfort level is not at issue. It hasn't affected your career here and has no bearing on your layoff."

"I hope not," Julianna returned. "I have friends at the Mass. Commission Against Discrimination. I wonder whether MCAD wouldn't be a little suspicious of a trans woman getting laid off by her devout Christian supervisor so soon after gender reassignment."

Roz resented the insinuation that she harbored some hostility toward Julianna. Any hostility had come from the other direction, from Julianna to her. She had never said a disparaging word about Julian's transformation. But neither would she celebrate it, and that fact might have been enough to get her branded as an enemy. A hater. She wished the culture warriors in her workplace could be as accepting of her presence as she was of theirs. Live and let live. That's what she'd always tried to do. But for some people, that would never be enough.

Roz was smart, but not always quick on her feet. If there were a way to defuse and deescalate the tension without denying her own convictions, she would have jumped at it. Unable to think of anything, she settled for saying, "I can't worry about what MCAD or anyone else finds suspicious. I've told you the truth."

"That's what you say," Julianna began. "But—"

"Yes. That's what I say." Interrupting people was out of character for Roz, but she'd had enough of this conversation. Hurt feelings made her sound angrier than she intended, and she regretted that. With an effort, she moderated her tone. "I also say that making implied threats is never a good career strategy for someone not looking to burn bridges." Julianna said nothing to that. "I think we're about done here. Make sure you see HR on your way out. They have a package for you. Good luck in your future endeavors."

While Julianna swished out of her office, Roz closed her eyes and willed herself to relax, rolling her neck and shoulders and taking a few slow, deep breaths. She knew she'd soon get over Julianna's bogus accusation and veiled threat. But she'd been losing sleep for days over the irony of these personnel moves. Senior management had ordered job cuts to boost the corporation's bottom line. According to the newspapers, the CEO's compensation package rewarded her for hitting certain profitability targets, and she would earn $20 million this year for making the numbers. To help ensure this, Roz had to terminate four colleagues, none of whom earned over $70,000 per year. It felt wrong. She realized with sudden clarity that, whatever she ought to spend her days doing, this wasn't it. She needed to find out what was.

But that would have to wait until this morning's unpleasantness was over. She'd delivered the bad news three times, but all these were the beginning of sorrows. The hardest exit interview still awaited.

Roz picked up the phone and called the one employee she considered a friend. Trina had graduated from Framingham North High School the same year as Roz. By chance, they had both attended Mass Bay Community College and majored in marketing. Roz had transferred to a four-year college to get her bachelor's, while Trina had not. But the two acquaintances reunited a few years later when they both landed entry-level jobs here at RHV Couture Corp. They'd renewed their connection over cafeteria lunches, sometimes daydreaming out loud about climbing through the ranks together all the way into upper management. Now Roz had to push her friend off the corporate ladder.

Trina stepped into the office wearing the gutted expression of a condemned prisoner walking the last few steps to the death chamber. All that was missing was a priest and a warden to accompany her. Looking at her face, Rosalyn's heart broke.

"I had a tiny crumb of hope until right this minute," Trina half whispered. "When you called me, I prayed it wasn't to fire me. I thought maybe you just needed a friend to vent to about what had happened with the others. I knew better, deep down, but I still had hope. Now that I see the look on your face, that hope is gone."

"I'm very sorry, Trina," was all Roz could think of saying.

"Nowhere near as sorry as I am. You're still employed, yes?" Roz didn't respond to that, so Trina continued. "When we last had lunch together, I told you that Steve and I had bought a house. We haven't even unpacked everything yet. And now this happens? Unemployment compensation won't replace my entire salary. How are we going to keep our house?" Her pitch and volume rose. She was almost wailing.

Roz squashed the urge to pat Trina's hand. "I know the timing is bad for you. Not that there is ever a good time to get laid off. If there is any good news here, it's that the economy is strong. Unemployment is low, and lots of companies are hiring. I'm betting you'll find something in no time."

Trina rolled her eyes. "That's our Roz; brings her own sunshine to every storm. If you had to walk barefoot on hot coals and horse manure, you'd still find a way to look on the bright side. But all your sunny optimism can't change how awful this is for me."

After a brief and awkward silence, Roz asked, "What can I do to help you, Trina?"

Trina looked at the floor for a long time. A thought seemed to seize her. "One thing you can do—for the sake of our friendship. Tell me you tried to talk them out of letting me go. Tell me you fought for me."

Roz couldn't say that, not without lying. This was worse than awkward. She tried deflection. "I'm sorry. I don't feel at liberty to discuss my conversations with the folks upstairs. If there's some way to help you navigate the process—"

"You wouldn't have needed to discuss anything, boss. All I wanted was a simple yes. You can't say it because you didn't fight for me." Trina was blinking hard. "Don't you even care that we've been friends since the ninth grade? We got hired here on the same day, like it was fate or something. The plan was to help each other make it. Be cheerleaders for each other's career. Be accountability partners. What's happened to you, Roz? You're not a helper, a cheerleader, or an accountability partner. I don't even think I can call you a friend anymore. Now you're just a . . . a corporate minion doing the dirty work for the suits so they can keep their hands clean. Maybe you can live with that. I know I couldn't."

Roz watched as Trina, red-faced and sobbing, fled the office. The face of the big wall clock was blurring, but Roz could still see it read 11:03. Six more hours before this work week ended. Six hours before she could go home, crawl into bed, and hide in a book. In the meantime, she had to keep up appearances for those employees who remained. A good leader wasn't supposed to go to pieces and start crying in front of the troops. She had to hold it together for them. Sniffling, she reached for a tissue, only to realize Trina had taken the box.

Security called a little after 4:30. Because a pair of the terminated employees had made a bit of a scene near the break room, HR sent a security guard to escort Roz to her car. In the central corridor, the guard reached for the call button on the elevator. But Roz gestured toward the stairwell. The guard's eyes widened for a second, but he wrestled his expression back to neutral and adjusted his course without comment.

No one ever expected her to take the stairs. People assumed she would take the path of least resistance. She was what her employer's catalogs called "plus-sized." Dating sites would say she was a bbw. Her doctor tarred her with the label *morbid obesity*. She knew it was a technical term, but it still felt like medical slang for *disgusting*. She thought of herself as a big girl, at least on happier days. On days like today, Roz settled for brutal honesty: she was just plain fat. To help alter that reality, she'd been taking the steps instead of the elevator for months.

On her way home, she stopped at the corner market for a pint of ice cream. Ice cream had been off limits for almost a year, though she had been planning to indulge on some yet unspecified special occasion. But tonight's mood called for comfort food. She knew she would berate herself in the morning for this dietary lapse tonight.

Once home, she spread the local newsweekly on the dining room table and ate the ice cream in lieu of dinner. The paper was full of the usual stuff: road construction projects, small business profiles, sports news. One article caught her attention. It was an analysis of a voter referendum in which her hometown had opted to become a city. Roz found this news almost as upsetting as the day's earlier events, which made no sense to her at all. She hadn't much cared about the outcome when she voted, so why should she sweat the results now? She sorted through the facts. With around seventy thousand residents, Framingham was the largest town by population in the whole of Massachusetts, and the largest municipality in the nation still governed by the direct democracy of town meeting. Now, by a mere 108 votes, the electorate had thrown away the very things that had made the place special. As a city, Framingham would be an also-ran, fourteenth largest of fifty-seven cities in the Commonwealth, with a mayor and city councilors, bureaucracy, and the usual political foolishness. This was not her idea of progress. Maybe she wouldn't care tomorrow, after the trauma of her workday had worn off. Besides, the newspaper was no place to look for solace. That's what books were for.

Books were an introvert's best friend. Roz had fallen in love with them as a child, and now her home was full of them. Every room in the house had at least one floor-to-ceiling bookcase in it. Entertainment, inspiration, education, and escape—especially escape—were never more than a few paces away. The historical fantasy novel in the dining room could deposit her amid the perilous intrigues of the emperor's court in Tang Dynasty China.

That crime drama in the living room could fill her with shivers of guilty pleasure as she experienced the fictional victims' terror from the safety of her recliner. Books were the world's greatest invention, the original teleportation device.

Truth be told, they were more than that; they not only whisked her away to other places and times, but they also held up a mirror to her soul. By learning what moved her, which characters she bonded with, which locations she felt most at home in, Roz could discover her true self in the pages of her books. Today's events had blurred her self-image. She hoped the right reading material would restore some needed clarity.

She got ready for bed early and sent a text message to her friend Shawna Bell, inviting her to meet at noon tomorrow. Roz needed someone to talk to, so she was glad when Shawna agreed to meet. As wonderful as books were, sometimes what you needed most was a flesh-and-blood friend to talk to.

Once in bed, Roz turned to four biographies stacked on her nightstand. She had always been one to read several books at a time and was partway through all four of them. On the top of the stack was *A Woman of No Importance*. It was the story of WWII spy Virginia Hall, an American woman who had spied for the British and helped ignite the French Resistance. Roz had always loved reading anything related to WWII, and the true story of an unlikely woman who played a significant role in helping the Allies defeat the Nazis had been irresistible. But tonight, she couldn't get into it, and she put the book down after reading a handful of pages.

Next, she tried a biography of William Wilberforce. Over twenty years of struggle, Wilberforce had been the primary driver of the movement to end the slave trade in Great Britain. But the sorrow Roz had been fighting all evening only deepened as she read about the life of this man who spent himself in the successful effort to make the world a more humane place for millions of people. Book two went back onto the pile.

She didn't bother picking up the biographies of Beethoven or Frederick Douglass. Biographies, it seemed, were not a good choice for a night like this, since they are about significant people who did meaningful things. Roz was not a significant person, and her life was not meaningful. These books would only sharpen the contrast between her and their subjects. A book about her, unlikely as that was, would have to bear the title *Minion*. It would relate the trivial tale of an errand runner for the suits, a corporate functionary who killed friendships and destroyed dreams on command. And with that thought, she turned off the light and cried herself to sleep.

CHAPTER 2
THE BODY ELECTRIC

Brandon had no love for thieves, so he hated becoming one. Not enough to dissuade him from his task, though. A man does what he must. On the plus side, the weather was ideal for his needs. The evening's fog and drizzle would decrease the typical Friday night foot traffic, and also hinder any security cameras pointed his way. The rain gave him a reason to keep his hood up and his head down. Anyone who passed by would be doing the same thing, so no one would get a good look at him.

The trick was not to look furtive. Skulking from shadow to shadow would only draw attention to himself. He needed to stride right up to this job and do it. He set his small toolbox down in front of the commercial van he had targeted. Opening the box, he eyeballed the license-plate bolts and surmised what size socket to use. A few turns of the ratchet did the trick. Brandon walked to the back of the van to repeat the process. He slipped both plates into the oversized pocket of his yellow slicker, closed his toolbox, and turned to go.

"Beautiful evening if you're a duck, eh?" Why did some people insist on talking to strangers about the weather? Brandon raised his gaze enough to see a stooped old man shuffling along the sidewalk and peering at him. He knew the man must have seen him removing the rear plate. Maybe this was a test of sorts. Brandon decided not to ignore it.

"Yep. Into every life a little rain must fall." Brandon tried to put the right mix of grumpiness and humor into his voice. He patted the plates in his pocket as if he had every right to them, and wished the old man a good night before walking away. Fatigue was setting in. It must be eleven thirty by now. He had one more place to go. He wasn't looking forward to it, but at least it was out of the rain.

Brandon clambered up the staircase at midnight, moving more by feel than by sight in the artificial twilight. The faint orange-red glow of an exit sign provided the only illumination. The wooden stairs were steep, like a stepladder. Halfway up, he paused, hearing a skittering sound off to his right on the floor below. Rats. He couldn't abide rats. City rats were too bold, too aggressive, and smarter than they had a right to be. At least their tiny footfalls were moving away, not getting closer. Thank God for small favors.

Reaching the top step, Brandon edged onto the landing, careful not to let the weight of his backpack unbalance him. He took a long stride over the square of sheet metal on the floor. He could not see it, submerged as it was in a deep pool of shadow. But memory told him where to place his feet to avoid jostling the steel plate or the cord that was fastened to it. Once clear of that obstacle, he swept aside the blanket that served as a make-shift curtain and stepped into the lightless interior of the place he hated most: home.

His fingers found the rotary switch that turned on the lamp. Darkness fled the room, but the pervading gloom did not. The light revealed a rough plank floor painted black, bounded by walls of unadorned gray cinderblock. It was a smallish space, cluttered with the evidence of life's unfairness. Along the wall to his left, stacked milk crates and plywood shelving held most of his worldly possessions. On the opposite wall, a mattress lay on the floor, with neither bed frame nor box spring to make it a respectable bed. Near the corner, blackout curtains covered the chamber's sole window. Not that he was missing out on any great scenery; the window overlooked a parking lot that served several drab light industrial buildings. By day, the lot was full of employee cars. By night, it teemed with street people who gathered to drink, shoot up, fight, and pass out.

From his backpack he withdrew dinner—a convenience store sandwich, a six-pack of Budweiser, and several bags of Goldfish crackers. Noise from the homeless hordes wafted up from the parking lot. He opened the first can and raised it in mock toast. To life in the Athens of America, the City of Champions, and the Hub of the Universe. Not that he wouldn't get back on his feet again; Brandon Heckler was nothing if not resourceful. He reminded himself of that several times each day to keep despair from setting in.

Motivational affirmations aside, it was impossible not to brood about his previous abode. He'd lost the Acton condo in the divorce after that accursed woman dealt him the wound that would never heal. He wound up couch surfing for three months at the homes of his few remaining friends until they ran out of sympathy and patience. Now he lived in this refuge of last resort, an off-the-books perch on the top floor of a warehouse near Boston's Methadone Mile. That made him not much better off than the addicts and crazies down there dozing in doorways and arguing with the voices in their heads. Preserving the slim distinction between himself and the urban campers cost five hundred dollars per month—cash only, please and thank you. Two big, beefy guys came around to collect the rent each month. They appeared devoid of both sympathy and patience, men it would be foolish to disappoint. Brandon always paid on time.

The "apartment" had no refrigerator, no stove, and no running water. The bathrooms were down on the lower floors, the ones occupied by the electrical supply company. Those floors were off-limits during business hours, so Brandon and the five other hard-luck cases who called the warehouse home had to take their daytime bathroom breaks at the McDonald's half a mile away on Mass. Ave.

Though life stank now, he didn't waste all his time on self-pity. He'd devised a plan to get back on top. Most of the required tools were on the shelf in front of him: a music playlist, four five-gallon buckets, a sink stopper, oversized hiking boots, a stout walking stick, and gloves. He added the final necessity to the collection, the purloined license plates. Tomorrow he'd put all these tools to use. Tonight, he'd allow himself to celebrate the changes that were coming.

One beer went down the hatch. A second one followed right after it. From beyond the entryway came a sizzle and a squeak. So, a rat had trailed him up the stairs after all. Brandon levered himself to his feet. Best to unplug the homemade trap and get rid of the carcass before it started smoking.

When he had disposed of the body and powered up the rat fryer again, he returned and considered the remaining four beers. He couldn't risk another. Drinking too much always filled him with melancholy and second thoughts. What he needed now was anger, not boozy sentimentality. Tended and fed with care, his anger would grow from sullen embers to a raging fire. That fire would power him through the coming unpleasantness. He needed unwavering commitment to see this through—for all he'd suffered at the hands of his ex, and also for what she'd done to the boy. Yes, most especially for that.

He paced around the perimeter of his room, rehearsing the steps he'd take. He stared at the floor as his concentration deepened, fingers interlaced across the back of his head, elbows forward. After several minutes of this, he was certain that he had overlooked nothing. The plan was risky; a high-stakes gamble if ever there was one. If he lost, the consequences would be harsh. But he had to take the chance. By this time tomorrow, that accursed woman would be choking on a jumbo serving of karma. And no one would suspect his involvement, not even her. His confidence grew. He could do this. He could *do* this. After all, Brandon Heckler was nothing if not resourceful.

CHAPTER 3
THE WEIGHT

The night had granted little rest to Roz. Now morning light filtered into her bedroom. The mild breeze fluttered the curtains and delivered the fragrances of pine trees and bee balm from the backyard. A chickadee greeted the day with his cheery two-note song. Most mornings, these things would have put a smile on her face. But now melancholy clung to her like a sweat-soaked garment.

If she could force herself to get moving, her rituals and routines might restore a sense of normalcy, snap her back to center. She had awakened ten minutes before her alarm went off. When it sounded at 5:45, she rolled out of bed at once, not even tempted to hit the snooze button. She might be tired and unhappy, but the day's work would not do itself. Best get to it.

Face washed, teeth brushed, and long braids corralled, she put on her workout gear and was out the door by 6:15. Her morning power walk through the neighborhood always covered the same circuit; down Elm Street to Central, and a series of right turns until Pinewood took her back to Elm. This early on a Saturday morning, there would be few people out and about, so Roz would not have much of an audience. She'd lost a lot of weight since the nightmarish events of last fall had given her a grim resolve to get fit, but she still preferred not to be the object of people's stares.

There was one person who was sure to be up and about. *Contact in five . . . four . . . three . . . two . . .* Roz rounded the corner onto Elm Street.

"Good morning, neighbor!"

"Morning, Mrs. Grimm!" The lady calling from her front porch was of unknown age, but looked old enough to be a great-grandmother. She had blue eyes, blue-gray hair, and the same dependable cheerfulness that Roz aspired to. She was also the only neighbor Roz had met. Between work and church, she hadn't had time to meet the others, despite having lived at her current address for years.

If Mrs. Grimm thought Roz looked ridiculous performing her daily exertions, wearing a skirt on top of sweatpants and sneakers, she had never said so. In fact, she had made it a point of calling out encouragement over the past few months. They'd taken to spending a few minutes chatting each morning. The older woman seemed to look forward to it. She'd disclosed that she was a widow, and if she had any children, she never mentioned them. She had introduced herself as Judy, but Roz felt their age difference mandated calling her Mrs. Grimm. The tiny woman declined to call Roz by her first name if Roz couldn't reciprocate, so she settled for addressing her as "neighbor" in place of a name.

Roz was huffing, but not so much that she couldn't converse. Eight months ago, she couldn't have completed this one-mile circuit at all, never mind doing it at speed and maintaining the ability to talk. Progress was a wonderful thing.

"Are we still on for lunch today?" Mrs. Grimm inquired.

Stupid me! Roz had forgotten all about that. Now she'd gone and booked lunch with Shawna. She'd have to cancel with one of them. And she felt the need to unburden herself to Shawna. "Say, Mrs. Grimm, would you mind too much if we put it off until next Saturday? I feel terrible about it, but I'm afraid I've overscheduled myself today."

A brief shadow of disappointment crossed the older woman's face. But her tone remained unchanged. "Next Saturday at noon, my dear; I'll hold you to it!"

Roz waved her thanks to Mrs. Grimm. "Neither snow, nor rain, nor heat, nor gloom of night shall stay me from my appointed rounds." Her father, a retired postal worker, had taught her that famous line.

Back home, she showered and hit the scale. She had been looking forward to today's weigh-in. It would be her first use of this new digital scale. What made it special was that it was a regular bathroom scale, not the high-capacity model she'd had to use for years. Stepping up on it, she felt crushed to see that the display didn't show a number—only the word *Error* in bright red letters. Eight months of intense diet and exercise, all that weight lost, and she still hadn't cracked the three-hundred-pound mark. The memory of last night's ice-cream dinner mocked her.

After getting dressed, it was time for morning devotions. She inched her way through the fifth chapter of Matthew, hoping the Sermon on the Mount might point her toward something that felt like her life's purpose. Yesterday's conversation with Trina kept intruding on her thoughts. It even infected her prayers, making them feel unfocused, scattershot. After several fruitless attempts to quiet her mind, she cut the session short and moved on to the next thing.

On a weekday, the next thing would have been driving to work. This being Saturday, it was time for a few hours of housecleaning. Every hard surface in her home gleamed. Roz vacuumed every carpet, dusted every tabletop, and fluffed every pillow before placing it with precision. Having failed for so many years at keeping the pounds off, she spared no effort to be sure there was nothing else for which people could criticize her, especially with stereotypes of the obese. People could call her fat, but no one could call her a slob.

At last, it was time to go meet Shawna. Roz pulled her car out of the garage. The 2011 Lincoln Town Car was spotless inside and out, like her home. Still, she was eager to be rid of it. In jest, friends called it the Batmobile, because it was over eighteen feet long and black-on-black. To Roz, it would forever be the Fatmobile. A good friend in the car business had picked it for her, doubtless because it was one of the last cars on the market to offer front bench seats. He'd never said that, never hinted at it, but Roz was no dummy. She had appreciated Eddie's tact even more than his practicality. It had been the right recommendation at the time, but now she wanted something new. Having shed so many pounds, bucket seats might be workable, even comfortable. If so, she could ditch both the Lincoln and the emotional baggage that went with it. *What a day of rejoicing that will be.*

She arrived at the eatery ten minutes early, as was her habit with all appointments, despite knowing full well that Shawna always breezed in five minutes late. Making her way toward the entrance, Roz caught an odd movement in her peripheral vision. Someone who had been approaching from the left reversed direction and double-timed it around the corner of the building. Roz wasn't certain, having caught only a fleeting glimpse from the rear, but thought the woman might have been Trina. *I bet she's still too upset to deal with seeing me.* That was understandable. Maybe she'd give Trina a call in a few days, even though it was against company policy to do so. After all, they'd been friends before either of them got hired there.

Inside the restaurant, Roz studied the menu board and waited. Fifteen minutes later, Shawna blew in, as predicted. As they got in line to place their food orders, Roz noticed several people craning their necks at them. The two friends always caused a bit of a stir when they were out together. Shawna was gorgeous, with a curvy figure and an air of elegance. Roz had always turned heads for a different reason. Thankfully, it happened less now than in the past. Both women ignored the attention their appearances drew. And aside from the contrast in their silhouettes, the two were much alike. Friends called them "the twins." They had identical cinnamon complexions. They spent a hefty sum on their wardrobes. Both were quiet women with a contemplative bent, though Roz was better than Shawna at navigating social interactions. Both attended the same church and were accomplished vocalists who sang in the choir. They had been friends for years and roommates for a time. Each understood the other in that nonverbal way real twins often do.

They placed their sandwich orders and grabbed a tall table while waiting for their numbers to be called. Shawna perched on a stool while Roz stood. They dispensed with small talk. It had always been their style to dive right into the topic at hand.

Shawna said, "So I got your SOS. What's your calamity?"

"I said I wanted to talk," Roz said. "I don't think I said anything about a calamity."

Shawna put one hand to her forehead and closed her eyes in mock exasperation. "Whatever was on your mind was bad enough for you to break your normal Saturday routine, and bad enough for you to agree to meet at a burger joint instead of the library or the park. So, yeah. What do you need rescuing from?"

Roz compressed her lips. "Myself. Mediocrity. I know that's redundant. I want my life to have meaning, and right now, I don't feel it does."

"You're thirty-one years old. That's a little young for a mid-life crisis."

A voice over the loudspeaker called for customers 124 and 125. Roz and Shawna were 132 and 133. Well, they weren't in any hurry.

"Not a midlife crisis," Roz corrected. "It's not an age thing." She told Shawna about the layoffs at work, and how much Trina's parting words had stung. "What I could never in a million years tell Trina was the real reason she lost her job. Our department has another employee who's in a tough spot right now." Roz lowered her voice to be hard to overhear from the next table. "Bernice. She had just been diagnosed with leukemia. I know this only because she came and told me. She was worried about the amount of sick time she would have to take from work. She's a single mother with an eight-year-old daughter. The ax was supposed to fall on her, not Trina."

"That would have been a lot of misfortune to deal with all at once," Shawna said.

"Too much," agreed Roz. "I realized if she lost her job, she might lose her company-paid health insurance. Maybe she couldn't afford to continue it out of her own pocket. Even if she could find and pay for coverage on the open market, would it be as good as what she was losing? Would she end up deferring treatments or skipping them altogether for lack of money? What if that shortened her life? Where would that leave her daughter, besides orphaned?"

Shawna nodded. "Those are all good questions."

"Trina has an employed husband and no kids. She asked me if I fought the suits. You better believe I did—for Bernice.

And I won, Shawna. I won. They didn't lay her off. Still, they were adamant about cutting departmental payroll by $250,000. So they made me pick someone else to take Bernice's place on the altar of sacrifice. It had to be someone whose salary equaled or exceeded hers. In our little department, Trina was the only option. I threw my friend overboard to save the sick woman. And the rules around confidentiality meant I couldn't tell her." She paused, gathering her thoughts. "The worst part is Trina was right. I'm a cog in the corporate wheel. I helped the CEO qualify for an eight-figure bonus, while helping four colleagues out of their jobs and losing a long-time friend."

Shawna thought for a minute before replying. "I understand why Trina was so hurt by what you had to do and by what you couldn't say. But you were a great blessing to Bernice. You spared her what might have been an unbearable amount of stress. You might have saved her and her daughter from tragedy. Does that not count for something?"

Roz considered that while the loudspeaker called for order numbers 126 and 124. A few seconds later, it was 127's turn.

"I guess it does. But I hope most good deeds aren't such a two-edged sword. More than that, I just can't see myself ever finding real satisfaction in this job anymore. I mean, I've given this company eight years of my life. And for what? So my obituary can read, 'She was marketing manager for the More to Love plus-sized fashion line? We could count on her to do the dirty work?' That's not how I want to be remembered. There must be a worthwhile mission for me somewhere. It's high time I figured out what I am supposed to be doing with my life. But I don't know where to start."

"Ah," Shawna said. "Sounds like the curse of potential." She looked away, gazing past Roz at something in the middle distance only she could see. It was one of Shawna's peculiarities that some found off-putting. The sudden silences and averted gaze made her appear bored or disengaged. But Roz knew it was Shawna's way of focusing, following every thought down whatever rabbit hole it led to. When she ran that thought to ground, pinned it down, and dissected it, she would retrace her steps and rejoin the conversation where she had left it. Shawna's thoughts could be odd. But they were often insightful enough to be worth waiting for.

Roz waited in patient silence. The loudspeaker blared again. "Order number 129 is up. And number 124, your order is ready for pickup; fourth call for order 124." Roz looked around the restaurant out of curiosity. That's when she saw them. Right across from her and Shawna sat a pair of young people at a table for two. They looked to be in their late teens. The pretty blonde girl was chatting with a gangly boy who hung on her every word. His expression bordered on worshipful. For a brief second, Roz felt tempted to chuckle at the cuteness of adolescent love. But a pang of envy smothered that impulse. No man had ever gazed at *her* round face with such adoration.

Catching the boy's eye as the PA system was announcing the last call for order 124, Roz made a head gesture toward the cash registers. The young guy rose with a sheepish expression and headed for the counter to get their order, a wave of knowing laughter rippling through the crowd in his wake.

Shawna returned to the conversation. "I knew this kid named Richie in high school. Nice guy, but not an intellectual powerhouse. He almost didn't graduate. I heard he took a job driving a forklift. I'm sure there were days he didn't like his job. Who doesn't have those? But I'll bet you dollars to donuts he didn't waste one minute wondering how life would have turned out had he become a brain surgeon."

She continued. "It's different for you. You had strong grades in every subject. Not to mention you had music skills. You could have had any of a dozen careers, but there wasn't enough time in the world to pursue all the possibilities. So, you picked one and went to work. Nothing wrong with that. But unlike the forklift driver, you wonder whether you would have been happier as a teacher, an engineer, a journalist, or a singer. It's a question nobody can answer. That's the curse of potential. All things being equal, I think Richie must be more content than either of us."

The counter help announced the order numbers Roz and Shawna had been waiting for. After getting their trays, they blessed the food and took up the conversation again.

"Okay, that's part of it," Roz conceded while removing the bread from her veggie burger. "But not all. What about gifts and callings? I don't imagine Mozart wondered if he should have been a schoolteacher. And William Wilberforce didn't get to the end of his career and wonder whether he'd wasted his potential or missed his calling. That's what I want. To find certainty about my purpose. Somewhere out there is the one thing God called me to do. I want to know I'm doing that, even if I don't like it every day."

"Ants!" Shawna's exclamation was emphatic. For a startled second, Roz looked around the table for a conga line of insects advancing toward her plate. Understanding arrived an instant later. There were no bugs; this was Shawna being Shawna.

Her quirky friend confirmed it. "You are saying that you want to be special. So does every ant in the anthill. But most ants are interchangeable. People aren't much different. How many of us can be special before that word loses all meaning? Mozart and Wilberforce have books written about them because they are flukes—people so unusual we all notice they were here. Trying to be like them is like trying to win the lottery. Bad idea. Bad odds."

The bleakness of Shawna's vision caught Roz off guard. It was one thing to fear you were missing your calling; it was quite another to infer you were an idiot for believing you *had* a calling. Did Shawna think of herself as nothing more than another ant in the anthill? Talk about a dark worldview; old Mrs. Grimm would have offered more encouragement and inspiration than dear friend Shawna here.

"I don't think I buy that. On the one hand, you say I have all this potential, all this talent. But you also suggest that I'm just another worker ant with no statistical hope of standing out. Aren't you trying to have it both ways?"

Shawna smiled. "Well, maybe a little. What I'm saying is that you have lots of great attributes, but you're also asking a lot. You want both a noteworthy life and personal fulfillment in the bargain. A few lucky people might get one or the other, but I can't imagine many people get both."

"And what made you come to that depressing conclusion?"

"Ecclesiastes."

"There's your problem," said Roz. "That's not the most motivational book in the canon."

"Motivational, no. But still true. Most folks just can't handle what it says. It doesn't fit with the narcissism of our current culture. But it speaks to your quest. Here's a guy who set out to discover what people were supposed to do with their lives. He brought a lot to the table: wealth, power, wisdom, all that. By the end, he'd seen it all, done it all, and had it all. Did any of it make him happy?" She didn't wait for an answer before continuing. "You know his conclusion as well as I do: 'Forget trying to find fulfillment or satisfaction under the sun. Fear God and keep his commandments. Everything else is vanity and vexation of spirit.'" Shawna sounded almost fierce, as if daring Roz to say otherwise.

Roz tried not to let hurt feelings add to her woes. She'd come here for a shot in the arm and found a wet blanket instead. But maybe Shawna was right. Why get invested in reaching for the unattainable? Still, that idea still felt wrong. Nobody achieved greatness by lowering their expectations. Life was more than a lottery governed by chance and dumb luck.

Both women stared at the faux wood grain of the tabletop and thought their own thoughts. After a few minutes Shawna brought up a new topic: "Have you heard anything from Eddie Caruthers?"

As if I needed something else to feel bad about. Eddie Caruthers was missing in action. His disappearance dated back eight months and eighty pounds ago. Roz had been crossing the street in front of the church last October when some crude man had hurled humiliating insults, fat-shaming her. Eddie had jumped to her defense and told the guy off. That should have ended it, but it hadn't. The trouble escalated until there was bloodshed and death. And none of it would have happened if she hadn't been so heavy. That knowledge was the greatest weight she carried. She felt guilty every time she thought of Eddie, and she thought of him almost every time she got into the big black car with the bench seats.

"No, I haven't," Roz said. "I always figured if he got in touch with anyone, it would be with you."

"Don't I wish! He's changed his phone number, changed his email address. I've heard he's gone down to Florida, but no one can get in touch with him. If his own family knows where he is, they're not saying."

"You miss him?"

"Not like that. But I worry about him. I feel he's not doing well."

Not like that. Everyone knew Eddie had liked Shawna "like that." Maybe Shawna had never noticed. Maybe she was so accustomed to male attention that it no longer made an impression. Must be nice to have such problems. But Eddie was a great guy who deserved someone to reciprocate his feelings more than dear, distant, immovable Ms. Bell.

Shawna had the faraway look in her eyes again. "I asked the pastor about him. I wanted to know whether he had any ideas for trying to draw Eddie back home. He expressed surprise that I asked. And he made it clear he saw Eddie as a problem he was glad to be rid of."

Roz didn't know what to say to that. She knew she could not bear any more bad news right now. She also knew she was tired of standing. Her feet hurt. She crumpled her sandwich wrapper and looked around for the trash receptacles. "On that sad note, I'm going to bid you farewell. Thanks for meeting me today. You've given me some things to think about."

Shawna still looked distracted. "Okay. Have a blessed day." She hesitated. "Look Rozzie, I know what I said earlier was not what you wanted to hear. I'm not saying you can't make a difference in the world. You can. Look to be special to someone, not to everyone. Don't insist on a calling. Find an opportunity. It won't be somewhere over the rainbow. I bet it's right down the street. There is still beauty in that."

Now that was patented Shawna. And it was hopeful. Roz smiled in gratitude and headed toward the exit. The summer heat hit her hard as she stepped outside. It had become much warmer than it was this morning, warmer even than when she first entered the restaurant. Spring was her favorite season, because summer's hot temperatures presented a greater physical challenge for well-insulated individuals like herself.

Reaching her car, she discovered that someone had keyed it. Deep gouges in the driver's door spelled out the word *fat*. The scratches went down to bare metal. The crosspiece of the letter T stretched all the way to the taillights. "Oh, poo!" Like many people who didn't swear, Roz struggled to find interjections that conveyed her displeasure without sounding irreligious. A walk around the rest of the car showed no additional damage, so she refrained from further euphemisms.

Back in the quiet of her home, dark clouds overshadowed her emotional landscape again. Had the defacing of her car been the work of some random teenaged vandal who'd watched her arrive? If so, how cruel must he be? And if it wasn't random . . . had she been correct in thinking that was Trina she saw earlier? She didn't want to believe her former friend would stoop so low. Friends came into your life, stayed awhile, and departed. That was normal. She wished Trina's departure hadn't been so traumatic. Maybe the timing of seeing the woman who might have been Trina and having her car vandalized was sheer coincidence. *Yeah. Sure it was.*

CHAPTER 4
INTRUDER

At five o'clock Saturday afternoon, a white commercial van backed up to the garage door of an Acton townhouse. Its side panels bore the name and logo of Spectrum Plastering. So did the lone occupant's T-shirt. Neither the van nor the man had any connection to the company. Brandon had purchased the magnetic signs online two months ago and affixed them to his personal vehicle this morning.

He dismounted and walked to the rear cargo doors. This was the dangerous part, being out in the open at the height of rush hour. But he was confident that looking like a typical trades-man doing his job was camouflage enough. No one was likely to give him a second glance. But even if his former neighbors peered out a window at him, Brandon was sure they would not recognize him. He hadn't been here in over a year, and in the interim he'd grown a beard, shaved his head, and deliberately packed on twenty-five pounds of junk food flab. He let his hips sag forward to alter his normal walk. Dark sunglasses completed the disguise.

Inside the van's cargo bay were four five-gallon buckets with lids. Two quick trips saw the buckets deposited by the side entrance to the garage. Phase one was complete. Brandon closed the back of the van. Time to go away and come back after dark.

A ten-minute drive took him to a movie theater in the neighboring town of Maynard. The attractive young woman in the ticket booth flipped her hair and gave him a shy smile. He did not smile back. Let her save her flirtations for someone more gullible. A pretty viper was still venomous.

After settling on a ridiculous cop buddy flick, Brandon sat in the back of the theater and managed to endure the movie all the way through. Afterward, he returned to the van and changed clothes in the windowless cargo bay. The plasterer's T-shirt and painter's pants made way for black jeans and a gray short-sleeved shirt. No need for the sunglasses now. He tied a leather jacket around his waist. The jacket was a bit of an odd look for a night in June, but he hoped the last two items he grabbed—his backpack and walking stick—made him look like a hiker coming home from a day spent trekking through higher, cooler elevations. A canvas fisherman's hat completed the ensemble. Transformation complete, he stepped out of the van and began the two-mile walk back to his former home. It was dusk now and would be dark soon. Tonight's half-moon was an acceptable compromise. In an ideal world, he'd have the darkness of the new moon for now, and the light of a full moon when he needed it in a couple of hours.

As he walked, he buttressed his resolve by thinking about the crazy, upside-down world of the gender wars. He'd had lots of time to study the facts after his divorce, and the fact was women had almost all the advantages. Seventy-six percent of public school teachers were women, giving them an outsized impact on the lives of school-aged boys. More girls than boys graduated from high school. And college. Women earned the most master's degrees and doctorates. More women than men enrolled in law school and medical school.

Their advantages weren't limited to education. Most corporate managers were women. Single women purchased homes at twice the rate of single men. For men with only high school diplomas, real wages had been falling for thirty years, while the wages of high school-educated women rose over the same period. There were, of course, a few areas where men led the way: Men were twice as likely as women to become alcoholics, and twice as likely to die of a drug overdose. Men committed 77 percent of all suicides and made up 90 percent of the inmate population. And to top it all off, the average man would die five years before the average woman.

What did women do with these advantages? They claimed to be oppressed, that's what. They moaned about "male privilege" and yammered about "the patriarchy." All this while they cleaned up in the divorce sweepstakes. That was how Brandon had come to call a warehouse home while that accursed woman occupied his condo.

Brandon's thoughts wandered to the man who should have been his father. His mother's husband—the guy he and everyone else assumed was his father until a DNA kit from some online genealogy company had proved otherwise—had a head-on collision with a bridge abutment after learning the truth. If he hadn't died on impact, the resulting fireball finished the job. No one knew for sure whether the crash had been a tragic accident or suicide. If it was suicide, the poor idiot had killed the wrong person.

That was not a mistake Brandon would have made. No, his only mistake had been being naïve enough to think his own marriage would fare any better. Their union hadn't been free of drama, but whose was? He'd been content to stay married, and assumed she was too. She wasn't. She didn't want him and hadn't for some time. When she'd dropped the d-bomb on him, it all came into focus. What the woman wanted was his home and as much of his money as she could get her grubby little paws on. It had all been a bunch of lies, including the lie she told the cops to make sure she won the divorce. She had won, all right; the female family court judge had given her everything she'd wanted.

The litany of resentments had the desired effect. He was seeing red by the time he approached the condo that he had purchased with his own money and improved with his own hands. The townhouse would never be his again, not even after he had served justice to the usurper. He couldn't undo any of the evils she had done. But he could present her with the bill for damages, payable on demand.

Brandon looked at the townhouse. Most of the interior lights were off, as expected. She got home late on Saturdays. Brandon had staked out the place every Saturday for weeks, watching the condo from the parking lot of the Mexican restaurant on the corner. It looked like she was sticking to her usual routine tonight.

Stepping off the sidewalk, he cut a path across the lawn, a meandering route chosen to avoid triggering the motion-activated outside lights. He reached the side door, out of sight of the other units, and saw that his buckets were still there, undisturbed. Good. He put on the leather coat, donned a pair of nitrile gloves from his backpack, and fished his old house key out of a pocket, confident that she would not have changed the locks. He was right. Brandon was a locksmith and a home security expert. Not even she was dumb enough to waste her money on new locks.

Swinging the buckets inside, he closed the door behind him and exchanged his floppy hat for a ski mask from the backpack before climbing the stairs and pausing at the door that opened into the main hallway off the kitchen. *Last chance*, whispered the voice of an occasional visitor he recognized as his conscience. *You should walk away.*

No way. Brandon stifled a snort of derision and opened the door. He saw the greenish-white glow of a keypad mounted on the wall opposite. The keypad emitted an insistent beeping. She'd had an alarm system installed! Probably used her last shred of initiative doing it. He recognized the brand of equipment and knew there would be one or more cameras hooked into it. A quick glance to his right revealed nothing in the front hall. That meant the camera would be somewhere off to his left, in the living room, probably positioned to see both the keypad and the front door. He angled the basement door so it would block the line of sight from the living room and shield all but his extended arm while he shut off the system.

The magic number would be four digits. That made things less unwieldy. Still, a four-digit code using the numbers zero to nine had ten thousand combinations. The default settings would give him sixty seconds to enter the right code. A few of those seconds were already gone. He was glad he had given this scenario a lot of prior thought. And deep in his gut, he had known what her choice of code would be. Without hesitation, he punched in 0-2-0-5. No good. The display remained unaltered, and the keypad continued beeping. He changed the sequence to 0-2-2-1. Still no good. His hands felt sweaty inside the gloves. There was time to try one more sequence before things got complicated. When he input the third arrangement of numbers, the beeping stopped. The silky voice of the system's artificial intelligence spoke from the base station somewhere to his left: "Alarm off."

Heart pounding, Brandon pumped his fist in triumph. But the feeling of elation was short-lived. It galled him to be right about this. Guessing the code had confirmed once again what kind of person she was. Not that he needed any more proof. She'd once told him she'd remember the date their divorce became official as the happiest day of her life. And her eyes had glittered with savage enjoyment of the pain those words had inflicted. That's how he'd known she would be twisted enough to want to relive that moment every day. His only challenge had been getting the formatting right: 2521, for February 5, 2021. It was a good bet that his pesky conscience wouldn't have anything else to say tonight.

With the immediate danger past, Brandon fought down a growing disquiet as he considered the implications of the alarm system. This brand came with an app that would allow her to manage the security system from her phone. She could check the system status, toggle it on and off, watch the camera feed, or see the running timeline of system activity. That timeline would show her the most recent system deactivation, the one he'd just accomplished. If she saw that, the next people to arrive at the condo would be a couple of cops with guns drawn.

He'd already planned for the possibility. If cops arrived, he'd be able to hear one or more cars pull up to the house. None of them would sound like that accursed woman's Volkswagen. Brandon might have enough time to exit his hiding place, open the slider to the rear deck, and go over the railing before the police made entrance. Or he might not. It wasn't optimal. He'd have to abandon his buckets, so there would be no hiding the fact that he'd been inside. Once outside, it was a long walk back to the van. They'd be searching for him in the meantime. His choices were clear. Possible capture and arrest if she used the app, saw the system history, and called the police; or probable success if she wasn't thinking about the security app, skipped the phone, and instead went for the keypad when she got home. He'd made his decision long before he got here. Fortune favors the bold. No risk, no reward.

He took a deep, calming breath and drew his playlist from the backpack, scanning the songs.

TITLE	ARTIST
Where the River Flows	*Collective Soul*
Blue Collar Man	*Styx*
Cinema	*Yes*
Dirty Water	*The Standells*
In the Dark	*Billy Squire*
The Waiting	*Tom Petty*
Love Is Like Oxygen	*Sweet*
Home and Dry	*Gerry Rafferty*
Who Are You	*The Who*
Ride Like the Wind	*Christopher Cross*
Ode to Billie Joe	*Bobbie Gentry*

It was a to-do list, a set of instructions. He'd taken the extra precaution of disguising it as a playlist in case he accidentally left it somewhere. There was no point in writing anything incriminating. Brandon's list of memory jogs was subtle enough. For five consecutive days, he'd rehearsed tonight's sequence, cementing the link between each song and what he needed to do. He was sure those connections were too tenuous for anyone else to make out.

The first three items were already complete. Next up was the Standells song, a regional anthem he could barely resist singing as he worked. He went to the laundry room, put his stopper over the drain in the utility sink, peeled the lids off the four buckets, and upended their contents into the sink. The water was brownish, rich with sediment and the scent of algae. Brandon had filled the pails in the Assabet River spillway behind nearby Damon Mill that morning, in accord with the first song on his list.

The Billy Squire tune reminded him to throw the circuit breakers on the electrical panel to disable all the lights on the main floor. He did not move the switches that powered the lower level; the garage-door opener needed to work, as did the lights inside the garage.

Now it was time to wait. Summoning the required patience might prove difficult, as Tom Petty said. He went back to the keypad and pressed AWAY. The disembodied voice from the other room said, "Please exit now." Brandon pushed the door to the garage stairway shut, stepping back into the kitchen as the door closed. He had chosen a hiding place from which he could monitor her arrival home without being seen himself. No cameras or motion sensors could detect him here. All he had to do was bide his time.

Though his body was at rest, his mind raced—not because of what he was about to do, but because of giddy visions of how life would be afterward. With some sense of justice restored, he'd reboot his life. He'd start his own business instead of doing the low-paying day-labor gigs and temp jobs that had sustained him these last months. He'd get paid enough to live somewhere decent. What more could a man ask of life but the opportunity to work with his own hands, earn fair pay, and be respected for his competency? Not so long ago, he would have added the love of a good woman to the list of things to be desired. He knew better now. A woman's love was always a high-stakes gamble, a financial game of Russian roulette that cost the losers a hefty sum. Sometimes that love was nothing but a mirage in the desert. Either way, he'd pass. Not interested. He almost smiled to himself, but the sound of the garage door opening interrupted his train of thought.

He heard the car pull in. He recognized the lumpy idle of her four-cylinder engine. The engine cut off. All was silent. He should have heard her getting out of the car. Why was she sitting there instead of getting out? Was she looking at the alarm system app? Calling the police? He had no way to see, no way to know. Part of him wanted to run, to get out while the getting was good. He wrestled that impulse down, forcing himself to stand rooted to the spot. *Wait.*

The computerized voice in the living room said, "Alarm off." He closed his eyes and sucked in his breath. She hadn't gotten out of the car yet, meaning she had used the app. If she scrolled down the page a smidgen, he would be toast. The sound of her car restarting would be all the warning he'd get. She'd flee the scene, and the cops would arrive in no time flat. The police station was only an eighth of a mile up the road.

After a heart-stopping delay, he heard the garage door closing, followed by the sound of her car door opening and shutting. A few seconds later, she was climbing the steps. Alone? Yes. Only one set of footfalls. It was showtime. As his long wait ended, he stood motionless behind louvered doors, a shadow hidden in the deeper darkness of the walk-in pantry.

CHAPTER 5
PEG

Almost everyone left the gym right after the class ended. Margaret Brewster dawdled, hoping to manufacture an excuse to chat with the hot guy she'd been admiring for the last three weeks. His chiseled good looks came straight out of central casting for soap-opera leading men. Instead of noticing her, however, he was busy texting someone and looking perturbed about it. When she could wait no longer without being obvious, she swallowed her disappointment and headed for her car. As she was tossing her gym bag into the trunk, he strode up to the car parked next to hers, still looking distracted. His ride was a gleaming silver Porsche, the low-slung kind with two doors, a sloping roof, wide tires, and a big wing on the back. It made her aging Volkswagen sedan look decrepit. *Beefcake boy's got money.*

"Hey there," she called to him. He looked up. "I couldn't help but notice you hardly broke a sweat in there. Any chance you're a professional athlete?"

His answering smile was at once dazzling and self-deprecating. "No, nothing like that. I have a cosmetic dentistry practice."

Margaret imagined her voice coming over an intercom: *Dr. Heartthrob, you're wanted in reception . . .* "Oh, so you know how to achieve peak fitness and a brilliant smile too? You'll have to share the secrets with me. Maybe over drinks? Something healthy, of course." She giggled and hoped she didn't sound overeager.

The dreamboat shook his head. "I appreciate the offer, but I don't think my wife would approve."

So don't tell her. Was this guy slow or what? She hid her exasperation behind an apology: "I'm so sorry. I didn't notice a ring . . ."

"That's because I never wear one." He flashed that megawatt smile again. "I don't like any jewelry on my hands. Occupational hazard. Don't fault yourself for asking. No harm done. Have a good night!" And with that, the dashing dentist folded himself into his pricey sports car and roared away.

And that was pretty much how the entire week had gone. As pickup lines go, she had to admit the one she'd tried was clumsy. Or maybe she was losing her edge. Not so many years ago, men would fall all over themselves trying to get a date with her. She had been married in those days, so she'd had to dash their hopes. Most of the time, anyway. Sometimes, when the attraction had been mutual, she'd allowed herself the occasional dalliance. But these days, she was the one doing the chasing—and coming up empty too often.

It wasn't fair. Driving away, she considered her plight. She'd suffered through a ten-year stretch hitched to Mr. Wrong. Mother and Dad had been against the union from day one. And they had a point; girls like her weren't supposed to marry into the lunch-bucket class. She'd married him because he was strong and brimming with self-confidence; because he could make things and fix things; because he had laughing eyes, like he was privy to some great inside joke. But the main reason she had married him was to spite her controlling parents. It had taken her years to realize the depth of her error. All those Ivy League boys she'd spurned would someday rule the world. They'd be judges and governors, investment bankers and CEOs. The privileged class would inherit the earth, while her blue-collar husband wouldn't even inherit the scruffy little shop that employed him. And he had been okay with that. No ambition at all. By the end, all she wanted was her freedom, even if her parents never took her back into their good graces and wrote her back into their will. Thank goodness a family court judge had commuted her sentence and set her free. Only now she realized being free wasn't half as good alone. She was facing another Saturday night at home, watching stupid romantic comedies until she fell asleep in front of the TV. It wasn't fair.

Margaret, called Peg by her small handful of friends, pulled into the parking lot of the twenty-four-hour pharmacy. She'd already been there once today, picking up a refill of her prescription antiaging cream. She'd meant to pick up a birthday card for her brother while she was at it. Now she would remedy that oversight and maybe pick up a little ice cream to keep her company during whatever movie was on. She got out and checked her reflection in the store window. *Stupid dentist. I bet I look better than his wife.*

Inside, she browsed through the cards and tried to imagine Mr. Right. Maybe he'd be from one of the old families whose names graced street signs all over the Bay State: Winthrop, Hancock, Conant, or the like. He'd have the impressive social and political connections that came with such a name. He'd work in downtown Boston but live in one of the pricey suburbs, like Weston or Wellesley. There would also be a summer place on Lake Winnipesaukee, or maybe out in the Berkshires. She pictured a country home in Lenox. She'd always wanted to take in the Boston Symphony Orchestra at Tanglewood. Imagine being able to walk home afterward!

She settled on a card and took it to the checkout counter, only to realize she had no cash. She handed the clerk her debit card with an apologetic shrug. Receipt in hand, she headed back to her car, still lost in reverie. What else could she foresee about her next husband? He'd be ten or twelve years her senior but would still look good for his age. And unlike the Ken-doll tooth-puller with his midlife-crisis car, Mr. Right would know a good catch when he saw one. She was still young, fun, and unencumbered. No issues, no baggage from her first marriage. Mr. Right would show his appreciation by taking excellent care of her. A man that successful would stay busy, leaving her with plenty of free time to spend his money. It was going to be a wonderful life, unfortunate ten-year detour notwithstanding.

Home loomed in her headlights. She rolled up the driveway and paused long enough for the garage door to open. That was when a wave of unease hit her. Something was wrong . . . but what? She eased the car into the garage and peered around. Nothing was out of place. The disquiet was probably because she had let herself dwell too long on unpleasant things from the past. Having purged that awful man from her life, it was high time to evict him from her thoughts. Maybe she'd start by changing her alarm code, so it wasn't a daily reminder of things best forgotten.

Speaking of the alarm—she fished her phone from her purse and fired up the security app to check the alarm status. The display said the system was on, so all was well. She tapped the OFF button. Still, she couldn't help feeling a bit creeped out. She looked around the garage again. *This is silly. Pull yourself together.*

Peg slipped the phone into her purse next to the birthday card and mounted the steps to the main level. When she opened the door to the hallway, darkness greeted her. That was what was wrong. She always left a light or two on so she didn't have to return to a darkened house. Her subconscious mind must have reacted to the absence of light from the windows as she drove up. The light switch on the wall beside her was in the up position, meaning it was on. The power must have gone out earlier in the evening.

Peg walked past the pantry into the kitchen, setting her purse on the counter. That's when it hit her: the power couldn't be out; the garage had lit up when the overhead door rose, the way it always did. She'd had light coming up the steps, and she could still see the light from the stairwell shining under the door. Another surge of foreboding washed over her as she tried to make sense of the inconsistency. Something must have tripped the thingies—what were they called? Circuit breakers. That was it. She only had to open the box and reset the switches. Why, oh why, was there never a man around when you needed one?

The panel was on the wall next to the laundry room door. She'd need some light to see it. Where did she keep the flashlight? Was it in the pantry? She turned toward the pantry and reached for the door pull before remembering the flashlight was on the other side of the kitchen in a drawer full of odds and ends. She stepped that way, still trying to shake off a case of the willies.

A spot in the center of the kitchen floor always squeaked when stepped on. The sound was sinister tonight, what with the darkness and her jangly nerves and all. She scolded herself for being a scaredy-cat, for acting like a child who was afraid of the dark. She felt around in the junk drawer until her hands closed on the flashlight. Pushing the button on its barrel produced no more illumination than had the light switch on the wall. The batteries must be a decade old. Wait, didn't her cell phone have a built-in flashlight? Duh, of course it did. She reached for her purse.

The floor squeaked again. Behind her. *Oh no, oh no, oh no, oh no.* A half-dozen conflicting certainties shot through her mind in an instant. *It's a burglar. A rapist. A murderer. It's just my imagination. I should have trusted my gut. Oh no.* Peg spun around in time to see a shadowy masked figure an arm's length away. A gloved fist smashed into her chin. She heard the crack of the impact and saw points of light like stars against the darkness. The world tilted. The floor rushed up to meet her, and the stars winked out, extinguishing the last vestiges of her awareness.

CHAPTER 6
TAKE ME TO THE RIVER

Exploding into action felt good after hiding in the pantry for so long. Brandon strode to the service panel to restore the lights and returned to stand over the crumpled form of the woman he had once loved. *Hi honey, I'm home.*

A handful of seconds ticked by. Peg moaned. Brandon took a surprised step backward as she grimaced and reached up to touch her chin where he'd cracked her. This shouldn't be. He'd assumed she would stay unconscious. But he hadn't known how hard to punch her, since he had never struck a woman before. Hitting her too hard risked breaking her jaw or knocking out teeth, and he couldn't take that chance. Now it was clear he had been too gentle. She was coming to after less than a minute. And she lay sprawled in such an awkward position he couldn't chance clocking her again. Not without bouncing the back of her head off the floor, which would be as bad as knocking teeth out.

Brandon paced back and forth several times, interlacing his fingers behind his head and staring at the floor, trying to concentrate. He needed to figure out his options, and fast. Maybe he should get out of there while she was still groggy. She'd think she'd interrupted a burglary in progress and thank her lucky stars that nothing worse had happened. There would be no evidence it was him, even if the lack of forced entry and the defeat of the alarm system made her suspect him. She'd feel compelled to take greater security precautions in the future. He might not get this chance again.

"Brandon!" Her voice was weak, but she sounded certain. He turned to face her, saying nothing. "I know it's you. You can hide behind a mask all you want, but I don't need to see your face to recognize you." She struggled to a sitting position with her back against the kitchen wall. "What are you doing here?" A brief pause, then, "You hit me!" Her speech was slurred.

None of this was going according to plan. She wasn't supposed to see him, let alone recognize him. He had to regain control of the situation. "I'll tell you what I'm doing here. I'm here to collect a debt." Now that he had spoken, there was no going back. Even if she had only been guessing before, she knew it was him now.

His ex frowned. "No way. I don't owe you anything."

"Oh, but you do. Only your debt to me isn't monetary. We still need to settle accounts, nevertheless. You can start by telling me why you lied."

She didn't answer right away. Her eyes darted around the room as she tried to get her bearings. Searching for an escape?

Or maybe searching for something she could use as a weapon. A set of knives stuck up from a butcher-block storage unit at the far end of the counter.

"Don't even think about it," he ordered her. "Make a move, and I'll hit you so hard, it'll hurt for the rest of your life. You sit right where you are and answer my question. Why did you lie?"

She let out a heavy sigh. "Fine. Because I didn't think the cops would take me seriously. Our last fight . . . the way you treated me . . . That was abuse, whether or not you realize it. You scared me. That's why I called the police."

"And the welt on your face? How'd you conjure that? You know I never touched you."

"It was a paperweight from my desk. Look, the police department is a male-dominated institution. I hit myself to make sure the cops didn't brush off a woman's concerns. I'm not proud of that. But I swear I didn't know they would arrest you. I felt bad about it. That's why I didn't press any charges, didn't cooperate with the DA's office. You can at least give me that."

"I still spent three nights in jail for nothing."

"Well, this time won't be for nothing. You've really done it now."

Brandon smiled behind his ski mask. "Ironic, isn't it?"

"You think it's funny? You broke in here and assaulted me. I'll press charges this time. You'll go to jail, and for more than a weekend."

"Maybe. Maybe not. Time will tell. But we're getting ahead of ourselves. Bad as your little charade was, that's not the lie I was talking about. I was talking about the boy."

"We're not going there."

"Yes, we are. If you didn't want to raise my child, I would have raised him by myself. You didn't have to do what you did." If he expected an apology, none was forthcoming.

"My body, my choice." If she were a cat, she'd have her claws out, back arched, and ears back. She all but hissed when she said the words.

"It wasn't your body that got mutilated. It was his." That thought filled him with fresh grief for his lost son.

His ex-wife's face contorted. "I hate you, Brandon. With all my heart." Her voice was regaining some strength. And volume. "You want to know why I lied? I lied to spare your stupid feelings. I shouldn't have bothered. Now I hate you enough to tell you the truth. The truth is, I ended the pregnancy to spare the world another you. Even one Brandon Heckler is one too many." She lurched forward, trying to get to her feet.

He hit her again, hard, a short right hook to the jaw. No question, she was out cold this time. He had to catch her as she slumped forward to make sure she didn't do a face plant. He stared down at her for a moment. Peg—it was hard to think of her as "that accursed woman" when she looked so small and helpless—was petite, barely five foot two and 110 pounds soaking wet. Long ago, this observation had inspired protectiveness in him. Not anymore. And speaking of soaking wet, it was time to get things back on track.

He hoisted her onto his shoulder so her legs dangled over his back and her head slumped over his chest. He'd rehearsed this in his mind a hundred times, but it still took a while to get her positioned right. A shift of the arm here, a hitch of the shoulder there, and the position was perfect. His right arm encircled her waist while his left hand held her wrists. Carrying her to the laundry room, he tipped her into a more vertical position, tightened his grip, and plunged her head-down into the utility sink.

The water revived her, and she began struggling. But with her arms held fast and her legs unable to push against anything solid, her efforts to free herself accomplished nothing. Brandon tried to imagine how she felt: blind, disoriented, terrified. The irresistible need to inhale warring against the stark certainty that inhaling meant death. He almost felt some sympathy for her. But the boy had died an even crueler death, head crushed, pulled limb from limb in the place he should have been safest, butchered at the direction of his own mother. There had been no mercy, no escape for the boy, and there would be none for her now.

She twisted and thrashed as she tried to get her nose and mouth clear of the water. A large air bubble broke the surface, and she stopped struggling after a few seconds more. Wary that she might have partially exhaled to trick him, he held her fast for another minute, long enough to sing several tuneless choruses of "Love Is Like Oxygen" under his breath. He finally lifted her clear and laid her limp body face up on the floor. Her eyes were wide open. He averted his.

Time was of the essence now. Rigor mortis would set in between two and four hours after death. He needed to complete the mission before that. Brandon retrieved his playlist and reviewed it yet again. After all, he had written it to guard against the risk of mistakes. Under time pressure, under the influence of anger, adrenaline, or guilty fear, he might overlook something important. This was no time for winging it. He scanned down the page until he found the first unfinished item.

Right under "Love Is Like Oxygen" was "Home and Dry" by Gerry Rafferty. This was his cue to take care of the sink area. Drain it. Wash it out along with the buckets so no sediment from the river remained. Get a used towel from her hamper. Wipe up any spillage from the floor. Dry the excess water from her face and hair, as well as the water that had splashed on his own clothes. He hadn't expected the need, but he closed her eyes while he was at it. Rinse the towel, wring it dry, and put it back into the hamper. The cleanup took fifteen minutes. Brandon made himself take two paces back to look it all over, because he had once read that the male of the species could see well at long and middle distances, but was prone to overlook things right in front of him.

Satisfied that the laundry area looked as tidy as when he had first entered, he thought of the next song on the list. It was there to remind him to secure her ID. He grabbed her purse from the counter and confirmed that her wallet and driver's license were in it. When the time came, her license plates would tell the authorities whose car they had found. But her purse and wallet needed to be inside, or they'd suspect she wasn't the last person to drive it. Before closing the purse, he fished out her cell phone and stuffed it into the front pocket of her jeans.

Song ten, "Ride Like the Wind," meant it was time to go. Brandon stowed his backpack and her purse on her VW's passenger seat and laid the stacked buckets in the trunk. His walking stick went onto the back seat. He saved the heaviest burden for last. Picking up Peg's lifeless body, he reflected on the inadequacy of both rage and adrenaline. The problem was neither one lasted long. And when they were spent, all that remained was a sense of . . . futility? Regret? Nothing he had done would change much. It wouldn't get him his alimony back or expunge the record of his arrest. It wouldn't bring back his son. No, it had never been a question of "fixing" anything. The only point of all this had been justice for the boy. And justice, so long awaited, had been done. It was only now that Brandon understood that justice anticipated was sweeter than justice served.

He carried his former bride across the threshold for the second time, taking her down to the garage with a gentleness bordering on tenderness. While placing her in the trunk alongside the buckets, he fiddled with the position of her body, as if he didn't want her last ride to be uncomfortable. The thud of the trunk lid closing snapped him out of the sentimental fog. The clock was ticking. This wasn't over yet.

Back upstairs, Brandon reset the alarm before descending to *his* garage for the last time. He tied his leather jacket around his waist and exchanged the ski mask for the fisherman's hat from his backpack. Getting into the driver's seat of her car was a tight fit. He resisted the urge to adjust it for more legroom. He raised the garage door, eased the car out, and pushed the button to lower the door behind him again. His destination was sixty-five miles away.

He passed the time by talking to his ex. He couldn't remember ever getting to have the last word with her and couldn't pass up the opportunity now.

"I really loved you once, Peg. And I thought you loved me. It took a while for me to realize you married me for the sole purpose of sticking it to your folks. After they cut you off for it, you had second thoughts about missing out on their money. I would've kept you comfortable, but never rich, and comfortable wasn't good enough for you."

After a few minutes of silence, he resumed his discourse. "I will not miss all the subtle digs, the little put-downs you directed at me. You liked to imagine they went over my head. They didn't. I was too tired to respond. I didn't have the energy to fight for your respect, woman. And I shouldn't have needed to. I had already earned it."

He knew the day would come when none of that mattered. He'd get over it. Let the past fade, forget about it, and move on. But there were two days he knew he would never forget: the day he learned he was going to be father to a little boy, and the day he learned he wasn't.

The pregnancy had been unplanned. Still, when the ultrasound revealed a boy, Brandon had spent nearly every spare moment trying out names, tentatively settling on Bronson and hoping Peg would like the name enough to agree to it. Bronson Heckler would someday learn to hit a baseball, throw a football, change a tire, and rewire a lamp, because his old man would teach him all those things. Brandon hoped that working together with his wife to raise a son would help their marriage by giving them each a purpose beyond themselves.

But it was not to be. A short time later, she informed him that the marriage was over and that nothing he could do or say would change that. Brandon resigned himself to having a broken family and shared custody. Thereafter, they slept in separate rooms, hashing out the timeline for disentangling all the threads of their lives.

One Friday when he returned home from a four-day security expo, she told him she'd lost the baby. Devastated, he'd done his awkward best to comfort this life partner turned enemy and grieved for the son he'd never know. Until the letter from his insurance company came, a standard explanation of benefits that listed payment to Planned Parenthood for a procedure called a D&C. That was when the horror hit him. She hadn't lost the baby. She'd killed it.

What followed was the mother of all confrontations, a screaming match in which he'd called her every vile thing he could think of. She'd retreated to the bedroom, sobbing. Ten minutes later, someone knocked on the front door. Brandon opened it to find two police officers, both wearing black face masks, as the pandemic-era mask mandates were in full effect then. Brandon figured a neighbor had heard the shouting and complained. He was about to apologize for the ruckus and promise the cops that it wouldn't happen again. But the officers said they were investigating an allegation of domestic violence, and they needed to see his wife. She had come downstairs sporting a big swelling under one eye. Brandon stared at her, mouth agape, and the cops arrested him on the spot. Because his arraignment had to wait until Monday, he'd spent the weekend in jail.

He swerved slightly as a new realization struck him. "You always made the same old mistake—thinking I couldn't see through your lies. What you said about the boy tonight was another lie. Killing him wasn't about sparing the world another Brandon Heckler. You thought being childless would improve your chances of marrying into money. Still, I'll give you credit for this: you made me what I am today. You showed me what it means to want something bad enough to kill for it. I followed your example and became as stone-cold ruthless as you were. You said we weren't compatible, but in the end, I think you understood. We're as alike as two peas in a pod. Well, except I'm alive and you're dead." Brandon tried and failed to stifle a guffaw. He gave in to it, laughing so hard it brought tears to his eyes. It was a giddy, floaty feeling, like the first seconds of succumbing to nitrous oxide.

The laughter stopped when the rearview mirror showed the silhouette of an SUV behind him. It had a light bar on top. Brandon was westbound on Route 2 in Fitchburg. He had been careful to obey all the traffic laws, even setting the cruise control to match the speed limit. Startled and a little alarmed, he wished this cruiser would pass him already. Cops usually camped out in the left lane, driving five or ten miles per hour faster than the civilian traffic. Why was this one ghosting along behind him?

None of the VW's headlights or taillights appeared to be out. The registration sticker on the license plate was current. So was the inspection sticker on the windshield, not that anyone could see it in the dark. His seatbelt was on. There was nothing about him or the car that should interest a cop. Unless—but how could anyone know? They couldn't. No way. Still, few things focused your attention like having the law on your tail while hauling a fresh corpse in the trunk. Brandon felt a film of sweat developing on his forehead.

The blue lights atop the police cruiser flared to life. Things were now much more complicated. The sudden surge of adrenaline made his heart pound. He felt a tremor in his hands. What should he do? What could he do? No way this car could outrun the law. Pull over and hope it was a routine stop? Try to come up with a plausible answer to why he was driving with a woman's purse on the seat? The questions turned out to be moot a split-second later when the police vehicle pulled into the left lane and rocketed past him. The speeding cruiser took the exit for Route 68 in Gardner, and Brandon was in the clear.

He needed to calm down and gather his thoughts. Focus on the list. Almost done. Only "Ode to Billie Joe" remained. He was heading for the woodsy fringe of Franklin County, the least populous county on the Massachusetts mainland. His target was the stretch of this road that ran from Erving into Gill, two small towns that rolled up the carpets at sunset.

Brandon knew there wouldn't be much traffic out there at this time of night.

The French King Bridge came into view, and Brandon reduced his speed. A bridge had been part of the plan from day one. He'd thought long and hard about which one to choose. The Zakim Bridge in Boston wasn't high enough, among other problems. Both the Sagamore and the Bourne bridges across the Cape Cod Canal were high enough, but plagued with heavy traffic at all hours on weekends. The French King Bridge carrying Route 2 across the Connecticut River was perfect. Higher than the others, little traffic, and no cameras. Brandon had read about plans to install cameras later this year, because this bridge had a reputation for attracting jumpers. Authorities said that installing cameras would give them real-time alerts when someone climbed over the railing. But the planned installation was several weeks away, so the coast was clear for now.

This was the deciding factor in his timetable. Submerged bodies always floated to the surface because of gases released during decomposition. A body would stay submerged longer in cold water than in warm because the cold decreased bacterial action. It was now June, so she would pop up sooner than he would like. But waiting for cold weather was not an option; he had to do this before the cameras arrived.

She'd been dead less than two hours, so rigor mortis should not be a problem. He brought the car to a stop near the center of the span. A quick check fore and aft revealed no approaching headlights. It took only a few seconds to pop the trunk, scoop up the body, run to the railing, and heave it over. The river was 142 feet below the bridge deck. Research on skydiving websites had told him she'd hit the water at fifty miles per hour in a little over three seconds. He was back at the car in less time than that.

He drove the rest of the way across the span, did a U-turn, and crossed back to park in a small lot near the east end of the bridge. During the day, people parked there to walk out to center span and take in the view up and down the river. At this time of night, hers was the only car.

His legs pained him. They were stiff from making the long drive with the seat all the way forward in the woman's preferred driving position. If he had adjusted it to his own comfort, he might have forgotten to put it back. The pain was worth the certainty that no such mistake would trip him up.

The last step was to offload his gear. He put on his jacket, shouldered the backpack, retrieved his walking stick, and got the buckets out of the trunk. After a last look around the vehicle, he put the keys in her purse and stuffed the purse into the glove compartment before locking up the car.

This had been a point of internal debate. He had considered leaving the keys in the ignition in hopes some enterprising young criminal would steal the car. With no one to report it stolen, it might disappear for good. When Peg's body washed ashore, those seeking to identify her wouldn't know where to start. That might delay identification of the body, giving the case more time to grow cold. Or maybe the unlucky criminal would get pulled over while driving her car. He'd have no registration in his own name. With the stolen car recovered and the owner missing, maybe the thief would take the fall for her murder once the body turned up. It was an intriguing possibility, but it felt sleazy, given his own experience with false accusations. He decided that having the car found at the bridge was the best way to bolster the suicide narrative.

That narrative was key to everything. If the police suspected foul play, the ex-husband would always be their prime suspect, especially when that ex-husband had a previous arrest for domestic battery. They would come after him with an entire team: detectives, crime scene technicians, pathologists, forensic scientists, and prosecutors. That team would have nearly bottomless financial resources, advanced technology, and all the time in the world to build a case against him. Brandon had to see to every detail all by himself, and before two hours elapsed. Given such time constraints, he felt he'd done well.

Time to go. His destination was one mile to the east. It would be easy to walk up the road, but at least a few cars were bound to drive by in the fifteen or twenty minutes it would take him to cover the distance. Someone might stop to ask if he needed help. A passing police officer might want to know where he was going on foot at this time of night. The cop might demand ID. It would be hard to explain how he'd gotten way out here without a car, or why he had a leather jacket and gloves in summer. The safe choice was to make for the woods beyond the parking lot. As he went, he put on the ski mask again to protect his face from any stray branches he might run into.

It was slow going. At first, he stayed a few feet inside the tree line, abandoning the buckets there and walking parallel to the road. When he reached the French King Restaurant and Motel, he swung wide around it, heading deeper into the woods both to skirt that property and to avoid the Erving Police Station located half a mile to the east. On the other side of the restaurant was a utility road that ran north and dead-ended at a large cell tower. Brandon strode down this lane to the end. At that point, he knew it was safe to walk east through the woods again. He'd pass north of the cop shop, well out of sight and earshot.

He'd spent hours studying topographical maps of the area. He'd walked these woods twice before in practice runs. But those had been in daylight, and the woods at night were a whole other animal. *Animals.* He wondered if any dangerous creatures were nearby. Black bears and moose were not uncommon in these parts. He'd be in a world of hurt if he blundered into either of those. The sounds of nocturnal creatures in the underbrush struck him as louder and more threatening than they had a minute ago.

Navigation through the thick growth required both hands. He used the walking stick like an insect uses its antennae, probing the air and the ground in front of his feet. If he stayed on course, he'd eventually run into Scots Brook. A few yards past that stream was a set of railroad tracks he would follow back south to the highway. From there, it would be an easy couple of minutes to his next goal.

It took almost two hours, but he rejoined Route 2 a mile east of where he'd left her car. He was sweat-soaked and breathing hard. His feet were wet from crossing the brook. His pant legs were muddy at the knees. He hadn't eaten since lunch and had felt for the past hour as if his strength was fading. At least he could take off the suffocating ski mask. His destination was a few yards ahead on the left.

Brandon headed for the combination bowling alley and self-storage center. Despite his nervousness and fatigue, he grinned as he approached it; only out here in the boonies would such an unlikely mishmash of businesses exist. He'd rented a storage unit there months ago. Waiting inside was an old motor scooter he'd purchased for this occasion. He marched up to the gate, punched in the code, and accessed his unit. Inside, he stripped off his boots and clothes. He'd laid out a complete change of clothes on the floor. Clean and dry never felt so good. He unscrewed the end cap from a short PVC pipe and dumped a couple of granola bars and a small apple into his hand. It wasn't much, but it made him feel a little less spent. After eating, he balled his dirty clothes and boots into a trash bag. All that remained was to put the bag into a random dumpster on his way home.

Two hours later, he was back at the Maynard lot where his van waited. It was 4:30 a.m. on Sunday. Dawn would come soon, so this was cutting things kind of close. Newspaper carriers, elderly dog walkers, and insufferable morning people were liable to be up and about as soon as it was light. He wanted to be out of town before anyone saw him. The scooter went into the back of the van. Next, he removed the magnetic signs and stowed them inside to be destroyed later. Finally, he replaced the stolen tags with the proper registration plates, stuffing the stolen ones into a storm drain. Finished, he cranked the ignition and let a wave of giddiness wash over him.

He assured himself again that the deception would hold once her body washed up. Everything depended on that. The best way to avoid getting caught was to stay off the police radar. He'd given himself an excellent shot at that. There were regular patrols of the bridge parking lot. They'd find her car, ticket it, and tow it. It would sit in some impound lot until someone connected it with a missing person report or a death investigation. Authorities would consider the circumstances and figure she was yet another jumper. After all, an autopsy would find river water deep in her lungs. No one would dream she'd inhaled that river water in her own laundry tub. And she'd have the broken bones and shattered organs that were typical of a fall into water from a great height. It was perfect.

And even if someone suspected foul play, there was nothing to tie Brandon to it. He'd left no fingerprints in the house or car. Even the boots he'd worn hadn't been his actual size or brand. In a few days, he'd take one more step to distance himself from all of this. He'd mail her the alimony payment that was coming due. Meanwhile, if anyone asked about his whereabouts the last few hours, he'd say he was at home. He'd be back there by sunrise. His cell phone was there now, streaming one of the longest videos on YouTube; one more layer in an alibi he hoped never to need. The other residents of the warehouse were sleeping off their Saturday night chemicals of choice and wouldn't witness his return. All he had to do now was get back to Roxbury without incidents, accidents, or traffic tickets. Feeling almost euphoric, he began whistling a melody. It took him several repetitions of the same snippet to register that it was from the Bobbie Gentry tune, the last song on his playlist, the line about tossing something off the Tallahatchie Bridge. He started laughing again and didn't stop for a long time.

CHAPTER 7
VOICES

On her Sunday morning power walk, Roz was still replaying yesterday's conversation with Shawna. She wondered whether she was approaching the problem of personal fulfillment all wrong. A career wasn't the only place in life to pursue meaningful activity. "Down the street," Shawna had said. Roz figured Mrs. Grimm's house was an obvious place to start. Maybe more than lunch was in order; maybe she could be of real help to her elderly neighbor. What might the woman need? As Roz approached the turn onto Elm Street, she tried to think of how to broach the subject. It turned out to be unnecessary. Although the weather was nice, Mrs. Grimm was nowhere to be seen. *Oh, well. There's always tomorrow.*

A few hours later, Roz was in her usual spot in the sanctuary of Solid Rock Church. Having felt so dispirited since Friday, she compounded the emotional burden by reproaching herself for feeling bad. If today's service would help her find her lost wellspring of contentment, she'd be oh so grateful. As she settled herself on her bench, Vera Robinson came bustling up. She was the choir director, and she looked flustered. "Sister Pitts, there has been a change. We need you to sing lead in place of Sister Bell, who won't be joining us today."

Roz smiled. "Sure, no problem. It's not like I don't know the songs."

Vera relaxed enough to let her shoulders drop a couple of inches. "Thanks for being so flexible." She hurried away, no doubt thinking of a dozen details to sort through before the top of the hour.

But Shawna Bell wasn't out sick this morning. She was sitting in her accustomed seat. And if she had planned to sit out the choir selection, she should have said something yesterday at lunch to give Roz time to prepare. This change in the program today might have been as unexpected for Shawna as it was for Roz. Did she have a sudden sore throat? Or was something else going on?

If something else was afoot, Shawna had been her usual tight-lipped self. There would be time to get the scoop later. Right now, it was time to find her place in line for the choir processional.

The processional had become one of her favorite parts of the service. It was a triumph to march in with everyone else in the choir. Not so long ago, Roz had had to use a different entrance to the sanctuary and position herself on the risers while the choir marched to her. In those days, the walk down the aisle would have made her too breathless to sing. And the two canes she'd once needed to take the pressure off her knees made for bad optics. But since she had lost so much weight, and the canes along with it, Roz was the choir's proudest member, besides being its second-best voice.

The service began. An assistant pastor read the invocation and prayed. Organ music filled the air, and the choir marched in. Roz glanced at Shawna, but her friend's expression betrayed no feelings about sitting out the song she'd been working so hard on in rehearsals. Roz felt bad for her, but had to shove such thoughts aside. It was time to thread the needle.

Threading the needle, walking the tightrope, hitting the bullseye—all were different ways that she conceptualized the same challenge. Solid Rock had a diverse congregation with disparate tastes in music. The challenge was to make the song connect with everyone.

The oldest attendees wanted to hear hymns from the now disused hymnals. They said the old standards such as "It Is Well with My Soul," "Great Is Thy Faithfulness," and "Amazing Grace" had a depth of thought to them that was not to be found in the praise and worship songs that were now in vogue. The old folks, traditionalists all, derided modern fare as "7-11 tunes." The reference was not to the convenience store of the same name, but to the fact that so many modern songs were trite six- or seven-word catchphrases repeated eleven or more times in a row. Composers of the old hymns served up theological nourishment, not musical cotton candy.

The millennial cohort took the opposite view. They had grown up on secular pop, rock, and country. Lyrics were for encapsulating a feeling, not presenting a theological dissertation. Take a good lyrical hook, add a catchy melody, and couple them to a beat that made you want to clap your hands and move your feet. You could enjoy church music like that. It was infectious and motivational. Who on earth could get excited about the stuffy formality of old hymns? King James English was obsolete before any of their great-grandparents had been born. Why would anyone want to sing such museum pieces? Even the happiest of old hymns sounded funereal to millennial ears.

The generational divide wasn't the only fault line in the musical culture of the church. There were also issues of Black and White. For around 20 percent of Solid Rock's membership, the phrase *gospel music* meant arrangements with a high melanin content. The sound might be hard to define, but it was easy to recognize. On top of the standard chord progressions and rhythmic features, vocal gymnastics and stellar technique were the order of the day. Gospel fans reasoned no one went to an NBA game to see high school-level play. And if you went to Symphony Hall, it was to hear some of the best musical compositions of all time interpreted and performed by some of the best musicians in the world. You wanted to stand in awe of those performers, not to think you could have done as well yourself. Why should church be any different? Soloists in church were not only ministering to you, they were presenting a musical offering to God. It needed to be of the finest possible workmanship.

Roz had to connect with all these factions in under five minutes. The selection was "Jesus, You're the Center of My Joy." The song harked back over three decades, old enough for the traditionalists to have fond memories of it. Country gospel listeners would know it as a Gloria Gaither composition. Black gospel fans would remember Richard Smallwood's rendition. A song with cross-cultural appeal like this made her job easier.

The pianist played the intro. Roz delivered the first verse straight, without embellishment. Instead of vocal gymnastics, she counted on her signature timbre and immense dynamic range to do the heavy lifting. She could sing whisper-soft, so that people practically leaned forward to hear, or she could project so much power that her microphone was superfluous, even with all the other voices in the choir and the electrified instruments in the rhythm section. Regardless of volume, she had a smooth, rich vocal tone. Strangers sometimes remarked on it when they heard her speak. That timbre was even lovelier when she sang.

As each verse went by, she added additional elements to her delivery—an improvised bit of melody here, a subtle pitch bend there, a controlled vibrato whose speed and depth she could vary at will. She could leap large intervals without bobbling a note. Listeners with discerning ears would clap or shout after her more impressive feats. But the best thing about her technique was how she made it all sound effortless. Everyone in Solid Rock's congregation found something to like in her singing. She could feel it. More than anything, people responded to how she never let her performance upstage the material. The message was more important than the messenger.

She became so lost in the song it was as if she was singing to an audience of One. And in presenting her musical offering, she felt the peace that had eluded her for days. It was almost hard to remember why she had been so upset. Her singing ministered to the listeners and to herself—the best possible outcome.

At the midpoint of the service, the choir members returned to their seats and Pastor Bowers came to the podium to preach. Roz realized she was holding her breath as he finished reading his scripture text. She knew the service would either go higher from here or take a sharp turn downhill. The last few messages had been edifying. But that only meant Bowers was overdue for a meltdown. As with bear markets, wars, and natural disasters, the longer the man went without an outburst, the more inevitable an outburst became. Maybe Russian roulette was a more apt metaphor. If nothing went *bang* on a given pull of the trigger, everybody knew it wouldn't be long.

Attuned as she was to the nuances of tone, Roz picked up on the preacher's every inflection. He exuded confidence and calm. His deep baritone and professorial delivery were reassuring, encouraging her to open her heart and mind to learn. She steeled herself anyway; she'd been a member here long enough to know initial impressions could be wrong.

Sure enough, Roz felt the mood darken as the message wore on. Now Bowers was hammering the importance of unity, a state he said was best achieved by everyone doing what they were told.

He expressed dismay that there were some in the congregation who were resistant to letting him "speak into their lives." As the thrust of the message changed, so did the pastor's tone of voice. What had at first sounded like confidence and reassurance took on undertones of something less attractive.

Voices were funny things, Roz mused. When tightly controlled and carefully managed, a voice could disguise its owner's true nature. That was how the most venal and self-serving politician could sound like a noble leader when reading a prepared speech. But Solid Rock was not a church where preachers scripted out their sermons and read them. Roz knew they most often spoke from an outline, using the bulleted points as a road map to keep their otherwise extemporaneous remarks on course. With lots of room for improvisation, for flowing in the Spirit, the preaching was often the most exciting and dynamic part of the service. But as with singers and musicians, a preacher's freedom to improvise was a mixed blessing. The chosen words and their delivery shone a spotlight on the heart of the speaker. Sometimes they revealed love and compassion. Sometimes they revealed pettiness or spite. It was not a rarity for both laudable and lamentable sentiments to inhabit the same message.

More than anything else, the pastor sounded tired. He might try to hide it behind a geyser of vehemence and indignation, but to Rosalyn's ears, it was clear as a bell. She had come in search of encouragement. And she'd found it, if only for a few minutes. What followed was an exercise in long-suffering patience. Maybe God knew that was what she needed most. Rather than be angry that the preacher was spending yet another Sunday morning berating people, she offered a prayer on his behalf. He might have had an even harder week than she'd had. *Let him find respite from whatever is making him so sour.*

After the benediction, Shawna made her way over to Rosalyn's bench. "Excellent job, Roz! You really sang that song today."

"Thanks, sis. You'd have done better, but I was happy to help. One thing is confusing me, though: I'm guessing you knew yesterday that this was coming, right?"

"True. I thought you had troubles enough of your own to deal with."

"I guess I did," Roz agreed. "But I'm feeling better now, in case you need an ear or a shoulder."

To Roz's surprise, Shawna flicked her gaze in the direction of the side exit and courtyard. She headed in that direction with Roz following close behind. Most people would exit the sanctuary from the main doors. There would be fewer people in the courtyard, so the two friends could talk there without being overheard.

Once they were standing among the trees and benches of the courtyard, Shawna said, "This was punishment. The pastor sat me down from the choir."

"For what? What could you have done that was so bad?"

Shawna pursed her lips and sighed. "So how do I talk about this? I mean, you're not supposed to talk about the pastor, right?"

"Pastors everywhere say that's true. Even the ones who don't mind talking about you. And I suppose they're right,"

Roz conceded. "Why don't you talk about a fictional character instead? Tell me a story about this made-up person."

Shawna allowed herself a tight smile. "Clever. And what kind of story should I create?"

"High fantasy. This courtyard and the architecture of the building cry out for it."

"You are totally silly. Do you know that? Okay, I'll play." Shawna took a few seconds to think. "Once upon a time—a few days ago, actually—a fair maiden ventured to speak with her liege lord. She wished to petition him concerning another of his subjects who had left on some foolish quest. She asked what was being done to locate her wandering friend and bring him home. I believe you already know this part of the tale, yes?"

"I do. A dear friend told me only yesterday, though I fear she left out key details."

Shawna waved her hand in dismissal. "It's a rather short story, not much to tell. The nobleman became irate. Maybe *wroth* is the more period-correct word. He reminded the maiden that he had advised her to erase the missing knight errant from her thoughts. He, therefore, wished to know why she had broached this subject a second time."

Roz thought calling Eddie a "knight errant" was a brilliant double meaning.

But Shawna was becoming animated now and dropped the high-fantasy construct. "Let me tell you straight, sister: beware of tyrants in servants' garb! Most people know what advice is. Advice is when someone gives you an opinion or a recommendation to be considered. That man"—here she rolled her eyes toward the pastor's office—"that man sees no difference between giving advice and giving orders. He thinks his advice is to be obeyed, not merely considered."

Roz glanced around the courtyard. There were a few people about, but none were close by. Still, she was concerned their words might carry farther than intended. She lowered her voice a bit, hoping Shawna would take the hint and do the same. "It's a well-known conceit among those in the minis—er, I mean the minor nobility. You must have noticed that, given the years you've spent in the Kingdom." She chuckled at the unplanned wordplay. "The attitude must come with rank."

"I have noticed it. And I agree it's pretty rank, which brings me to my second issue. To put it in terms of our little fantasy tale, several of this man's retainers are determined to court me."

"I see. Forgive my utter lack of experience with having multiple suitors, but would you explain why that's a problem?"

Shawna looked impatient. "It's a problem because that man is mentoring them, training them to follow his example. They're learning to both think and act like him. Look, I'm more than ready to get married, but none of those guys are what I want in a man."

Now there was a revelation. Shawna was more than ready to marry. Lots of guys had made a play for Shawna, but the church's most pursued woman had never paid much attention to any of them. She'd shown no interest in the game. Maybe that was a false front. Shawna had always been hard to read, even for those closest to her. She kept a lot to herself, making it feel as if she knew her friends better than they knew her. While she would do almost anything to help or comfort you, she had a way of keeping you at arm's length even while giving you a hug. Roz had always thought of Shawna's guardedness as a kind of armor; a learned response to a social environment where a confidence whispered in the ear today might reverberate from the pulpit tomorrow. Whatever the reasons, such forthrightness was an unexpected gift. Careful to mask her surprise, Roz asked, "What do you want in a man?"

"For starters, I want someone who respects my intelligence and can keep up with it. Beyond that, I've got a whole wish list of attributes, starting with kind and humble and ending with handsome and successful."

The two friends laughed. Roz resisted the temptation to yell, "Ants!" even though wish lists like Shawna's must be common to every ant in the anthill. "Surely you didn't say any of this in your audience with the lord of the manor. So why did he relieve you of your duties?"

"Ego. He knows Christ is King, but he sees himself as regent in the Lord's absence."

Roz winced. "That was harsh."

"Maybe I should put it this way: it was for giving him an honest answer to his question. Like I said, he asked why I revisited that conversation about Eddie. I told him it was because of the parable of the lost sheep. I pointed out how the man in that parable didn't say 'good riddance' when he lost a sheep. He left the ninety-nine to go seek the one that was lost. And he rejoiced when he found it."

"Ouch. I imagine that didn't go over well."

"Like a Trump sign at a Bernie Sanders rally. I don't think you'll be seeing me up on the platform again."

"Fear not," Roz said, trying to reassure. "This, too, shall pass."

Shawna gave her a searching look. "Whatever career choice you make, Roz, stay away from meteorology."

"Pardon me?"

But her friend said nothing else. The animation vanished from her features. If the eyes were, indeed, the windows of the soul, Shawna Bell had drawn the blinds and closed the curtains. There would be no more revelations today.

Contact in five . . . four . . . three . . . two . . . Roz rounded the corner onto Elm Street. But the voice she most wanted to hear was nowhere to be found. No cheery greeting came from the ranch house on the right. She bit back disappointment. It was unlike Mrs. Grimm not to be out fussing over her potted flowers, taking in the fresh air, and shouting, "Good morning, neighbor!" when Roz hit the final straightaway on her power walk. Mrs. Grimm rarely missed a day, not even in the cold, damp weather of early spring. Now she had missed four days in a row. Why should she be indoors on this beautiful Wednesday morning in summer?

Roz stopped and considered ringing the bell, but thought it might be impolite at such an early hour. Maybe Mrs. Grimm was sleeping in. Fatigue must be a fact of life at her age. Roz went home and looked up her neighbor's phone number online. She dialed the number during her lunch break that day. Although it rang many times, there was no answer and no voicemail. *I hope nothing's wrong.*

CHAPTER 8
THE OLD MAN DOWN THE ROAD

Everybody in Roz's department at work had been tight-lipped and grim-faced all week. People talked less than usual, and when they did talk, it was often to snap at a colleague over something trivial. Roz knew letting employees go wasn't the most unpleasant thing about layoffs. In the aftermath, the responsibilities of the laid-off employees had to be reallocated among those who remained. Everyone, including Roz, would have to pick up the pace and get more done, all for no more pay than they had been making before the layoffs. It was the white-collar equivalent of factory foremen speeding up the line. Roz tried to smile through it all, to stay upbeat, and to shrug off the resentment that was aimed at her. Still, between the emotional stress and the physical fatigue, she was glad the work week was over.

Saturday morning found her looking for the perfect gift. She settled on a tea-tasting assortment, hoping it was something Mrs. Grimm would like. They had agreed to meet in an hour. The more she thought about the nice little old lady who she hadn't seen all week, the more worried she became. At 11:55, she marched up to the woman's door and rang the bell.

She looked around the front porch while waiting for a response. Given her neighbor's age, it might take her a minute to get to the door. The mailbox on her left overflowed with mail. That suggested her neighbor was away and had forgotten to suspend her mail delivery. But Mrs. Grimm's car was still in the driveway, where it always sat. Roz wondered whether the car ever got driven.

A second push of the doorbell drew no more response than had the first one. A scratchy male voice said, "Wrong time of day for you, isn't it?"

Roz looked over to see a man with a ruddy face, a short white beard, and thick eyeglasses. He was standing in the yard next door. She smiled through her anxiety and answered, "I'm not sure what you mean."

"I only mean that I recognize you from your morning walks. I see you go by the front window most mornings before seven. And I know you're in the habit of chatting with Judy"—here he nodded toward Mrs. Grimm's door—"but it's the first time I've seen you around in the afternoon like this."

Roz shifted the decorative tin from one hand to the other, stepped off the porch, and took a few uncertain steps in the man's direction. "Yes, she and I are supposed to have lunch. But I haven't seen her all week. Have you?"

"Can't say that I have. I know she was bustling around last weekend. Even when I'm not looking this way, I can hear her hollering her good mornings to you. That woman's voice really carries." The old man's face twisted into a mischievous smile. He raised his hands in placation. "Not that it isn't a lovely sound, first thing in the morning."

Roz said, "I'm getting worried about her. She hasn't answered her doorbell or her phone. If her car were gone, I'd assume she was away, but since it's right there . . ."

"Yeah, her car never leaves that spot except on Friday afternoons. She does her banking, goes grocery shopping, and runs the car through a car wash before coming back home. At our age, I guess that's enough excitement for one week."

Roz looked more closely at the vehicle. She saw an accumulation of dust, pine needles, and bird droppings on the windshield. In no way did the car look like anyone had washed it yesterday. She looked at the overstuffed mailbox again. "I'm probably overreacting," Roz said to reassure herself, "but I'm going to call the police for a well-being check." She reached for her cell phone, only to realize she had left it at home. "Silly me. No phone. I'll need to run home to call."

The man objected. "Nonsense, there's a phone right inside the door here at my place. You can make the call from here and see when the police arrive."

Hesitating for a fraction of a second, Roz concluded the old fellow couldn't pose much of a threat. And his offer was the good neighbor thing to do. She nodded her gratitude. "Lead the way."

Inside his front door was a sunroom with windows on three sides and potted plants everywhere to take advantage of the abundant sunlight. They lined the windowsills, sat atop bookcases, and even peeked out from the gutted interior of what had once been a big console TV.

A second door led to the main part of the house. In the living room, an old corded phone sat on a TV table next to a reclining chair with worn upholstery. The man gestured to the phone. Roz didn't want to call 9-1-1, fearing a wellness check didn't qualify as an emergency. But without her smartphone, she had no way to look up the police department's business number. She explained her quandary to Mr. Schroeder, who looked amused and pointed to a phone book sitting next to the phone. *And it isn't even Throwback Thursday.* She put her gift box down, found the number on the cover of the phone book, and relayed her concerns to the dispatcher. Dispatch assured her an officer would swing by to check on Mrs. Grimm.

"Thank you, Mr. Schroeder," she said after she'd hung up. "My name is Rosalyn, by the way. Rosalyn Pitts. I'm your neighbor three doors down." She pointed toward her house.

"Pleased to make your acquaintance," he said, running a hand over his thin white hair. "But how did you know my name?"

Roz laughed. "It's on the mailbox at the end of your sidewalk. I've been walking past it every morning for months."

Something was making a jingly sound, and it was drawing nearer. A small puffball of a dog, mostly Pomeranian by the looks of it, came in from another room and marched right up to Roz.

"Don't mind Sarge," Mr. Schroeder said. "He thinks it's his duty to inspect anyone who comes over. He's self-important, but he's also an old softy who loves everybody." The dog sniffed delicately at Roz's knee, let out a single shrill bark, and wagged his tail before turning and marching back whence he had come.

"Looks like you've passed muster," the old man announced.

"He's the cutest little thing! And I love the name." Roz giggled while Mr. Schroeder beamed.

"He was my wife's," he explained. "I wanted a real dog, a man's dog, like a German Shepherd or an Akita. But the missus insisted on this little half-pint rescue dog. Once he got here, he took over the place like he was the senior officer. Calling him Sarge seemed to fit."

Roz caught the use of the past tense—"was my wife's"—and inferred that the man was a widower. The silence stretched on for a bit, so she asked, "How long have you and Mrs. Grimm been neighbors?"

"Half a lifetime, I guess." He sighed, perhaps an old man's acknowledgment that the road ahead was now much shorter than the road behind. "Laura and I bought this house over forty years ago. Judy and her husband Eric arrived in the neighborhood a year or two after we did. We got to be great friends, the four of us. We were birds of a feather, so to speak."

From the corner of her eye, Roz saw a Framingham police cruiser drive past the house. "Here they are," she said. She and her newest acquaintance went out and crossed the lawn to hail the officer as he exited his vehicle.

"I'm the one who called," Roz told him.

After listening to her explain her concerns, he advised Roz and the neighbor to stay where they were while he investigated. He went to the front door, rang the bell, and announced himself. He also tried the door, which was locked. After a minute passed with no response, he circled the house, peering in the windows. When he got to the window at the corner near the back, he said something into the radio mic on his shoulder. Roz picked out the code phrase 10-54, but did not know what it meant. Nor could she make out the rest of what he said. The cop disappeared around the back. A sharp crack suggested he had broken open the back door.

Within minutes, an ambulance arrived, along with another police car. The patrolman in the house opened the front door and let them all in. Roz and Mr. Schroeder stood beside the driveway while the minutes crawled by. Another vehicle arrived, this one a van bearing the words Office of the Medical Examiner on the doors. After the driver went inside, the first patrolman walked over. He lowered a handkerchief he'd been holding over his nose and confirmed what both neighbors already knew: Judy Grimm was inside, and she was dead.

The officer asked them whether Mrs. Grimm had any known medical conditions. Once he determined that Roz hardly knew the woman, and that Mr. Schroeder had done little more than wave at her in the years since his own wife died, he didn't keep them long. Schroeder told the officer there was no family to notify; Judy had been an only child and a widow, and she had never had children herself. He hadn't known her to have company in recent years. The cop sighed. "That's rough," he said. "At least she's in a better place now."

That was a comforting thought. Not at all comforting to Roz, but both the officer and Mr. Schroeder seemed to appreciate the sentiment. Roz saw it as one of those things people said, because who knew what to say in the presence of death? Sometimes people said the words with heartfelt conviction. Other times it was rote formality, the perfunctory fulfillment of perceived social obligation. Either way, when someone died, people rushed to assure all and sundry that the deceased was in a better place.

Roz assumed they meant heaven. Perhaps they imagined heaven as the destination of all good people, or at least people who were not horrible. Except for genocidal dictators, serial killers, or child molesters, they figured everyone spent the afterlife in a better place. Roz half wished she could share in the comfort of that notion. Blissful ignorance must feel so much better than dreadful uncertainty or sad knowledge to the contrary. Roz knew heaven wasn't the reward of the decent or the good, because no one could be good enough. Heaven was reserved for the redeemed. Was Mrs. Grimm redeemed? All Roz could do was hope.

But if she was not . . . well, best not to dwell on it. There was guilt enough in the problem of the postponed lunch. From the sound of things, Mrs. Grimm had led a solitary existence. Was she lonely? Was that why she had extended herself to chat every morning? A shared pot of tea and an hour or two of small talk wasn't much to ask. It might have been the woman's last request in this life, and Roz had been too caught up in her own troubles to grant it.

After saying goodbye to the officer and her neighbor, Roz turned homeward, eager to be gone before she had to see a body bag on a gurney. Mr. Schroeder rushed inside to retrieve her gift box. She thanked him, though she took no joy in getting it back. It was now a pretty little box of regrets. If she kept it, it would always remind her of this day. But it would be wasteful to throw it away. Since Roz couldn't abide wastefulness, she knew she'd have to find something useful to do with it.

She would have liked to turn to one of her church friends to share the day's sorrow, but that would only result in another measure of guilt and regret being added to the load she already bore. Someone from church might ask, "Did you witness to her?" Or "Did you invite her to church?" These were two versions of the same question, both with the same awful implication: that Roz had failed in her most basic duty, perhaps with eternal consequences for the neighbor. If the poor old lady hadn't known the Lord, it might have been Rosalyn's appointed task to make the introduction. That's what her friends would think, even if they said nothing.

Their silent disappointment could sting as much as any rebuke. That kind of pressure might be what turned so many Christians into dogged proselytizers of the unwilling. These were the folks who would steer every conversation into a discussion of your immortal soul. They'd talk about God to the most uninterested people. They'd offer to pray for situations in the lives of militant atheists. Besides wearing their faith on their sleeve, they proclaimed it on T-shirts, coffee mugs, bumper stickers, and lapel pins. They thought every disaster, from wars and earthquakes to stock market crashes and bad weather, was proof that Jesus was coming back within weeks, if not within days. When their singlemindedness made them social outcasts, they didn't care. They thought themselves near kin to the martyrs, suffering for the Gospel and wearing it like a badge of honor.

Rosalyn had never been one of those people. She didn't hide her beliefs, but she had no interest in forcing them on anyone. Everywhere were vegans, yoga fans, keto dieters, and multilevel marketers in full missionary mode. Not to mention the flat Earthers and the conspiracy theorists who said 9/11 was an inside job, and that the Boston Marathon bombing was a hoax featuring amputee actors. In the end, most people didn't want to hear any of it. They preferred you to keep your enthusiasms and your more-enlightened-than-thou revelations to yourself. They wanted to be left in peace, and Roz was content to oblige them. Most days, that felt like wisdom. But some at church would call it dereliction of duty. Today, she worried they might be right.

An hour later, Roz sat in her oversized leather recliner, sipping a glass of ice water, lost in thought. She would never have an answer to the question of what had happened to the soul of Mrs. Grimm. But it was plain to see that the woman had died in the manner Roz most hoped to avoid—alone, with no one to grieve her passing or keep her memory alive. Dying like that was like never having lived.

The mystery of what to do with her life loomed even larger than before. Perhaps Shawna was right to think the problem had no solution. Maybe Roz was behaving like an ant or a worker bee with implausible ambitions. As she tried to sort it all out, the environment shifted around her. Impossible though it was, she was now standing in an unfamiliar stairwell. It was the type with two parallel stairways joined by a landing halfway up or down between floors. The stairwell stretched upward and downward as far as the eye could see. This must be an enormous skyscraper; was she in Boston's Prudential Tower, or maybe the Hancock? No, even they couldn't be this tall. Besides, wasn't she at home in her favorite chair? This was disorienting.

Wherever this stairwell was, multitudes of other people thronged its steps. Some headed up, and some were going down. Roz struggled to remember where or when she had first gotten onto the stairs, and what direction she was supposed to be going.

She headed up. The sea of humanity surging around her was wondrous to behold. Men in well-tailored suits climbed alongside guys in bib overalls. There were women in high heels and miniskirts, as well as those wearing kaftans, kimonos, and camo fatigues. Some were traveling in groups, talking in at least a dozen different languages. A gaggle of preteen children, shrieking with laughter, came charging down the stairs and almost bowled over an old lady who was tottering her way up.

As she looked to see whether the woman would keep her feet, Roz noticed that the walls of the stairwell had changed. She was positive they had been cinderblock, painted in that bland institutional beige used in so many public schools and parking garages. Now rich paneling and recessed lighting surrounded her. Bewildered, she resumed her climb, looking down at her feet to avoid any missteps.

When she next looked up, the walls were different again. And not only where she stood; the change continued seamlessly above and below. A distant corner of her mind informed her that this was a dream, so things didn't have to make sense. That thought wasn't as reassuring as it might have been. She wasn't one for naps and didn't remember having gone to sleep.

Roz climbed ever upward. The landing on each floor had an exit door. She planned to exit on the next floor, as it might help her figure out where on earth she was. But as she drew closer to the door, she felt increasingly wary of it. She couldn't bring herself to push on the crash bar and walk through. It wasn't exactly fear, more like a gut feeling that she shouldn't be in a hurry to discover what lay beyond. Many other people ascending and descending the stairs also took care to stay well clear of the doors. Maybe they felt the same instinctive aversion Roz did. Maybe they knew something she didn't.

Roz took a moment to catch her breath, surprised that climbing imaginary stairs was so taxing. When she resumed, she saw something unexpected on the next landing. A youngish man was lying face up on the floor, stretched out in front of the door. A couple of uniformed paramedics knelt over him, performing CPR. Although she was no medical expert, it didn't look as though they were having any success. She could see the downed man's face. The appearance of his skin and teeth testified to a life lived hard and fast. He looked dead. *Probably a drug overdose*, Roz thought with genuine sympathy. She quickened her pace and kept climbing.

Three floors higher up, she watched as an old man staggered against the crash bar. The door flew open as if spring-loaded. She tried to peer through the opening but saw nothing beyond. Better to say that it was nothingness she saw—not an empty hallway or a darkened room, but the complete absence of anything at all. She got the impression of an immense and impenetrable gray void. The old man shrank back from it. A barely perceptible entity, like a will-o'-the-wisp, detached itself from the man's body. A mirror image of its container, a gossamer luminescence that seemed wrought of smoke and moonlight, it shot out through the door. The man himself collapsed to the floor of the landing like a discarded husk.

Horrified, Roz could do nothing but continue her climb. On floor after floor, the same scene replayed itself. Some unfortunate soul touched the crash bar, whereupon the door sprang open, and the doomed person's doppelgänger left the stairwell and whooshed into the void. The door slammed shut while the corpse fell to the floor. Roz didn't let her gaze linger. It felt wrong to gawk at the last seconds of some stranger's life. But even as she turned away from the latest wisp of soul and/or spirit that was leaving the material world, she caught an odd flicker of movement so creepy it made her shiver. She turned to look, but whatever had caught her peripheral vision was gone. The entire scene was fading away, and her living room was coming back into view.

She again felt disoriented as she lost her immersion in the stairwell and the real world displaced it, pushing it almost beyond recall. Still, she could have sworn . . . yes, it was right before the last door had banged shut. Something was different about that one. She was certain the movement she'd seen had been another of those ghostly apparitions crossing the threshold. Only this one had been coming *in*.

Returning to herself felt like breaking the surface of a pool after coming up from a dive. There was time for one indrawn breath before the shock of realization hit her: this could not have been a dream, because she hadn't been asleep. She was sitting upright in her chair, still holding the glass of ice water. She hadn't spilled a drop.

Because she didn't know what to make of it, Roz decided not to tell anyone about her experience. Could this have been a vision from God? If it was, she didn't have any new understandings or illuminations to show for it. And why should she—she was no prophet, nor had she ever been given to spiritual dreams and visions. A brief online search convinced her she'd had a waking dream. The clinical term was *hypnagogia*, a word she found preferable to the more disreputable *hallucination*, though it meant the same thing. Principal triggers included recreational drug use, narcolepsy, bipolar disorder, stress, and anxiety. Roz ruled out the first three things, so she concluded she needed less stress and anxiety in her life.

Coming home from church the next day, Roz noticed Mr. Schroeder and his dog out in their front yard. She had a few questions she wanted to ask him, so she walked over. After an enthusiastic greeting from Sarge and some cursory pleasantries with the neighbor, she got down to business.

"If Mrs. Grimm had no family, who is going to handle her funeral arrangements?"

"I'm told the county has a department that handles that sort of situation. When someone dies alone, there are people who'll go through the house, search for any contacts, that sort of thing. If there are no heirs to be found, the county will figure out how to dispose of her stuff."

"Do you know if she was a religious person?"

"She didn't belong to a church, if that's what you mean. As for her beliefs—well, folks as old as Judy and me aren't too quick to broadcast our innermost thoughts the way young people today do. I don't know what she believed in. But don't you worry. If she has a connection to some religious tradition, the county will dig it up. They'll get the right person to officiate at whatever funeral services they have."

Wondering who would officiate at Mrs. Grimm's funeral was the least of Rosalyn's concerns. But her reason for asking would not be easy to explain to Mr. Schroeder, so she let the matter drop. Instead, she thought about trees that fell in forests where no one was present to hear any sound. "It's such a shame to live an entire life and have no one who will miss you or honor the fact that you were here," she said.

"Let me show you something," her neighbor urged.

He turned and walked back toward his front door while Roz followed. Inside, he gestured her to the chair next to the phone she had used yesterday. He held up his index finger in the universal gesture for "wait a minute," and disappeared around the corner.

Roz glanced around while his footsteps receded down the hall. As at her house, books were everywhere. Unlike at her house, the furniture was all mismatched, and there was a smattering of vintage electronics sitting around: an old console TV, a classic shortwave radio, and a stereo receiver with a built-in eight-track player. The man returned in a moment with a military uniform in a dry-cleaner's plastic bag.

"Corporal, U.S. Army," he announced. He stood a little straighter than before. "I got my honorable discharge in 1975 after seeing active duty in Vietnam. The morning after I close my eyes for the last time, whoever finds me should call the honor guard agent for the Army. They'll arrange my funeral with military honors. I keep the contact info around here somewhere," he said, "but you can always call the local VFW hall. They'll know how to get things rolling." He laid the bagged uniform out on his orange crushed velour couch before sitting in an armchair opposite Roz.

"I'm like Judy Grimm," he said, shrugging. "No living family—at least none that I'm in contact with. But the Army will take care of me. And now that it's fashionable to run around saying 'thank you for your service' to those who wear the uniform, I bet I'll even have a few strangers show up for my funeral. Probably the adult children of the people who spat on us back in the day."

The Vietnam War had ended fourteen years before Roz was born, but she had read about the often-shameful treatment visited on returning servicemen by protesters and antiwar activists. No one did nasty quite like an activist, no matter what the cause *du jour* was. Of course, today's activists were more likely to be part of a mob of keyboard warriors on Twitter or Facebook than to confront actual warriors in person, one-on-one.

"Well, it may be forty-some-odd years late," she said, "but thank you for your service."

Her neighbor nodded in acknowledgement. "Eh, that stuff was a long time ago, like I said. I ought to be over it by now."

Roz looked around again. "I see you've surrounded yourself with a lot of military-themed books," she said.

"Yeah, war is fascinating. It brings out the extremes in people—love and hate, bravery and cowardice, heroism and . . . well, you get the idea. From the Battle of Thermopylae to Desert Storm, the technology of warfare changes, but the people never do. Every war is different, but still contains the same stories as all the others. It's an awful business, but there is nothing like combat to teach you who you are. Yeah, I used to love my military history books."

Roz wanted to ask him to elaborate on how war had taught him who he was, but she decided against it. It wasn't as if she could find her purpose by running out to join the Army Reserve. She focused on his last statement. "You used to? You don't now?"

"The old eyesight isn't what it used to be. I can read the spines if I stand right next to them, but I can't make out much of what's on the pages."

Roz stood and walked to the nearest bookcase. "You can get audio books now, you know. Professional narrators read them to you." Roz figured a man who owned a cathode-ray TV and an eight-track player might not know about downloading audio books to a cell phone.

She chose a random book, opened to the first chapter, and began reading aloud. After hearing a few sentences, the old man said, "*Escape from Colditz.*" Roz doubted that he'd been able to read the title from across the room. She tried another.

"That's an easy one: *War and Peace.* And you have a wonderful reading voice, by the way."

Roz read from the opening pages of half a dozen books, and he quickly identified each one. This man was sharp as a tack. When Mr. Schroeder mentioned that he especially liked the last book she picked up—*All Quiet on the Western Front*—Roz carried the book back to her chair and continued reading. The old man sat back and listened. Sarge came over carrying a chew toy, and without so much as a by your leave, jumped up and wriggled his way into a comfortable position on her lap.

After she had been reading for a while, her neighbor interrupted to say, "I could happily listen to you read the nutrition information on a box of cereal. You'd make it enthralling."

Roz offered her best aw-shucks laugh. From that day forward, she came over every Saturday to give Mr. Schroeder the gift of his own books. She'd read for thirty to forty-five minutes, and the two of them would discuss the material. Once, she brought her own favorites for a change of pace. It surprised her to discover that her neighbor appreciated good poetry. He closed his eyes and sighed deeply upon hearing *Lake Isle of Innisfree* by Yeats. Her rendition of Poe's *The Raven* earned a round of applause. He sat with a spellbound expression through her reading of *The Destruction of Sennacherib*, though his apparent enthusiasm for that war story cooled a bit when he heard the last line, and Roz explained that the whole account was based on a Bible passage in 2 Kings 19. Still, he listened politely, and Roz pretended not to notice his ambivalence about the source material.

During their weekly discussions, he dispensed random bits of wisdom garnered over a lifetime and delivered with the placid certitude of the elderly. Thus, he told her that Heinz was the only real ketchup; that of all the musical genres, only country songs had proper moral underpinnings; and that there was no judge of character so perceptive as a dog. On that last point, at least, they both agreed.

CHAPTER 9
COME TOGETHER

Two middle-aged men disembarked a dark Ford SUV and walked toward Brandon as he left The UPS Store with his mail. He'd never seen them before. They wore dress slacks, Oxford shirts, sport coats, and ties. Their attire was unusual for this part of town. It was not natty enough to be the uniform of investment brokers or fund managers from the Financial District who sometimes visited the South End's trendier restaurants. Doctors, nurses, and orderlies from the nearby hospital on Harrison Ave. would be in lab coats or scrubs. Local workers and shop owners favored casual dress. These two didn't have the look of Jehovah's Witnesses going door-to-door to pass out literature and corner people into unwanted conversations about the end of the world. Their facial expressions broadcast the weary skepticism of people who had seen and heard it all, mixed with the hyperalertness of hounds eyeing something they might get to chase. They were still a few feet beyond the distance at which polite conversation usually takes place. Brandon beat them to the punch.

"Good morning, detectives."

If his powers of deduction surprised them, they didn't show it. "Brandon Heckler?" The speaker was the older of the two men, a jowly guy with salt-and-pepper hair and a face that sagged like a bloodhound's. His gaze darted between a photo he was holding and Brandon's face, as if confirming they were a match. "I'm Detective Genetti, and this is Detective Ambrose, Mass. State Police." The two men waved badges and ID cards in his general direction. "We'd like to have a word with you."

The self-satisfaction Brandon had felt when he made them as cops vanished. Two detectives had come looking for him, and there could only be one reason. His pulse quickened, as did his breathing. He wanted to be anywhere but here. And unless they planned to detain him, he had the right to walk away. But he was also curious. Satisfying that curiosity would require some amount of conversation.

"I see," Brandon said. "And what business might the State Police have with me?" He thought there might have been a slight quaver in his voice. He hoped the cops hadn't noticed.

Ambrose spoke this time. "Nothing that will take too long. Is there somewhere we can talk?" If Genetti was a bloodhound, the smaller Ambrose was an Airedale terrier, leaner, sharper of eye and ear, quicker of movement. He'd be the more aggressive of the two, the one who would play bad cop in the good cop/ bad cop routine.

Brandon noticed how the two had stepped apart from each other so they were almost flanking him. It was probably a cop reflex; the urge to make neutral ground feel more threatening. It reminded him of how much he disliked cops. They always played these stupid mind games. He had no reason to feel threatened; if they were going to arrest him, they'd have gone straight to the cuff-and-stuff, saving their questions until they had him in an interview room. He took a few unhurried steps to the side and placed his back against the wall of the building he'd exited. That would keep them both in front of him. "This is as good a spot as any," he said. "How can I help you?"

"It's about Margaret Brewster."

Genetti again. Brandon hoped the two of them would not play the conversation like a ping-pong match. He frowned. "What about her?"

"When was the last time you saw or spoke with her?"

"It's hard to say. You must be aware we're no longer married. We don't talk much."

That answer was a little slippery, but the question bothered him more than his deliberate nonanswer. As did the way the cops were watching him after asking it. Their mannerisms confirmed his initial unease. This had the look of a full-fledged investigation. Brandon had often tried to envision the events that must have followed the woman's death. Her coworkers would have worried when she didn't show up for work or call to explain her absence. When they couldn't reach her by phone, maybe one of them stopped by the condo. Nobody home. But none of that demanded a police investigation; people had an absolute right to quit their job, disappear, and start over somewhere else. She'd never kept in close touch with her family, so none of the relatives would have been hounding the police for a well-being check. Someone must have found her and identified the body already.

If that were true, the cops must have their doubts that it was suicide. Why else would they track him down? He had to find out what they knew. Not that they would volunteer much information. That wasn't how they played the game. They were there to get him talking, hoping he'd make their job easy by incriminating himself. The safest thing was to say nothing. But if he didn't talk to them, he couldn't discover where things stood. He decided he could play along if he kept his answers vague and avoided stupid mistakes, like referring to that accursed woman in the past tense.

The Airedale was talking again. "Well, would you say it's been days? Weeks? Months? Give me a ballpark."

"As far as I can recall, she hasn't had the pleasure of seeing my face at all this year. And we never talk on the phone, not since the divorce. Why? What's she accusing me of now?"

"She isn't." Genetti talking. "Mr. Heckler, I'm sorry to have to inform you that Margaret is dead. A hiker found her body in Turner's Falls. That's a village in the town of Montague, out in Franklin County. Are you familiar with that area?" Both detectives scrutinized him as they delivered this news. Or was he imagining that?

So the corpse had traveled only four or five miles downstream from the French King Bridge. Peg had been dead about a month. Brandon had been hoping she'd make it at least into Connecticut, if not all the way to New York Harbor. He also wondered why the Smokies were here. Didn't little Montague have its own police force?

Shelve that. Concentrate on getting through this. He ignored their last question. "When? How did she die?"

"She drowned. We'd have notified you sooner, but you haven't been easy to find."

"Wow, drowning is a bad way to go."

"That it is." Genetti again. "We believe she went into the water off a bridge a few miles upstream from where she washed ashore. The coroner said her injuries were mostly consistent with a fall into water from a great height. Sir, I need to ask: did you ever know your wife to be suicidal?"

Brandon frowned. "*Ex*-wife," he corrected. "And no, I can't say I did." The detectives said nothing, so Brandon continued. "Look, I appreciate the notification. But I'm not exactly next of kin anymore. Last I heard, both her parents were still alive, and she has a brother in New York. Shouldn't you be talking to her family instead of me?"

"We have," the Airedale assured him. "We're hoping you can help us tie up some loose ends."

That didn't sound good at all. He remembered the care with which the detectives had chosen their words: her injuries were *mostly* consistent with a fall into water. "We believe she *went into the water* off a bridge." Not quite the same as saying she jumped.

Brandon asked the obvious next question. "What loose ends?"

"Well, as you might expect, we are investigating her circumstances as best we can," Ambrose said. "None of her family, friends, or coworkers thought she seemed out of sorts. There is no evidence she was experiencing depression or other major health issues. No legal or financial troubles that we can find. So people are wondering why she would kill herself."

Genetti took over the story. "We've been retracing her steps. She was alive on the evening of June 11th, because she shopped at a drugstore near her home that afternoon, and again that evening. Her car was at the bridge by dawn the next morning, according to the company that towed it away. We asked ourselves why she would she pick up her prescription beauty cream if she was planning to kill herself. Why would the smiling woman on the store security video decide to throw herself off a bridge a few hours later? Can you shed any light on that?" For a guy seeking Brandon's help, this cop's tone sounded mighty accusatory.

Brandon shrugged. "Nope. It's been a long time since I could explain much of anything about her."

Ambrose asked, "Did you know she owned a gun?"

That was news to Brandon. And it threatened to make the suicide-by-bridge theory look rickety. "Nope again. She must have gotten it after I moved out."

"Yeah, she did. All legal, above board. It was in her nightstand. So if she wanted to end it all, the gun was close at hand. She could have done the deed in the comfort of her own bed, quick and painless. Instead, she leaves the gun at home, drives an hour to Erving, parks the car, walks out onto this high bridge, climbs the railing, and takes a swan dive into the darkness. It takes a lot more effort and physical courage to cash in your chips that way. You can see why this all looks a little odd to us."

Both cops were eyeing him closely again, as if they were half expecting him to take off running. This was all wrong. The plan had assumed no one would suspect a crime had occurred. These two not only suspected it, but they had also brought their suspicions and insinuations straight to him. If this went south, he might have already spent his last full day as a free man. He felt sweaty. Forcing himself to take a deep breath, he spoke in slow, measured tones. "All I see is that you're searching for logic and reason in a suicide. Suicide must be the world's most unreasonable act."

"You may be right," Genetti admitted. His voice was sympathetic, but his expression was not. "We're trying to make sure that suicide is what it was; that she went into the water of her own volition. We'd like to rule out any other possibilities. For starters, can you tell us where you were from the evening of Saturday, June 11th, through the following morning?"

Brandon's anger was unfeigned. "Let me see if I've got this straight." He struggled to keep his voice down. "You can't explain why she killed herself, so you speculate maybe she didn't. Then, with no evidence a crime even happened, you ask me for an alibi to prove I didn't do it. My respect for the police is growing by leaps and bounds here."

"Your sarcasm is duly noted. But put yourself in our shoes," Ambrose countered. "We know you and Margaret had some amount of conflict in your marriage. Yes, the prosecutor dropped the spousal battery charge. But it wasn't a friendly divorce, right? Add to that the fact no one in her circle believes she would have killed herself. And her death saves you a lot of future alimony payments. Last, but not least, you didn't look all that heartbroken when we gave you the news. Those things may not mean anything, but it's our job to make sure. All we're saying is this: show us you were somewhere else, and we'll know you're in the clear."

"Oh, so I didn't look heartbroken enough to you? Did you want me to dissolve into tears? Is that what Janet Brewster did?"

According to Peg, her mother had always displayed iron self-control. She was a Brit with the stereotypical stiff upper lip, and Brandon suspected she wouldn't have shed a tear even if she'd been slicing onions when she got the news.

Growing angrier by the second, Brandon continued. "You know what? Never mind about my favorite ex-mother-in-law. I don't care what she did. I care about this: I'm an American citizen, and that means I don't need to prove my innocence. If you're accusing me of something, you need to prove my guilt. I'm done answering questions. Enjoy your day." He edged past the cops and began walking away.

"Sure, you're free to go," Ambrose said, as if Brandon had asked his permission. "But first, give us an address and phone where we can reach you if we need to talk again."

Brandon fished in his wallet for a business card, which he handed to Genetti. "This is my lawyer. If you want to talk again, talk to him."

The bloodhound looked exasperated. "Do you really want to go down that road? All we want is to straighten this out. We're trying to give the family some closure, you know? If you've got nothing to hide, what's the problem? You should want to get this cleared up as much as we do. Lawyering up looks bad."

It was the tired old ploy depicted on a hundred TV shows. Cops tried to shame people into waiving their rights by implying that innocent people shouldn't need lawyers. But guilty or innocent, anyone being questioned by the police needed legal help. That was Civics 101. Brandon snorted and said nothing in response.

He felt shaky as he walked away. Rage, fear, or the predictable aftermath of an adrenaline dump? Probably all those things. He wondered how much danger he was in. He wished he hadn't talked to them at all. Curiosity had led him to break a cardinal rule, and now the cops had all but accused him of killing her. How many times had he reminded himself that you could only talk yourself into an arrest, never out of one? All his careful planning hadn't kept him from making a bonehead mistake.

The gun was an unexpected problem, assuming it existed. It was illegal to lie to the cops, but it was perfectly legal for them to lie to you. Peg had never wanted guns in the house when they were married, but she might have changed her views. There hadn't been time to search the house, even if he had thought to look for something like that. Still, he hadn't lied, so they couldn't catch him in one. He was positive he had left no evidence at the condo, in the car, or on the bridge. And he had kept nothing potentially incriminating. He'd terminated the rental on his storage unit and disposed of the contents. There might be video of him entering and leaving the self-storage facility. But he probably wasn't recognizable on the video anyway, although that wouldn't matter if the license plate on the scooter was legible. He hoped it would not be. Or that the facility hadn't kept the video long enough to matter.

What if they had? Video of him on the scooter near the bridge would prove he was nearby on the night she died. That didn't make him guilty of anything, but it would be too much of a coincidence for the detectives to ignore. Things would get ugly from there. What options did he have?

He could run. Taking his last bit of money out of the bank would fund a one-way road trip of maybe fifteen hundred miles. That could get him to Miami, or Little Rock, or Kansas City, or North Dakota. But which way should he go? Would it be better to disappear into the crowd of a big city, or hide in some remote rural area? Either way, he'd have to invent a backstory for himself, move to unfamiliar surroundings, find a place to live, and find work or start a business, all while looking over his shoulder for pursuers. Running would cement his guilt in the eyes of the cops. Getting pulled over for any minor traffic infraction could mean getting arrested on a warrant out of Massachusetts. So he'd need a new identity along with everything else. Could he pull it off?

Notorious Boston gangster Whitey Bulger had managed sixteen years on the lam before they caught him. There was also that guy from Lynnfield, Thomas Randele. Turned out his real name was Theodore Conrad, and he had fled to Massachusetts in 1969 after stealing $215,000 from the Cleveland bank where he worked. He changed his name and reported age, found a career selling cars, got married, had a kid, and died surrounded by friends and family at the ripe old age of seventy-one. Fifty-two years hiding in plain sight and the law had never caught up with him. So it could be done. But Brandon knew he wasn't up for spending his life jumping at shadows and wondering if each day of freedom would be his last.

He could go on as though nothing had changed. Those two bozos didn't have a case against him, or they would have arrested him. They had their suspicions, but that was all. Brandon could get on with his life, such as it was. But what if they found more evidence, built a case, and came for him? He'd need a good criminal defense lawyer, not the useless hack whose card he'd handed the cops. That guy had done nothing for Brandon except siphon off most of the money that hadn't gone to the baby killer. He'd be no help in a homicide case.

The problem was a first-class murder defense would cost way into six figures. Brandon didn't have anywhere near that kind of money. If he did, he wouldn't be spending his nights with the residents of *La Casa de Ratas*. People with lots of money could hire a legal dream team. That's how O.J. Simpson had walked. Poor folks got saddled with public defenders. Public defenders were a wink and a nod to due process, but not a real help. They had too many cases, too little time, and too few resources. Only an idiot would entrust his future to the so-called justice system's weakest link. Brandon was not an idiot. But he was almost broke, and he needed to fix that in a hurry if he were to have a chance of beating any charges. So how could he find a quarter-million dollars needed to fight for his freedom in the event he got arrested for murder?

Thanks to the racket that was family court, his biggest asset was gone. He had neither the credit nor the collateral to borrow enough. What options did that leave? Bank robbery? Binge-watching detective shows had taught him that the average take was small. The FBI got involved, and robbers almost always got caught. Knocking over an armored car was out too. He'd need partners in crime for that job. That meant more ways things could go wrong. Drug sales? He wouldn't know where to start. And there was a good risk of getting shot by your competition. No, none of those things would work.

What he needed was a benefactor; someone with money who knew him and didn't hate him. That, of course, left Peg's family out. Her parents were loaded. But they had declined to even meet him before the wedding and had disinherited her after it. After she pulled that little stunt that got him arrested, Peg had probably convinced them he was the devil incarnate. And while he had killed that accursed woman, they had no way of knowing that. Still, there would be no help there.

His own mother was a lost cause. Last he knew, she had crawled into a bottle and never come out. She wouldn't have any money, and probably wouldn't help him if she did. There was no other family except Uncle Al. Al was his mother's half-brother.

Brandon remembered childhood visits to Al's house. It was a nice ranch house with an enormous yard. Mom always teased Al about his frugality. He had an engineering degree and a cushy state government job, but a house full of chintzy furniture and outdated appliances. Al's wife disliked the teasing, and his mother hadn't much liked Al's wife, so the visits grew fewer and farther between. By the time Brandon had grown up, they had all fallen out of contact. Brandon decided it was high time to remedy that. This was his last surviving relative. Who could you turn to in time of need if not family? Uncle Al was sure to feel the same way. *He'd better.*

Brandon walked a circuitous route back to his warehouse loft to pack up his crates of gear. It was a precarious business getting them down the steep ladder to the third floor, and from there to his van. On his third trip back down the hallway, he ran into Vinnie, an on-again off-again resident of this, the city's least desirable rental.

"Bran the man! You leavin' us? Tired of the ambience here?"

"Yes to both questions," Brandon said. "I think I'm going to get some better digs." He put down the crate and fished in his pocket, pulling out two Ben Franklins to hand to Vinnie. "Just in case . . . do me a favor, would you? I may have to come back here if things don't work out. Could you make sure nobody takes my spot for a while? If I'm not back in a week, it's a safe bet I won't be coming back."

Vinnie pocketed the money and nodded. When he reached for the cash, Brandon noticed the skinned knuckles on Vinnie's right hand. "How's the leg-breaking business?"

Vinnie smirked. "You got it wrong. I'm in communications."

"Communications?" Brandon asked with a knowing grin. "How so?"

Vinnie held his right hand up, as if he was swearing an oath in court. "I'm a freelance communications facilitator." He made a fist and rubbed his knuckles. "Suppose a guy in Providence needs to send a message to a guy in Boston. He hires me to deliver the message loud and clear."

"Sounds like work that should pay pretty well. If you don't mind my asking, why live here in poverty's penthouse?"

"I don't live here, not most of the time. But sometimes we all need to get away, you know? This is a good place to drop out of sight for a few days. It's off the radar. And I'm not too picky about the amenities."

"I hear you. Hey, is there any way for me to get in touch with you . . . in case I ever need to, you know, send someone a message?"

"Sure. Call the guy that runs the shop downstairs. Ask to speak to Vinnie in Communications. He can put you through to me. If I take the gig, I'll deliver your message anywhere in New England. But I'm a busy guy and I don't work cheap, so only reach out to me for priority work, if you know what I mean."

"Understood. Thanks, Vinnie." Brandon walked away, congratulating himself. It couldn't hurt to have friends in low places.

The photos were everywhere—on the bookshelves, on the end tables, on the mantel, and on the walls. The numerous pictures of the woman who must have been Mr. Schroeder's now-deceased wife were the only photographs displayed in his home. With the day's reading done, Roz finally asked him about her. How long had they been married?

"Forty-five wonderful years," came the answer. "She was my first, last, and only wife. Marrying her was the smartest thing I ever did. She really was my better half." He declared they were a matched set, perfect together. He extolled her beauty, her work ethic, her fierce loyalty, her no-nonsense ways, and her love for him and the home they shared.

When he finally wound down, *wow* was the first word that came to Roz's mind. "It must be difficult to be parted from her."

The old man smiled. "Well, there's the secret: we're not parted. Not really."

Roz didn't know what to make of that. It was a strange thing to hear from a man who had heretofore spoken like such a clear-eyed realist. Being sentimental was one thing, but . . . not really parted? What did that even mean? Not wanting to say anything that might spoil his mood, she said nothing at all.

Mr. Schroeder must have understood the reason for her silence. He thought for a few seconds, as if weighing whether to explain himself. "Look," he said at length. "That's not as nutty as it probably sounded. When you meet a stranger, your relationship consists entirely of the present moment. When you live with someone for many years, the accumulation of moments turns into a mountain of memories. That mountain dwarfs the little sliver of 'now' you're experiencing." He pointed toward various parts of the house. "My Laura and I ate breakfast at that table every day, danced in this living room, slept in that bedroom, talked our hearts out—for decades. If I can't see her at this moment, what's that against so much history? Unless my memories desert me, I'll still have most of what I loved and cherished before she died. She's still here," he said, pointing first to his head and then to his heart. "That means we're never truly parted."

On her way home, Roz thought about his words. They were beautiful. They were heartfelt. And they were hiding something. She knew voices, and Mr. Schroeder's voice had carried an unmistakable note of misdirection.

She flashed back to her one and only date, which was more years ago than she cared to admit. Shawna had talked a friend into taking Roz on a blind date. The man said all the right things at the end; he'd had a good time, he enjoyed her company, they would do this again sometime, and so on. But he never asked her out again, even though they had run into each other a few times since. He volunteered that he was super busy at work, which she understood was both true and beside the point. It was easier and kinder of him to make an excuse than to confess he had no interest in a second date with the fat girl. Roz had internalized a valuable lesson: telling the truth was not the same as telling the whole truth. Over the years, she'd become adept at hearing the difference. She couldn't imagine what Mr. Schroeder's unspoken truth might be. Not that it mattered; everyone must have a few of them. None of her business.

When she reached her own house, she grabbed the mail from the box and headed up the walk. Her hand was inches from the doorknob when she froze. "Oh, poo!" The door handle looked to be caked with mud. The smell reached her nostrils a second later, and she realized the burnt umber smear wasn't mud at all. In fact, she had unwittingly summed up the situation with her euphemism. Who would do such a thing? Disgusted, she walked around to the rear door, but found someone had likewise defiled it. There was no way in.

First someone had keyed her car, and now this. She needed to figure out who her new enemy was. It had to be one of the people she'd laid off. She was sure she could rule out Phil. But Pam had been her habitual brooding, silent self. Julianna had made accusations and a none-too-subtle threat, and Trina had expressed feelings of betrayal. And hadn't Trina made some wisecrack about hot coals and horse manure? Was the filth on the doorknobs horse manure? Any of those three might be guilty. Or all of them.

She was going to have to get a doorbell camera to monitor the premises. The more immediate problem was getting into the house without grossing herself out. The solution was a walk to the nearest convenience store to buy trash bags. She'd wrap her hand in a bag to open the door and get in.

An hour later, the hardware on both doors gleamed again, all shiny and disinfected. Her mood was as noxious as the doors had been. She went to church on Sunday, but work concerns and worries about who was messing with her house kept her from focusing on the service. Shawna didn't attend, which was unusual. Roz made a mental note to call her as soon as she could recover her own equilibrium.

From the looks of things, that was going to take a while. That afternoon a songbird crashed into her kitchen window, and the loud report startled her into an almost scream. She went out to tend to the poor fellow. It was a chickadee, the sweetest and cheeriest of backyard birds. It lay motionless on the ground with its head and neck so twisted around that she knew at once it was dead. She buried it in the perennial garden. Poor little broken-necked birdie would never know what a fright it had given her. Her heart was still pounding when she went back inside.

The extra hours she put in at the office kept her too busy to brood much about her personal problems. The rest of the week was uneventful, a fact she welcomed. Before she knew it, another Saturday had rolled around. Time for her reading appointment with Mr. Schroeder. Roz made her way there at the usual time, eager for pleasant company and the chance to share the experience of his books.

She was reading from *The Iliad* when the front door opened, and heavy steps thudded across the sunroom floor. Sarge growled, leaped from her lap, and retreated to a corner behind Mr.

Schroeder. A muscular man in work boots and cargo pants walked in carrying two bags of groceries. He was of indeterminate age; older than Roz, but whether by a few years or a dozen, she couldn't tell. The man didn't speak. In fact, it looked as though he would ignore her and her host while making his way toward the kitchen.

The old man held up a hand. "One minute, please. I think introductions are in order." He looked at the newcomer and gestured in Rosalyn's direction. "Brandon, this is my neighbor and new friend Rosalyn Pitts. Rosalyn, meet Brandon Heckler, my nephew. He is staying with me for a while, so you two might as well get acquainted."

Roz stood and extended her hand for a handshake but retracted it when Brandon made no movement besides a curt nod. *Silly me. He's got bags in both hands.* She was about to apologize for the oversight when she found herself captured by his bone-chilling gaze. While his facial expression betrayed no emotion, looking into his eyes called to mind the abyss—dark, cold, and empty, as if something had sucked the soul out of his body. She suppressed a shiver. Still huddled in the corner, the dog whimpered. *Yeah, Sarge . . . my sentiments exactly.*

PART TWO
GHOST IN THE MACHINE

CHAPTER 10
YOU DON'T BELIEVE

A Monday in August

Roz set to work installing the doorbell cameras she had ordered online. She could think of little besides how creeped out she had felt over meeting Mr. Schroeder's dead-eyed nephew last weekend. But her mood lifted when her phone lit up.

"Hey, sis! What's up?"

Shawna said she was in the neighborhood and wanted to stop by with some news. Roz told her she was more than welcome and silently lamented the fact that she had no snacks to set out. But having company was a rare event these days, and she had long ago stopped keeping empty carbs in her pantry.

When Shawna arrived, they sat in the living room. Her friend got right to the point. "We talked about my thoughts on marriage recently. It wasn't theoretical or hypothetical. Truth is,

I've met a guy. He's asked me to be his wife, and I've said yes. I'm hoping you'll bless us with a song when I plight him my troth."

Roz emitted a giddy shriek. "Shawna! Fantabulous! Congratulations!" Her inflections were more melodious than ever as she almost sang those words. "Yes, of course I'll sing—I'll be honored. Goodness, you must be the first person in history to use the phrase 'plight my troth' outside of the wedding ceremony. That is so like you. But wait, who's the lucky man? And when on earth did all this happen? You never even mentioned dating anyone. You need to go back to the beginning and tell me everything I've missed."

Had her friend chosen that moment to assume the lotus position and levitate above her chair, Roz would have found it less surprising than Shawna's unabashed gushing about her new man. His name was Marcus. They'd met at her workplace. Shawna was certain this handsome man ranked in the 98th percentile for IQ. He was soft-spoken, but in a way that projected thoughtfulness and confidence rather than shyness or reticence. He was kind to animals, respectful of his mother, and patient with restaurant waitstaff, whose names he never failed to remember. To top it all off, he owned a home, drove a nice car, had impeccable grooming, and was hardworking, but not a workaholic. Shawna made it sound as if she'd won the grand prize in the matrimonial sweepstakes. She was over the moon.

Half in jest, Roz asked, "Does he have any imperfections at all? More to the point, does he have a twin brother? And why haven't you brought this good-looking paragon of virtue around to meet your friends?"

"Mostly because I didn't want people all up in my business before it was time. Also, because of the shock factor at church."

"I totally get the first reason. The second one, not so much."

Shawna explained. "His branch of the theological tree is some distance from ours."

So that's the sound of the other shoe dropping. Roz felt a little of the air go out of the room. "Okaaaay. How much distance are we talking?"

"How far is it from the Apostolic Faith Mission to the St. Pierre Cathedral?"

Roz couldn't place the reference, though she felt she should know it. The names alone made the two points sound worlds apart. Still, Roz wanted it spelled out. "No riddles, please. Make it plain."

"I'm saying his church roots don't run through Azuza Street. Geneva, Switzerland, is closer to home for him. Think less William Seymour and more John Calvin."

"You're saying he's a Calvinist?"

"He's not a full-blown, Five-Point Calvinist. But he's not far from that. He's a Reformed Baptist."

Roz felt a sensation like a mild case of vertigo. By strenuous effort, she avoided looking as bewildered as she felt. "Correct me if I'm wrong, but doesn't that mean he rejects half of what you've always believed? Like the existence of free will, for starters? Spiritual gifts? Does he even think being Spirit-filled is a thing?"

"What it means is that we both believe in the Bible, understand parts of it differently, and will work out our differences over time."

Roz was trying to tally just how many significant differences there must be when another thought occurred to her: "Holy moly, you must know Pastor Bowers will have a conniption over this. What's he going to say?"

"As my mother likes to say, 'That don't confront me.' Last time we talked, you asked me what I wanted in a man. Do you remember what I said?"

Roz remembered it well. "You said that, for starters, you wanted someone who respected your intelligence and could keep up with it."

"Bingo," Shawna said, smacking the arm of the chair for emphasis. "And I want the same thing in a pastor too. Rev. Bowers is not that man. Even worse, he opted to punish me for giving an honest answer to his question. I deserve better. Everybody deserves better. That's the main reason I'm done there. I'm not going back. What Reverend Bowers says no longer concerns me."

"I don't know what to say, Shawna. I never would have seen this coming."

"I know," Shawna answered. "That's why I made that comment about meteorology before. I apologize for that. It must have sounded snide, and I didn't mean it that way. When you said, 'this too will pass,' you couldn't know which way the wind was blowing. You're such an optimist, and I love that about you.

But rose-colored glasses don't let you see storm clouds as they are. That's all I meant."

"No worries. I hope I'm not as Pollyanna as all that. But if I must err, I'd rather err on the side of hopefulness. I didn't feel offended, then or now."

"Good. I know you wish I didn't keep such a tight lid on things. But if I've learned anything in a lifetime spent in church, it's to keep most of my thoughts to myself. People make their own guesses about what I'm thinking or doing. I'm content to let them guess."

"So, about Marcus—I'm surprised you went so far afield in terms of beliefs. But we're all adults. If you love him and your conscience is clear, I won't rain on your parade."

"Thank you. And to state the obvious, I'm not violating any biblical prohibitions here. If you're thinking I'm about to be unequally yoked, remember he's not an unbeliever, only someone whose beliefs about some things differ from ours."

Roz considered this for a few seconds. She wished she could feel as happy for her friend as she had a minute or two ago. "You have so many choices, Shawna. Why opt for such a challenging situation?"

"I have lots of choices, but not a lot of good ones, and not a lot of time. Look, I'm twenty-nine years old. I want to have kids while it's still safe. I don't have forever to find the right man. Give me a great guy with some erroneous beliefs rather than some Bowers clone with sound doctrines and a nasty attitude. That's a harder problem to fix."

Shawna continued, "I think you have a tougher row to hoe than I do." She was slipping into her patented hundred-yard stare. "You know that once your pastor finds out about this, he won't want you to attend the wedding, let alone sing in it. He'll make it personal. He'll force you and everyone in the congregation to choose sides. And he'll ostracize anyone who chooses mine. Are you ready for that?"

Roz thought about it for a couple of heartbeats. "Honestly, no. I've avoided getting on his bad side so far. I'm not looking forward to experiencing it. But I'm also not the type of person who would abandon her best friend on one of the biggest days of her life. I'll sing at your wedding. Pastor Bowers will get over it. Or he won't. I'll deal with whatever happens." *Or I won't. When the time comes, I hope I'm half as brave as I made myself sound.*

Four days later, Roz sat at her dinner table making a list of potential wedding songs. At the same time, she wrestled with her mixed feelings about the engagement. On the one hand, she was thrilled that Shawna had found love. Weddings were joyful occasions, and both Roz and her best friend could use a little more joy. On the other hand, the trade-offs Shawna had made for love were hard for Roz to fathom. She tried to look at it in practical terms. Most people had to manage conflicting priorities from time to time. When Roz had been house hunting, her priorities were getting three bedrooms and two bathrooms, keeping her commute below twenty minutes, and staying within a certain budget. She soon learned she couldn't do all three. The budget was nonnegotiable, while the other things weren't. So she he settled for two bedrooms and one-and-a-half baths. Such was life.

When it came to conflicting priorities in moral or spiritual matters, fidelity to scripture was presumed to be nonnegotiable. But Shawna had given precedence to her feelings, and to the promptings of her biological clock. That path was fraught with potential heartache. Would she hold fast to her doctrinal convictions and end up raising children in a house divided? Would she abandon her own cherished beliefs for the sake of harmony at home? Neither course foreshadowed a happy ending.

Not that Roz had never forsaken something important in favor of something that felt urgent. But abandoning her healthy lifestyle to have ice cream for dinner after a bad day at work wasn't the same order of magnitude. Still, what if something of major importance created a tough choice in her own life? What if she found her calling and realized pursuing it meant quitting her well-paid job? Could she do it? If it turned out that financial security was her one nonnegotiable thing, then she'd have no high horse from which to look down at Shawna's choices. *I'll sing at the wedding, I'll pray for them both, and I'll wish them nothing but blessings.*

As if on cue, Shawna phoned. Roz wondered whether it was to convey more details about the wedding plans, or about Mr. Wonderful himself. But as soon as Roz said hello, Shawna asked, "Can you do me a favor and listen without interruption? No questions, no observations, just hear me out. Will you do that for me?"

This did not sound like the precursor to the cheerful chatter Roz had been hoping for. She settled into her chair and said, "I'm listening."

Shawna began: "First, thank you for being my friend all these years. For accepting me as I am and understanding me better than most. You'll never know how much your willingness to sing at my wedding meant to me. Especially considering your own uneasiness with my choice. I am always impressed by your kindness."

Roz noted how Shawna said *meant*, rather than *means*. Something was off here. And the delivery sounded canned, as if her friend were reading scripted remarks. This was out of character.

"Another thing," Shawna continued. "Things have changed. Marcus and I opted for a wedding without fanfare. We were married in a small private ceremony yesterday. Nobody there but us, the preacher, and two witnesses. I'm officially Shawna Bell-Wallingford. You don't have to worry about defying your pastor now.

"I gave this a lot of thought," she went on. "I believe you don't yet appreciate the price you would have paid for being at the wedding. Now that I've left Solid Rock, Bowers will try to make your life miserable for being my friend. If you doubt that, remember what he did to Eddie. I couldn't let you go through that for the sake of a song.

"I never told you this, but when Eddie left town last year, he sent me a last message before changing all his contact info and blocking me on social media. It hurt my feelings something fierce. I couldn't understand why on earth he would do that to me."

Those last few sentences didn't sound canned. The teleprompter vibe was gone.

"Well, I get it now. You can't walk down a new road with one foot still planted on the old one. You release one thing to embrace another. It's the only way."

A brief pause followed. Roz wondered if it was her turn to talk now.

But Shawna resumed. "This is me saying goodbye, Roz. I'm disappearing the same way Eddie did. None of this is your fault. I'm just saying this is how it has to be. For how long, I don't know. I hope this, too, will pass. I know a day will come when Bowers won't be able to threaten you, and maybe my choice of life partner won't cause you such discomfort. On that day, we can take up where we left off. I'll reach out to you. Somehow, I'll know the time is right. We'll be the twins again. Partners in crime. Kindred spirits. Until then, I'll miss you, Rozzie. I wish you all the best. Goodbye."

The line went dead. Roz stared at her phone in disbelief. Shawna couldn't be serious. Who suspends a years-long friendship like that? Roz had done what Shawna asked. She had listened and not spoken. But now it was her turn to speak. She dialed Shawna's number, but immediately heard an automated message: "Welcome to Verizon Wireless. The number you were trying to reach has calling restrictions that have prevented the completion of your call."

Roz threw her phone onto the couch and covered her face with her hands. She was running out of friends. Eddie had vanished. Trina had declared their friendship over. And now Shawna had cut her off after doing much the same thing, albeit in a kinder and more hopeful fashion. Soon, Rosalyn's only friend would be the septuagenarian bibliophile she read to every Saturday. And Sarge, of course. She reminded herself to be grateful for them both.

Brandon finished cleaning the gutters and put away the ladder and the pressure washer. He catalogued the tasks he'd handled over the last few weeks: keeping the lawn cut, edging the sidewalk and driveway, topping off fluids in his uncle's car. He'd landed a part-time job and contributed something to the household budget each week. It was a pittance, but it made him look like a saint. And while Al didn't need the money, it was plain to see how much he appreciated the help around the house.

It had been six weeks since he'd first shown up at his half-uncle's house with the tragic tale of his beloved Peg's suicide. He had hinted that she was probably bipolar or manic-depressive but had never received a formal diagnosis. The small business he worked for didn't offer serious bereavement time off, and he'd ended up losing his job while he was still in mourning. With the job gone, his condo went to foreclosure. Before he'd even processed his wife's death, he'd ended up living in his van. He'd borne up under that harsh reality for a time, but now found it unendurable. He needed a little emotional support, some human interaction. "Could you give me a place to land while I get back on my feet?"

Uncle Al had responded with an emphatic yes, along with a bear hug and heartfelt condolences. He showed Brandon to the spare bedroom and told him to make himself at home. Brandon rejoiced in all the little things, like the fact that the floor of his new room had carpet. And the house had a thermostat and central air conditioning. There was no sign of rats. No gangs of addicts would gather outside at sunset, and there were no rent collectors who looked like they'd wandered in off the set of a low-budget mob movie. A private bathroom and a full kitchen were mere steps away, available day or night. He hadn't lived this high on the hog for a long time.

In the first minutes of their reunion, Brandon learned that Aunt Laura—Aunt Lulu, as he'd called her in childhood—had died five years ago. Brandon spoke the requisite bromides, remembering to intone that she was in a better place. But he felt nothing. He hadn't seen or spoken to the woman in decades. Her absence meant there was no one to object to his sudden presence in the house. And one less person to persuade when it came time to make the big ask.

In the days that followed, the two men became caught up with each other's lives. Brandon learned how his uncle met the fat lady who read to him each week. He also explored the rest of the house. There was one room stuffed floor to ceiling with what must have been everything Aunt Lulu had ever owned. There were piles of clothes, magazines, a sewing machine, assorted cosmetics, costume jewelry, photo albums, scrapbooks, and who knows what else. It was as if Al couldn't bring himself to part with anything that had been hers. Such sentimentality five years after her passing was hard to understand.

All his snooping took considerable time. Sometimes he searched in the early hours of the morning when Al was sound asleep. Sometimes he snooped on Saturdays when Al was busy with the do-gooder story hour. Working around the house helped, as it gave him an excuse to nose around the basement while searching for tools and supplies. And he always took advantage of the rare occasions his uncle got in the car to run an errand, driving at a snail's pace down a road he could barely see. No way the old guy would pass the eye exam when it was time for his next license renewal.

Brandon had now gone through every room, every closet, every desk, and file cabinet. Some of them were locked, but that was hardly a hindrance to Brandon. He found a fireproof lockbox containing $5,000 in fifty-dollar bills. He was careful to leave everything the way he'd found it, even the writing tablet with a list of usernames and passwords he'd found near Al's personal computer. He snapped pics of these for use later.

He learned two things from all this spying. First, except for that one room, the place was well-kept and organized, especially considering the old man's poor eyesight. Second, his long-lost uncle had serious money. During his career, the man had earned far more than he'd spent. And given his generous state pension, he had spent none of his savings, even in retirement. The old man had financial assets totaling over $3 million.

I need some of that. Brandon figured one-tenth of the total nest egg would give him enough money to hire a top-notch defense attorney should the bloodhound and the Airedale come calling with more than mere suspicions. As soon as he had the thought, Brandon realized that was aiming too low. If Uncle Al gave him $600,000, he could set aside a quarter-million for his defense and still have $350,000 with which to buy another condo of his own. But why stop there? Al could afford to transfer a cool million to his only surviving relative, and still have two million he'd never live long enough to spend. It wouldn't affect the old man's dowdy lifestyle one bit.

But separating frugal Al Schroeder from a million dollars of his money would not be easy. And before Brandon could start, there was a crucial task to perform.

Roz approached the corner of Pinewood and Elm Street. She had doubled the length of her morning power walk by repeating the circuit, so she was hitting this intersection for the second time today. The extra distance was a strain on her body, but her joy over the achievement made up for it.

She turned the corner, eyes cast downward to avoid the sight of poor Mrs. Grimm's vacant house and its potted plants dying on the porch railing. That was when a man stepped from behind a tree directly into her path. Roz had to stop short to avoid a collision. She recognized him at once. It was Mr. Schroeder's nephew, the creepy houseguest with the black-hole eyes.

Without preamble, he said, "What's your business with my uncle? Why have you latched onto him?" The dead eyes bored into her. Roz felt breathless and a little weak, not all of it from her morning exertions.

She asked, "What are you talking about?"

"Don't play dumb with me. What's your angle?"

"For Pete's sake, I don't have an angle. I have not 'latched on' to your uncle. I'm trying to be a good neighbor. Is that so hard for you to understand?"

"What I understand is that before you befriended my uncle, you were trying to get close to the old lady who lived next door." He gestured at Mrs. Grimm's house. "Al told me how and when you met him. You must have a thing for ingratiating yourself with lonely seniors, one after another. I know your type. You're angling for his money. Well, we're both onto you now."

"You're wrong. You don't know me at all, never mind my so-called type." The accusations hurt, baseless as they were, and despite coming from a man she barely knew and shouldn't care anything about. "You are jumping to unfair conclusions, and I don't appreciate it."

"And I don't give a rip. Consider your visitation privileges revoked. Don't set foot on the property again. If you do, you'll be trespassing. I will not be kind to trespassers."

Roz was stunned. A few seconds ago, she'd been celebrating her fitness milestone. Now this. The sense of emotional whiplash was painful. She tried to counter it, to take back some of her power. "I'll need to hear that from Mr. Schroeder himself, since it's his house."

Brandon laughed, though there was no mirth in it. "I'm his caretaker. I have the authority to enforce his decision, and I intend to. If you fight me on this, you will lose. Be smart. Don't cross me. And don't darken our door again." He turned and strode back toward the Schroeder house before she could say another word. And faster than she could say, "What happened?" Roz lost two more friends.

The next day, Brandon came in from the garage and found his uncle sitting in his favorite chair. "Seeing as it's Saturday, it occurs to me I could read to you from your books, if you like. I'm probably not as skilled a reader as the double-wide do-gooder used to be, but I'll improve with practice."

Brandon had already told Al that they'd seen the last of Roz. The old man had been reluctant to believe it, so Brandon filled him in on the gory details: how she'd passed him in the street and given him the news; how her responses had been vague when he had asked her why. Brandon gathered that she'd met a senior citizen who was older and less healthy than Al, and who appeared to have deeper pockets. She had found greener pastures. When his uncle continued to insist it couldn't be true, Brandon had met his objections with irrefutable logic: wait for a week or two, he said, and see whether she comes back. She hadn't, of course. Al had even spoken of going to visit Roz to talk things over. Brandon scoffed, telling him he would look weak and needy if he did. It was important to maintain dignity in old age and not go hat-in-hand to a woman, especially one who was only out to take advantage of him. That worked. The old man swallowed his disappointment and moved on with his life. Brandon hated to lie. But he wasn't the type to shrink from unpleasant tasks. He did what had to be done. For his plan to succeed, the old man needed to know that he was alone in the world—all alone except for his devoted and indispensable nephew.

The old man scowled in obvious disapproval of the "double-wide" moniker, but didn't rebuke Brandon for it. "No thanks, you don't need to read to me." A brief pause. "She had a genuine gift for speaking, you know. Great voice and delivery. She would make a stellar voice-over artist or actor. She's that good." Al sounded wistful.

"Actor is right," Brandon retorted. "Didn't it strike you as funny that this talented stranger wanted to pay weekly visits to a man more than twice her age? Especially so soon after her first target died?"

"Somebody might as well befriend us old folks. It's not like we have family busting down the door most of the time."

"Touché. I must admit that when Mom drifted apart from you and Aunt Lulu, she pulled me along in her wake. What else can you expect of a kid? It took me a while to realize family should stick together. I'm doing my best to make up for lost time now. I hope you can see that my coming here is not the same as some woman with no connection to you."

"Of course, of course. Blood is the strongest connection there is."

"Truth is, even before my mother's husband died, you were the only other blood relative I had. I was still a teenager and could have used a little family outreach. I guess we both messed up. But hey, that's all . . . water under the bridge. The main thing is, we're both here for each other now."

Before his uncle could answer, Sarge interrupted the conversation. The dog had been sitting quietly at Al's feet, looking at the younger man with obvious mistrust. For no apparent reason, he jumped up and sprinted down the hall toward the primary bedroom, emitting a staccato fusillade of yips and yaps. Brandon put his hands to his ears.

"What's he barking at now?" Something had to be done about that ridiculous furball. He was always acting either hostile or fearful, though Brandon had never done a thing to him. And like most deluded dog owners, Al maintained that the little mutt was friendly to almost everyone. But this time Sarge wasn't barking at Brandon, and no one else was in the house.

So why was he kicking up such a ruckus? Brandon stood up to have a look.

"You probably won't see anything," Al said with a sigh.

"You mean Sir Barks-a-Lot has psychotic episodes and yaps his head off at nothing?"

"No, I didn't say there was nothing there. I said that you probably wouldn't see anything." When Brandon gave him a look of bewilderment, Al's expression became a mix of embarrassment and stubbornness. "Look, you might as well know this. Since Laura died, she sometimes . . . makes her presence known."

Brandon spoke slowly, not quite believing he had heard right. "You are saying the ghost of Aunt Lulu haunts this house? Like Jacob Marley in Scrooge?"

"I know how it sounds," Al said. "I didn't use to believe in such tales either. But seeing something with your own eyes has a way of changing your beliefs."

"But you said that whatever the dog is barking at couldn't be seen! So how do you know her ghost is haunting the place? What is it you've seen with your own eyes?"

"Does everyone your age have such poor listening skills?" Al was trying to pull himself out of the maw of the over-stuffed chair and stand up. "I said that you probably won't see anything. I didn't say I never have. She doesn't show herself often, but it happens from time to time. And it's always been to me alone, not to people she doesn't know or wasn't close to."

"Did you tell the book lady about this, by any chance?"

"No, of course not. She wouldn't have believed me any more than you do. Still, she's a smart one. She listens. Picks up on more than she lets on. But I don't think she had a clue about Laura's visits. I suspect her religious presuppositions wouldn't let her imagine such a thing."

Brandon held his tongue with difficulty. This entire conversation was nuts, but he didn't want to risk antagonizing the old kook further by saying so. The dog stopped barking. The old man settled back and let the chair almost swallow him again. And Brandon realized he needed a beer and a quiet place to think. Shrugging his shoulders at his uncle in a manner meant to imply, "If you say so," Brandon retreated to his room without further comment. *And I thought the stupid dog was the crazy one.*

There are moments when reality shifts in some fundamental way. This almost always happens without fanfare. A cougar trailed by hunters doubles back and begins stalking them. A camper realizes the woods have gone silent despite being filled with the chirping of crickets a moment before. Some guy in a bar goes from merely running his mouth to deciding to take a swing at you. Most people in these situations don't realize something has changed until too late. Only the observant few perceive such moments, understand them, and use that understanding to their advantage. Brandon's gut told him this was one of those moments.

His uncle had to have a few screws loose. That was obvious. This new reality called for a change in strategy. Brandon had been planning on finessing the man, conjuring up a mix of gratitude and guilt to cajole him into writing a check, the first of many. But now, better options were presenting themselves. All he needed was a little time to work out the details. Within two hours, a rough plan had taken shape. It wouldn't be easy to pull off. He reminded himself that he was nothing if not resourceful. He could do what had to be done. The hardest part would be creating the right playlist.

CHAPTER 11
HEAD GAMES

His uncle was always in bed by 8:30, and Brandon waited until thirty minutes after that. The first order of business was to retrieve the short-handled sledgehammer from the basement. He also picked up the well-chewed rawhide bone from Sarge's bed and made sure the dog saw him carry it out the back door. How had this little dust mop on legs gotten a name like Sarge? The old man should have called him Swiffer. Brandon plopped into a chair on the patio, dropping the toy on the ground beside him and maintaining a light grip on the sledgehammer as it rested on his shoulder. The little creature's attachment to his favorite toy was the only thing that would get him to venture close. Brandon heard the doggy door swing on its hinges but avoided looking toward it. He had every confidence he wouldn't have to wait long.

An hour after disposing of the body, he knocked on the old man's bedroom door to tell his sad tale. "I'm sorry to wake you, Uncle. I've got bad news, and I don't think it can wait. It's about Sarge." In somber tones, he relayed the details of how Sarge had gone out to the patio a few minutes ago, only to be attacked by a pair of coyotes that raced from the shadows and snatched him up. The poor little dog had emitted a pitiful yelp before being carried away. Brandon had tried to run after the predators but was of course unable to keep up. They had disappeared into the night with the little fellow in their jaws.

"There was nothing I could do. I even drove around the neighborhood hoping to see where they went, but it was no good. We can only hope he didn't suffer long." Brandon knew his story was plausible. According to the MSPCA, there were more than 12,000 coyotes in Massachusetts. They'd been spotted in every city and town. They were known to kill and eat domestic dogs and cats with regularity. There was no reason for the old man not to believe the story.

Al wandered around the house in forlorn silence for a long time. He found his way back to bed around midnight, wearing the mournful expression of someone who'd lost his last friend. Brandon was not without sympathy for his uncle. He understood how hard this loss must be for the old man. But he could not permit sympathy to derail his plans. His own jeopardy was too extreme. Since failure was not an option, he would not negotiate details with his conscience. For the next steps to have the best chance of succeeding, Uncle Al needed to be under maximum stress. From the looks of things, he was. *Good.*

Wednesday night Bible study had ended twenty minutes ago. Roz sat and waited while Pastor Greg Bowers steepled his fingers and looked thoughtful. They were in the preacher's office at Solid Rock Church. She'd requested this meeting, and wondered whether she should have done so months ago. There was a time when her pastor would have been the first person she turned to for advice. She thought it right and proper to ask his opinion, but knew she'd been dragging her feet about it. It wasn't that she was fearful; her only real trepidation had been about the office seating. There was no bench here like the one she always sat on in the sanctuary. She didn't want the embarrassment that would come from being unable to fit into an armchair. She need not have worried. The stout, armless chair in front of the pastor's desk accommodated her size and weight with no difficulty. When she heard no snaps, crackles, pops, or groans from the seat, Roz realized she could relax.

Once prompted, she laid out the issues at work that had brought her here. She described how the latest round of layoffs struck her as unjust, and how the role she'd had to play had cost her a friendship of long standing. She did not linger on the vandalism to her house and car, but emphasized how much the troubles at work had reinforced the feeling that she needed to find something meaningful to do. Something that felt like her calling.

Sister Connie Bowers, the minister's wife, sat next to Roz. She was there because of the pastor's oft-stated refusal to be alone behind closed doors with a woman who was not his wife. Roz approved of the precaution. While she could not conceive of this preacher doing or saying anything inappropriate, every congregation likely had people who enjoyed a little conjecture, innuendo, and gossip. The presence of the pastor's wife in meetings like this would forestall that.

After unburdening her heart, Roz glanced around. The big office made ample use of empty space, though every item in it exuded quality. The executive desk, the heavy drapes, the prayer bench with the large painting on the wall over it, the built-in bookcases full of hardcover and leatherbound books—all of it combined to give the room an aura of gravitas. The feeling was that she was meeting a consequential person in a sacred space, almost holy ground. The only thing that spoiled the effect was a bit of snark on the corner of the desk, a little plaque that read, "If at first you don't succeed, try doing what your pastor told you in the first place."

Upon reading that, Roz realized why she had put off asking for this meeting. She wished she could be talking with her *old* pastor today. She didn't mean this man's predecessor; she'd never met him. Nor did she mean a preacher at some other church, such as the one she'd grown up in. She meant the man Pastor Greg Bowers used to be. That man was caring, self-effacing, and wise. Listening to him was inspiring and talking with him felt safe. The main reason Roz had stayed at Solid Rock this long was the hope that her old pastor would make an appearance. Every once in a while, he did.

The barbed humor on the plaque was emblematic of how the atmosphere at Solid Rock had changed over the years. Roz's earliest memories here were mostly joyous. And it wasn't just because of the great music, the exultant worship services, the in-depth Bible teaching, or the uplifting messages this man preached. Even when conviction was the order of the day, she had received it with gratitude, because although conviction felt uncomfortable, it came packaged with its own cure. Repentance made everything right again, and the resulting sense of communion with God was a gift beyond measure. In recent years, divine conviction had been an infrequent visitor, replaced by near-constant ecclesiastical condemnation. Vitriolic scorn, ridicule, name calling, and guilt tripping were not like conviction. Conviction lingered no longer than it took to induce repentance. Guilt was designed to last, so that the accuser could wound you and pick at the scab for as long as it suited him. Picked at long enough, scabs became scars.

So which Bowers would Roz be dealing with tonight? Close up, the man before her looked several years older than he did in the pulpit. His once brown hair was mostly gray. His face looked drawn, a little pale. The silence drew out for a minute before the minister finally smiled and spoke. "I understand your dilemma. You've been a good hire for your employer. You've been promoted to a position of responsibility. Based on your tithe record, you're well paid. But it's not satisfying or fulfilling. That's because your career lacks eternal purpose. As the saying goes, only what's done for Christ will last."

Roz nodded. This preamble was not unexpected. She was curious to see where it would go. She would like nothing better than to do something with her life that mattered in God's eyes as well as her own.

He continued. "Your timing strikes me as a God thing. The leadership team has been thinking and praying about several needs in the church. We're looking to put the right people in the right positions to help us move the program forward. I won't make a specific recommendation right now, but I promise to get back to you as the Lord leads me. That said, I do get the sense that there is more on your mind than the search for meaningful work. What else is troubling you?"

Though she hadn't planned to bring up her dealings with Mr. Schroeder, she decided to tell him that whole story too.

"How many Saturdays did you spend reading to this man?"

"Six weeks? Two months? I hadn't counted, but that's a good ballpark."

"Had he expressed any interest in coming to church, or in having a home Bible study?"

Roz resisted the impulse to squirm. "No, not really. He doesn't seem too interested in talking about spiritual things. He enjoys the company, and he loves his books, especially the ones on military history. He's not all that comfortable discussing matters of faith. I don't know what his religious beliefs are, or if he even has any. He suggested it was a generational thing, that people his age liked to keep their personal lives to themselves."

"I see." The preacher closed his eyes and grimaced. "Sister Pitts, your compassion does you credit. But you are sidelining yourself, taking yourself out of the battle. The Bible says the fields are white unto harvest. Don't squander your limited time where the hope of a harvest is least. The key to spiritual productivity is applying your efforts where they can make the most difference for the Kingdom. Invest where the returns are greatest. Otherwise you miss out on reaching a hungry soul while you are entangled with an uninterested one. You have a tender heart, so I know it hurt your feelings when the nephew told you to stay away from this man's house. But see it for what it is—a blessing in disguise. The man did you a favor. You now have more time for finding and fulfilling your calling. Is there anything else you wanted to discuss?"

Roz was less than comfortable with the pastor's comments. Was he suggesting that being a good neighbor was worthwhile only as a recruiting tool? That kindness was a waste of time if it wasn't going to result in church growth? Didn't the Bible say to do good unto *all* men? She would have liked to discuss this further, but it was clear he'd said all he was going to say on this topic.

The pastor cleared his throat and shifted in his chair. "There is one issue I hope you will clarify for me. What on earth has been going on with your friend Shawna Bell? Her behavior is much changed of late, and it's a shock to everyone who knows her. And now she's missed service for a couple of weeks. I've reached out to her without response. This is all so out of character for her. I know you two are the best of friends. What can you tell me?"

Roz hesitated. "If Shawna hasn't seen fit to say anything of her own volition, I'm not sure I should try to speak for her. It would feel like gossip. Like I'm a talebearer."

Pastor Bowers closed his eyes again, as if in deep concentration or mild pain. "In general, being able to keep a secret is a good thing. But there are limits. If someone comes to you in confidence and says he is planning to commit suicide, your duty to save that person trumps your duty to keep their secret. You should go at once to someone who is equipped to help, and you should spill the beans. I am the guardian of this flock, but I can't be everywhere at once. I need eyes and ears in the congregation that will bring the important stuff to me."

The preacher had always demonstrated keen awareness of what went on in the lives of his church members. Roz had figured it was due to spiritual insight. The thought that he might have a network of church members serving as his "eyes and ears" was not a pleasant one, even if the suicide analogy had merit.

Choosing her words carefully, she gave him a brief overview. "Shawna told me she was . . . offended . . . by the turn her last meeting with you took. It intensified her desire for a change. I guess that desire had been simmering for a while. Plus, none of the brothers at Solid Rock who were pursuing her caught her interest. She found someone somewhere else who did. They got married and Shawna is attending his church now."

Rev. Bowers furrowed his brow. "How long have you known about this?"

"Not long," Roz said. "She didn't tell me anything until after it was a done deal."

"I'm more than a little disappointed at the way she changed up on me. After all the opportunities this church has afforded her, I would have expected more loyalty. I talked sense to her, and she's offended with me? It's one of the many burdens of ministry. We're called to speak into people's lives, and this is often the thanks we get."

Roz could think of nothing to say to that.

With a visible effort, Bowers let the anger drain from his expression and from his voice. "In any case, I don't hold this against you. You weren't conspiring with her. You didn't know until she'd made her choice. But this is the kind of thing you'll want to tell me as soon as you learn of it. If there is to be a more significant role for you in the church, I'll need to know I can count on you to keep the lines of communication open."

Roz nodded, acknowledging his spoken need, while not making any promises.

"Well, that about wraps it up. I'll get back to you after I've had a chance to meditate on the question of your calling and purpose." They both stood. "Oh, by the way," said Bowers, "I believe Shawna is a year or two younger than you. Did you feel at all bad that your good friend was getting married while you're still unattached?"

The pastor's question struck Roz as tactless, but she chose not to take offense. "Was I envious? No, not at all. Of course I wouldn't object to meeting someone one of these days. But I'm in no hurry. I've got so much going on right now that finding Mr. Right is nowhere near top-of-mind."

"Okay, good, very good."

Dismissed, Roz turned toward the door. As she did, she noticed Bowers and his wife sharing a knowing glance with each other. For a few seconds, she wondered what that was about. But by the time she was halfway across the sanctuary, her mind turned to the challenges of the coming workday, and the look was forgotten.

The playlist for Peg had been heavy on brute force. Uncle Al's was more about subtlety, and it required more attention to detail. The task at hand now was to prepare a couple of bottles, and Brandon knew he'd need the patience of a Zen Buddhist monk.

He lined up two amber-colored plastic containers from CVS. One held his uncle's atorvastatin, a cholesterol medication. The other contained pills that had been prescribed for Brandon. The immediate need was to get the pharmacy's label off his uncle's bottle so he could replace it with a counterfeit label of his own making. He'd spent days playing with a graphics program, trying to get every detail right. It was harder than it looked. Given Al's poor eyesight, this was probably overkill. It need not be perfect. Close was good enough.

Judicious application of a heat gun melted the glue behind the old label and let him peel it off. A few minutes later, the forged label was affixed. It differed from the old one in only one detail. Instead of describing atorvastatin as "a white, oval-shaped tablet imprinted with 114 on the front," the new label called it "a white, oval-shaped tablet imprinted with amb-10 on the front and 5421 on the back." Brandon's pills went into his uncle's pill bottle, and the bottle went back to the kitchen counter with the rest of the medications and supplements the old guy took. Tomorrow would be Sunday. In the morning, Uncle Al would take the last of a week's pills from his dispenser and refill it with a week's supply from his bottles. A day later, Brandon would know if this was going to work.

Sure enough, his uncle woke up later than usual on Monday, and stumbled about looking tired and disoriented. Brandon turned on the inside security cameras so he could monitor the live feed going forward. You never knew when the cameras might see something important.

On Tuesday, Al said he felt exhausted and dizzy, far worse than he had on Monday. Brandon assured him it was residual stress from the sudden loss of Sarge. It would pass. The cameras caught Al being unsteady on his feet, and even taking a mild fall as he was headed for his living room chair.

On day three, Al announced he was staying in bed. He raised no objection when Brandon presented him with a small stack of checks to sign. In fact, he expressed gratitude for the help. The payments were for utility bills, along with a few small purchases.

Brandon's inspired gamble was paying off. That was the funny thing about Ambien. Not everyone had the same response to it. But a little online research had informed him that older users of the psychoactive sleep aid tended to have more and stronger side effects than younger people. These could include daytime drowsiness, dizziness, a "drugged" feeling, memory loss, depression, and increased risk of falls. Oh, and sleepwalking. There were documented cases of people fixing a snack, taking a walk outside, and even driving their cars while sleeping with eyes wide open. Brandon had read that the so-called "Ambien defense" had even been used in a couple of murder trials.

The drug had proved challenging for Brandon to obtain because it was a Schedule IV controlled substance that presented a risk of addiction. He had gone to three different urgent care centers before he'd found a doctor who would prescribe it for him without a battery of tests first. It helped that he had stayed up all night before the appointment, making his exhaustion unfeigned. He'd done his research and said all the right things, so the reluctant physician relented. Still, he'd warned Brandon that there would be no refills. No problem. From the looks of things, a fourteen-day supply would be enough to do the trick.

A week later Brandon brought in the mail and sat his uncle down at the kitchen table. "Uncle, what is the meaning of this?" He held out a magazine that had come with the mail. It was an issue of *Woman's Day.*

"Not mine," Al said, chuckling. "Mailman must have put it in the wrong box. It happens sometimes."

"Not this time. It's got a mailing label with your name and address on it."

Uncle Al held the magazine cover an inch from his nose so he could read the label. "Well, I'll be doggoned. I don't know what to think about that."

"I think I do," Brandon said with a sigh. "Did Aunt Lulu used to read this magazine?"

"Why, yes," Al said. He wore a look of concentration, as though recollecting this detail of his wife's past was hard work. "She read that magazine for years." He hesitated, sounding uncertain. "Maybe the publishers don't know she's gone. Maybe they're sending a free sample to get her to subscribe again."

"A free sample for her addressed to you?" Brandon tried to make his voice as gentle as possible. "Maybe you got a little confused? You haven't been yourself lately. Maybe you'd like to see your doctor?"

Al reddened. "I'm not at all confused about the fact that my wife is dead. And no, I don't want to see the doctor. Fat lot of good he does. Fills my calendar with appointments. Keeps me shuttling around to specialists to check on every little ache and pain. Schedules endless follow-up consultations for as long as he thinks Medicare will pay for them. I'm not a patient to him; I'm an annuity!"

"Okay, okay, no doctor visits. Since you're quite clear that Aunt Lulu is gone, why don't you tell me about the first time you saw her here . . . after she died."

Al harrumphed and favored his nephew with a look of pure scorn. "I know good and well you don't believe it. It was all you could do to keep from laughing out loud when I first mentioned it."

"No laughing, I promise," Brandon replied with as much earnestness as he could muster. "No judgment at all. I want to understand."

His uncle seemed to take this under advisement. Brandon waited with what he hoped was a patient and sincere look on his face. After a minute or so, the old man began to speak.

"It was a few days after the funeral. I was walking into the kitchen to get breakfast. I had set out a plate and silverware the night before. That's the way we'd done it for years. Now the only strange part was having only one place setting. I walked into the room, turned on the light, and there she was, standing at the kitchen table. Right next to her accustomed seat. She was looking at the missing place setting. The look she gave me was like . . . how could you have forgotten me?" He paused for several seconds. Was he trying to maintain composure? Or trying to remember what he had been talking about? It was hard to tell. But he picked up where he had left off, though his voice was weak. "I was shocked. I asked her what she was doing here. That was a mistake I hated myself for making. It's not the most welcoming thing you can say to someone you've lived with for most of your life. As soon as I asked the question, she was gone."

"I convinced myself it was imagination. The stress of the funeral and all that. But she started showing up at random times, even though I had accepted her death. Sarge always knew when she arrived. He could sense it. In the early days, she would talk to me—mundane stuff, asking me to remember to get Sarge's nails trimmed, or telling me the grass needed cutting. As time went by, she no longer spoke—just looked at me. Sometimes she looked sad, and other times she looked irritated. I didn't know what was on her mind, or what I could do to make her happier. I wonder whether she's not stuck here somehow. Bound to this house. Bound to me. In her last months of life, she never left the house. Now it's like she has no idea where else to go, so she keeps showing up here. I wish she could rest in peace." Al wiped his eyes.

Brandon sat in awkward silence. After a minute he reached out and patted his uncle on the shoulder before retreating to the silence of his own room. Once behind the closed door, he took his phone from his shirt pocket and tapped the button to stop the recording. Today had been a productive day.

"This is highly irregular. I'm expecting an appointment with a seventy-six-year-old man. You don't look a day over forty. Care to explain?"

"You're right, Doctor. I am not my uncle Al Schroeder. But I live with him. Since he is pretty much housebound these days, I felt there are some things you needed to know. Things he won't tell you himself."

When the doctor said nothing, Brandon continued. "You may know he lost his wife five years ago. What you don't know is that he's losing his grip on reality. He bought her a subscription to her favorite women's magazine. Last month. And he bought her one of those gag gifts where you purchase a square foot of land in Scotland and get a certificate deeming you "Lord" or "Lady" So-and-So. Brandon opened his satchel and pulled out a framed certificate. "He made her "Lady Laura Schroeder. I suppose he intends to present it to her ghost."

The doctor raised his eyebrows and asked, "You don't mean that literally, do you?"

"I'm afraid I do. He's convinced she shows up at the house from time to time. 'Makes her presence known' is how he put it. Claims only he and his pet dog can see this ghost, and he claims she materializes out of thin air and talks to him. Here, I'll let him tell you in his own words." Brandon pulled up the recording on his phone and pushed play. The doctor listened with pursed lips and a concerned expression.

"Doc, I could go on all day with evidence of my uncle's deterioration. He's frailer than he used to be. He's fallen at least three times in the past two weeks. Part of his house looks like an episode of *Hoarders*. All this on top of the obvious delusions about the ghost of my aunt."

"I understand your concern," the doctor said. "But I can't diagnose him for you. I'd need to see him for a proper diagnosis, maybe refer him to a psychologist. Maybe with the right treatment . . ."

"He'll never come in for diagnosis or treatment. That's a fact. My main concern is that he can't take proper care of his house, his finances, or himself. I can help him, but first I need you to sign this." Brandon pulled a form out of a manila folder and held it out to the doctor. There were four crisp one hundred dollar bills paper-clipped to the top. Brandon explained, "The courthouse downtown gave me this form. I've already informed the court of my uncle's situation, but they need a doctor to confirm the obvious. All I need is your signature at the bottom. And since you can't bill my uncle's insurance for a consultation with me, I'm hoping this will be enough to compensate you for your time and assistance today. All I need is your signature at the bottom."

The doctor glanced over the form and looked at Brandon for a few seconds. Brandon felt himself holding his breath. Finally, the physician unclipped the money from the form and set it on his desk. He signed the paper and handed it back to Brandon. "Good luck to the both of you," was all he said.

Later that evening, Brandon was standing in the kitchen, mulling the next steps. He glanced at his uncle's pill dispenser and noticed the old man hadn't taken his nighttime medication for the last two days. Brandon frowned. He needed the old man sleepy and loopy for a few more days, after which it would no longer matter. Al was getting ready for bed, so Brandon rapped on his door and walked in carrying the pill dispenser and a glass of water.

"Uncle Al, I noticed you've been falling behind on your meds. You don't want to forget to take these."

"I don't want to take them. I think I've been having some kind of negative reaction to them. I'm starting to feel better now that I'm not taking them."

"Most medications can cause side effects in some people. It's something to take up with your doctor or pharmacist. But you can't stop taking your pills without medical supervision."

"Well, they never caused any noticeable side effects until recently. Maybe they changed the formulation of the pills. Maybe they gave me the wrong stuff, I don't know. Given how bad they make me feel, I see no sense in continuing to take them."

Brandon replied, "It's a cholesterol medication. However bad they make you feel, you'd feel worse if your arteries clogged up and you had a heart attack. And if you died, where would that leave me?"

Uncle Al said nothing to that. But the stubborn set of his mouth was easy enough to read. Brandon leaned over his uncle, stared into the old man's eyes, and let all the pretend warmth drain from his voice. "Al. Take the blasted pill. Now."

After a few seconds of hesitation, the old man complied.

Help me. Please help me.

The writing was spidery, the cursive written in large letters by what must have been a shaky hand. Nonetheless, the letter was neat enough for Roz to read, and the message was shocking. The envelope it came in had been hand delivered to her mailbox—no postage stamp, not even a street address. No return address. Only the word "Rosalyn."

Roz sat at her dining room table and read it all again.

Rosalyn,

My nephew told me you weren't coming back. I didn't believe him at first, but it seems he was right. I wanted to come ask you why, but he would have shamed me for it.

He is not what I thought he was. He was nice at first. Now he mistreats me. He says I'm incompetent, that I do things I don't remember doing. He may be poisoning me. He acts like I'm soft in the head, like my recollections can be dismissed because I'm old. He saunters around my house like he owns the place. I am afraid of him.

Would you please come back so we can talk? Best to visit when he is away. Late mornings or early afternoons. If his van is not in the driveway, it's safe for you to visit.

I know I'm presuming a lot to ask you this. I don't know what else to do.

Help me. Please help me.

Al Schroeder

Attached to the bottom of the note with two pieces of cellophane tape was a key. It looked like a house key.

So the evil nephew was even worse than she'd thought. The man had pretended that Mr. Schroeder had banished her out of distrust for her motives, but the note made it clear that Brandon had lied. He had his own reasons for wanting her gone.

Maybe it was as simple as keeping Mr. Schroeder isolated so no one could see and report what sounded like a clear case of elder abuse. She shuddered while trying to imagine the old man and his dog stuck in a house with that monster. But how could she help? She didn't know where to start.

Roz took the next day off work. She was no expert on the subject of elder abuse, but figured she knew who was. The local Council on Aging would have informational brochures that would bring her up to speed and direct her neighbor to whatever resources could best help him. After going to the COA, she drove by the man's house. No van. She pulled into his driveway but thought better of it a second later. She didn't want the dead-eyed houseguest to see her car if he came home while she was visiting. So she put the Lincoln back in her own garage and walked over to her neighbor's house.

She rang the bell and waited for an answer, but none came. A second attempt got no more response than the first. She used the key to let herself in.

She looked around the sunroom. "Mr. Schroeder? It's me, Roz. Are you here?" She at least expected Sarge to rush out to greet her, but there was no sign of the little dog. She called louder. "Mr. Schroeder?"

A faint mumble came from the living room. She walked into that room and found him sitting in his favorite chair, eyes closed, looking as if he'd just nodded off. He was still in his pajamas, sitting with a blanket spread over his lap. He looked haggard, as though he hadn't slept all night. Unshaven.

Maybe unwashed. Roz's hand flew to her mouth. "Are you all right?"

He turned his head toward her with an effort. "I guess you can say I've been better. Thank you for coming."

"Of course, of course," she said. "How can I help?"

"Tell me . . . a few things. You disappeared without so much as a goodbye. It's been so long. I can't remember how long. My nephew told me you were an opportunist, that you ditched me when you found someone else to con."

"Brandon lied. He told me that *you* said I was no longer welcome. He ordered me not to come back. Said he was enforcing your wishes."

Mr. Schroeder sighed. "I see. In that case, he lied to both of us." The old man sat there looking miserable. After a few seconds, a horrified expression crossed his face. "Maybe he even lied about Sarge."

"What about Sarge?" Roz asked, looking around. "Where is he? I was so looking forward to seeing him again."

"Sarge is gone . . . there was a whole story about . . . coyotes that carried him off. I believed my nephew at the time, but now that I see how mean he's gotten . . . and the business with the pills . . . maybe *he* did away with Sarge, not coyotes. He never liked the little guy any more than Sarge liked him."

"I'm so very sorry," Roz said. "But I have to ask you something. You once told me there's no better judge of character than a dog. I could see Sarge was afraid of your nephew. Why did you ignore your dog's instincts and let the man move in with you?"

"Because he is family. There are obligations that come along with that. I let that sense of obligation override my better judgment. Little fella tried to warn me. I didn't listen. I think Sarge paid the price for that." There were tears in Mr. Schroeder's eyes now. "But I need to ask you . . . why you didn't come back."

"Now, Mr. Schroeder, we just talked about that. It was Brandon. Brandon told us both a lie."

"Yes, yes, I know that now."

Roz struggled to keep her composure. This was not the quick-witted and engaged Mr. Schroeder with whom she had discussed military history and poetry every Saturday. His apparent mental decline had happened faster than she would have thought possible. She couldn't imagine an explanation for it.

"You mentioned the business with the pills. What pills? Is that the poisoning you wrote me about?"

Mr. Schroeder wiped his eyes with his sleeve. "Yes. He messed with my medication. I take all of my meds in the morning except for one. I take . . . I take . . . atorvastatin . . . for cholesterol . . . at night. Been taking it for years. All of a sudden, it makes me sleep really hard, but I still wake up tired. I can't remember any of my dreams in the morning. I half feel like I'm dreaming for hours after I wake up. I'm exhausted now, after ten hours of sleep. It takes me until afternoon to feel alert. I'm not steady on my feet anymore. I fall sometimes. He told me it was all due to stress about Sarge. But I know that's a lie. I stopped taking the pills for a couple of days and was starting to feel better. Last night he noticed and forced me to take one. *Forced* me. And now I feel like I've been hit by a truck."

Roz was outraged. "Why would he do this?"

"I have no idea."

"When did it start? You said he was nice at first."

"I think he changed after I told him something. Something about his aunt. It's a trivial thing. No need to bore you with it."

Roz doubted it was trivial if it had triggered Brandon's shocking behavior. But all she said was, "No pressure. You don't have to tell me anything you don't want to. I just thought if there was one thing that set him off, knowing what it was might help me help you."

Mr. Schroeder appeared to consider this. The moment stretched. Roz decided to break the tension. "By the way, I brought you some brochures on elder abuse. They're from the Council on Aging. Now that I look at them, I realize the print size is too small for you to read. Would you like me to skim them and read you anything that looks helpful?"

"Maybe. Probably. But first, do me a favor. Could you go to the kitchen and bring me my pill bottles? They're in the cabinet over the sink."

Roz put the brochures down and went to the kitchen. When she returned, he said, "Look at the one labeled atorvastatin. Do the pills look funny? Like they've been tampered with?"

"I'm not sure I would know. They look like regular pills. Oh, wait, I have an idea. Google is our friend." She pulled out her phone, opened the browser, and typed *What does atorvastatin look like* in the search bar. Soon she was on a site called drugs. com, looking at images of pills. The various photos of atorvastatin all looked the same, except for the stampings. There were different letters and numbers stamped on the pills in the images, depending on dosage; ten milligrams, twenty, forty, and so on. Roz tilted the bottle in her hand and tapped it until a solitary pill dropped out onto the end table. It did look similar to the pills in the picture, though the shape was a tiny bit different. But the imprints on the front and back of the pill weren't even close to those in the online images. "You may be on to something here. I don't think they look quite right. Why don't you throw these out and get a new supply from your pharmacist? We could see whether they look like these ones again, or more like the ones in the online photos."

"I suppose I could," he said. "But then I'd have no evidence against him."

"Well, I can take a pill or two to a drugstore for you. See what the pharmacist says it is."

"Oh, would you? I'd be grateful."

"No problem, Mr. Schroeder. I'm happy to help. I'd better take a photo of the pills and the label on the bottle. In case I lose these, or they crumble or something." She snapped the photos and slipped two pills into her change purse. As she turned toward the front door, he arrested her with his words.

"Okay, I'll tell you. You'll probably think I'm crazy. Brandon does. But if you're going to think it, I might as well find out now. My Laura died some five years ago, but her spirit still visits this house. I've seen her, and that's a fact. Sarge always knew when she was here. He didn't bark much indoors, but he would bark his little head off whenever she appeared. I only told Brandon because I wanted him to understand what was going on if it happened while he was here. That's when he changed toward me. He acts like I'm senile or something."

So that's what he was hiding. Roz sat down again. She remembered his long-ago comment about him and his wife not "really" being parted. He had tried to explain the remark away, but Roz hadn't bought the explanation. Well, this little revelation answered her question, but also complicated things. She'd need some time to figure out how to respond in a way that wouldn't upset or antagonize him.

The two of them sat in silence for a moment. Mr. Schroeder nodded toward her purse. "So you still plan to check out the pills and come back when you find out what they contain?"

"Absolutely." She smiled to convey reassurance. From outside came the sound of a vehicle pulling into the driveway. "Neither snow, nor rain, nor—"

"It's Brandon! He's back! Run out the back door. Don't let him see you."

"He won't be happy to see me, but I don't think I'll come to harm over it."

"*You* might not. But I might. Run!"

Roz didn't need any further urging. She went out the back door and hurried across the yard. A narrow strip of wooded growth separated Mr. Schroeder's lot from the back of a commercial parking lot with frontage on Nicholas Road. She could take Nicholas

Road to Water Street and circle back home from there, like doing her morning power walk in reverse. It would be a clean getaway.

"Having a good day, Uncle?" The question was innocuous enough, but Brandon made sure it sounded threatening all the same.

"A normal day. Not all that interesting. Why?"

"Have any company?"

"Well, you know my reputation for throwing parties. And for hosting them in my pajamas, which is why I'm dressed this way now."

"Glad your head is clear enough to make wisecracks for a change. Maybe you're sharp enough to solve a riddle for me: how did these pamphlets get here?" Brandon picked up the small stack of booklets from the end table and began leafing through them. "Facts about Elder Abuse. Five Things Everyone Can Do to Prevent Elder Abuse. Identifying, Preventing, and Reporting Elder Abuse. I'm sensing a pattern here. Is there something you want to say to me?"

"Not at the moment."

Brandon bellowed, "Good! Because if you've got anything to say to me, it had better be 'thank you!' I'd hate to think a half-blind man who talks to the dead is trying to tick off the only person on earth who is helping him. Who brought you this stuff?"

The old man said nothing. He sat there looking stunned, as if realizing for the first time what a predicament he was in.

Brandon suppressed a smile of satisfaction. He'd seen enough psychological thriller movies to know that emotional volatility and sheer unpredictability frightened people. Time to dial things down as fast as he'd ramped them up.

He lowered his voice and spoke with slow precision. "I'll make it clear for you. Since you spent the day in your pajamas, you didn't go get these. And they didn't come in the mail because today's mail hasn't arrived yet. So someone brought them here, yes? Who?"

Still Uncle Al said nothing. Brandon stood beside the old man's chair and put his hand on his uncle's shoulder. He squeezed a little, not enough to cause pain, but enough to convey the implied threat. "I'll do whatever I have to do to get you to answer the question. Somebody's stirring up trouble. That makes me angry. I need to know where to direct that anger." He squeezed a little harder. "Tell me who has come here trying to turn you against me."

"The only one turning me against you is you. You've been doing that since you started lying to me."

"Uncle, you wound me!" Brandon tried to convey both hurt surprise and mockery in his tone. "When did I lie to you?"

"For starters, you told me that Rosalyn Pitts decided not to come back. Now I know that's not true. You told her not to come back, and pretended you were conveying my wishes."

"Oh, is that what happened? Sounds like a case of he said, she said. And you've sided with a stranger rather than with blood. Such a shame. At least I know who to thank for these flyers."

"I didn't say they came from her," his uncle grumbled.

"Right. Who did they come from? Tell me who brought them if not her."

Silence. The old man looked away. "As I thought," said Brandon. "One last thing . . . she didn't come here out of the blue. Am I right? She wasn't coming back, ever. I refuse to believe she showed up uninvited with all this garbage in hand."

"It doesn't matter," replied Uncle Al. "It's not your concern. I'm going to ask you to leave. I'll go to court and get a restraining order if I have to. I won't be threatened or manhandled in my own home." He raised his eyes and stuck his chin out in defiance.

"Threatened? By *me*?" Brandon let his face fall in imitation of sadness. "If anyone has made a threat, it's you. And after all I've done for you! If I had any feelings, they'd be hurt. I guess that's the way of the world. That's why I had to go to court myself. I came straight here from there. They gave me this."

He produced a piece of paper that had been folded up in his shirt pocket. "It's a copy of a court order. I know you won't be able to read it, so I'll summarize what it says. I have been appointed your legal guardian. Your doctor believes you are no longer competent to handle your own affairs. He signed off on my application for guardianship. After reviewing the evidence, the judge agreed. The court has given me the burden of looking after you. So they won't be listening to an addled old kook yammering about restraining orders. From now on, I'll be making all the decisions around here. You'll do nothing without my oversight and approval. It's for your own good, you know. Now let's try to get along and make the best of it, shall we?"

At 5:45 a.m. on Friday, Roz rolled out of bed. She'd slept only fitfully, wondering about yesterday's conversation with poor Mr. Schroeder. He was clearly frightened and more than a little depressed, more than a little out of it. Understandable, considering his circumstances. The possibility that Brandon had switched out his uncle's meds was horrifying. She planned to stop at the drugstore at lunchtime to get the pills identified. Meanwhile, it was time to get moving. Maybe she'd change the route of her power walk this morning to avoid passing the Schroeder residence. Couldn't hurt to be prudent.

She headed for the bathroom. Upon reaching the door, she screamed. There were words scrawled on it in crayon. Or maybe it was lipstick. The dark red hue was the color of drying blood.

Stupid woman. U messed up. Move somewhere far away. Now.
Or stay and wait for my next visit. I almost hope you do.

CHAPTER 12
MY CITY WAS GONE

Roz ran back to the bedroom, slammed the door, and locked it. It was only a few steps, but she found herself gulping air like a hooked fish while her pulse hammered. Her body and mind both felt numb. It was a profound sense of disconnect, like knowing she was lost, but having no idea of where she even wanted to go. Only one thing was clear; evil had been in her house, standing in the darkness mere feet from her while she slept. The mental image was dreadful. She didn't want to dwell on it, but she couldn't tear her mind away. She stood gasping, rooted to the spot.

An even worse thought broke her paralysis. What if he was still somewhere in the house? "My next visit" suggested he was gone, but maybe he wasn't. It could be a sick game of cat and mouse, with him waiting to pounce from around a corner down the hall. That idea jolted her into action. Roz dashed for the phone on her nightstand, ready to call 9-1-1. But she hesitated. She couldn't let police officers into her house while she was dressed only in her pajamas. Dropping the phone on her bed, she ran to her closet for something to put on. She dressed hastily, then pulled down a suitcase and started stuffing it with random blouses and skirts—office wear, casual clothes, a mix of everything without rhyme or reason. When it was full, she jammed it closed, threw her phone into her purse, and after a quick peek down the hall, made a breathless run for the garage. Once in her car, she locked the doors, backed out of the garage, and called the police from the safety of her driveway, leaving the car running all the while.

After telling dispatch that she was the victim of a home invasion and that she didn't know whether the invader was still present, she didn't have to wait long. Two uniformed officers in separate cars arrived in less than five minutes. She told them about the note on the bathroom door and directed them to enter the house through the unlocked door to the garage. After several minutes, they returned to tell her the coast was clear. There was no one inside.

An unmarked police car arrived. When the driver dismounted, Roz noted he was wearing a jacket and tie instead of a policeman's uniform. He introduced himself as Detective McGlaughlin, though she forgot his name seconds after he said it. He asked her whether the garage door had been open or closed overnight. Assured that it had been closed, he and one of the officers circled the house, checking all the doors and windows.

The first officer dusted for fingerprints on and around the front doorknob.

After completing his circuit, the detective had Roz walk him inside and show him the note. He asked her when she had discovered it.

"A few minutes before I called. I saw it right after I got out of bed."

He said, "I assume you didn't sleep in those clothes. You weren't sure whether or not someone was in the house, but you got dressed for work before calling? That's a little unusual."

Roz tried not to feel offended. She didn't expect the man to understand her instinctive need for modesty and propriety, never mind the mental chaos that accompanied her awful discovery. "I remember thinking I couldn't have police arriving at the house while I was in my sleepwear. I got dressed in a hurry. Once I made it outside, I called from the driveway."

The detective nodded without comment. He looked again at the note scrawled on the door. Sniffed at it. Declared that it was lipstick, not crayon. Took a couple of cell phone pictures of it.

Roz told him she knew who had broken in and written it. "Who?"

She recounted her entire history with Mr. Schroeder's evil, dead-eyed nephew. He listened in silence, jotting a few notes as she spoke. When she was done, he said, "I haven't seen any sign of forced entry. All your doors and windows were closed and locked, and you said the garage was closed. Do you have any idea how he got in?"

"I was hoping you'd tell me."

The detective responded with a whole series of questions. Did she live alone? Any recent breakups with a romantic partner? Did anyone else have keys to the house? Was anything stolen? Yes, no, no way, and not sure. There hadn't been time to check. The detective accompanied her while she walked from room to room, looking around. She reported that nothing appeared to be missing.

He asked her to check her makeup supply to see if the lipstick used to write the note had been hers. She explained that she never wore lipstick, and, therefore, kept none in the house. His only response was a skeptical sounding "huh." When he asked her for a sample of her handwriting, she realized he didn't believe her report. He assured her it was standard operating procedure, a formality. *Yeah, right.*

Almost as an afterthought, he said, "I noticed you have doorbell cameras. Why don't we check the video feed now?" Roz had forgotten all about that. She felt a surge of excitement, knowing the video would vindicate her. But as the two of them watched the doorbell video at high-speed playback, they saw nothing. Just a couple of anomalous visual artifacts at the back door a little after 3:00 a.m. A few flecks and lines of green light that flickered for a moment and then disappeared. Other than a possum and a raccoon that wandered past, there was nothing to see. Nothing big enough to be human. Yet a human had gotten into the house and made threats.

The detective explained that most cases of B&E—cop shorthand for breaking and entering—were pretty straightforward. It was unsophisticated burglars looking for drugs, money, or portable items they could sell for quick cash. Domestic disputes with an ex-lover. On rare occasions, it was a rapist looking for his next victim. None of those things looked to be at play here. Instead, Roz's home had been invaded by an invisible intruder, who got in without forced entry, and neither stole anything nor bothered her. He only broke in to leave a note written with lipstick he brought with him for the occasion, and left as mysteriously as he had arrived. Was that about the size of it?

Frustrated, Roz explained again about her run-in with Brandon. How he'd warned her to steer clear of his uncle's property, but she had gone back anyway. The next morning, the writing was on her door. It couldn't be a coincidence. Brandon was the only logical suspect. The detective listened without giving any indication he accepted her conclusion. No evidence of a crime sometimes meant no crime had occurred. Sometimes "crime victims" were lonely people looking for a little attention. It was understandable, he said, but risky, since filing a false police report was itself a crime. Roz felt as if her head was going to explode.

In the end, the detective took down Brandon Heckler's name and address, promising to talk to the man. He warned her the suspect would have to confess outright, or there wouldn't be probable cause to charge him. If he opted not to talk at all, the investigation would be dead on arrival.

Once the public servants had all left, Roz once again felt vulnerable in the extreme. In a panic, she stuffed a satchel with some additional items she might want and headed out the front door. From her car, she made three calls. The first was to her office. She explained she'd been the victim of a crime and needed to take a week off. The second was to the church voicemail, informing the secretary, and through her, the pastor, that she had to go out of town and would miss some services. The last call was to her mother, to announce a surprise visit.

Within twenty minutes, she was on the Mass Pike headed west. She wasn't running away. At least that was what she told herself. The trip to visit her mother was an annual obligation. Making the trip two months earlier than usual was sheer coincidence. Try as she might, though, she couldn't fool herself. The fact she had stuffed the satchel with important papers such as her passport, original Social Security Card, checkbook, $2,500 in cash, mortgage documents, and even the title to her car, made the whole "I'm not running away" story ring hollow.

As she drove, she thought about Mr. Schroeder's scary situation to avoid thinking about her own woes in an endless loop. Messing with someone's medicine was extreme, but it looked as if Brandon had done just that. And he had lied about her. All that was bad enough; she hoped he hadn't stooped so low as to do away with Sarge. It took a heartless and depraved person to hurt a fuzzy little critter like Sarge on purpose. Given Brandon's straight-outta-Tartarus vibe, she'd have been more than willing to believe Mr. Schroeder's suspicions—but his tale of ghost sightings complicated things. Roz didn't believe in ghosts. The old man had sounded sincere. She knew he wasn't lying. Yet Roz had to admit that the most likely explanation was that he had an overactive imagination fueled by grief. Or perhaps he was suffering from mental decline, the beginnings of dementia. Neither possibility was encouraging, but she much preferred them to the one remaining alternative she could envision.

Roz turned onto I-84 and drove through Connecticut and New York. After crossing into Pennsylvania, she stopped at the rest area in Matamoras. A little kiosk displayed free literature listing places to go and things to do in the state. One brochure was about Beaver County, where she had been born and where her mother still lived. She flipped through it, shaking her head at a sentence that read, "We are blessed with a number of historical and heritage points that will peak your interest." *Peak*, rather than *pique*.

Perhaps the county was too cash strapped to spring for an editor. She felt a modicum of guilt for picking up on the error, as if noticing it proved she was pedantic or even a grammar Nazi. She took the brochure, along with booklets from neighboring Allegheny County and Butler County. Some of the information might come in handy if she moved back to the area. Not that she was running away or anything. Time to get back in the car. She'd been driving for over four hours, but the longest part of her drive was still in front of her.

By late afternoon, she was having a hard time staying alert. Route 68 West in Clarion gave her the opportunity to ditch the monotony of I-80. The up-close views from secondary roads felt less static than the distant views from highways, and the twists, turns, and rapid elevation changes made back roads more involving. Her big Lincoln was a highway cruiser, but enough was enough. This sometimes-scenic byway would take her the final seventy-five miles to her childhood home.

Her destination was in the heart of Beaver County, near Pennsylvania's southwest corner, nestled up against the Ohio state line. It wasn't a big place. The county's population was one-tenth that of Middlesex County, where she lived now. Not one city in Beaver County had a population of over ten thousand. The view out the window presented one tired-looking small town after another. Weeds pushed up through cracked sidewalks. Graffiti covered every overpass. Shuttered factories and boarded-up warehouses stood watch over heavy equipment rusting away on vacant lots. The county's industrial past was dead but still unburied. The carcass lay draped over the hills and valleys, a constant reminder of more prosperous days now long gone.

An hour-and-forty-five minutes more brought her at last to Fairport, at the confluence of the Ohio and Beaver Rivers. Fairport was home to about thirty-six hundred people, at least a few dozen of whom might still remember Roz. That thought filled her with embarrassment; she wished she had lost more weight before returning. She wished that every year.

Roz had lived in Fairport until the age of thirteen. Her parents' divorce when she was eleven pushed her down the path of stress eating. The more she anesthetized herself with food, the more weight she gained. The more she gained, the more her mother harped on her. As the criticisms and even punishments multiplied and intensified, so did the reasons to turn to the fridge for comfort. Her parents had rejected each other, and now her mother was rejecting her. The two butted heads until Roz couldn't take it anymore. She went to live with her father in Massachusetts. Other than the annual visits she felt were required of a dutiful daughter, she had not come back in sixteen years. Now, staying here was a possibility.

She parked in front of the house and grabbed her duffel bag from the trunk. The short walk up the sidewalk and the five steps to the front porch were as daunting a journey as the nearly twelve-hour drive from Framingham had been. Roz braced herself and rang the bell.

The door opened and her father's ex-wife blew outside like a leaf in a stiff breeze and fired off a barrage of comments and questions. "Rosalyn! Glad you made it safely. I was expecting you an hour ago. Come in, come in! How was the drive? You tired? Want me to take your bag? Look at you, have you lost a little weight?"

Each question followed so closely on the heels of its predecessor that Roz had no time to respond to any of them before the next one came barreling at her. At least she could answer the last question. "Yes, Mom, I've lost weight. A lot, in fact. Thanks for noticing."

"Well, good for you! I always knew you could trim down if you got serious about it. Get down another half-dozen dress sizes and you might land yourself a good man one day."

Some things never changed. Her mother had a knack for delivering backhanded compliments and insults with a thin veneer of politeness. This was still an improvement over Roz's childhood, when the woman hadn't bothered with the veneer. Every time she visited here, Roz felt like her preteen self—rejected, ashamed, awkward, powerless, and tongue-tied. Was winning the acceptance of her own mother too much to ask?

She had to remind herself she was no longer that preteen girl. Those feelings were nothing more than an echo of the past that still reverberated in this house. There was no need to take the bait her mother dangled in front of her. She changed the subject.

"How is life in Fairport these days?"

Her mother shrugged. "Same as always. Could be better. Has been better. Could be worse. Probably will be worse soon enough. Why?"

"I've been considering coming back to Beaver County. Thought I'd check out where the jobs are, what towns are growing, where I might get the most bang for my real estate buck—that sort of thing."

Her mother looked alarmed. "Did you lose your job? Didn't I tell you years ago there was no security working in retail?"

"No, Mom, I didn't lose my job. And you make it sound like I'm a cashier in some strip mall. I'm a marketing manager in the corporate headquarters of a company with $50 billion in annual revenue."

"So why on earth are you considering coming back here if things are so 'beautiful for situation' at home?"

Roz caught the partial quote from Psalm 48. That her mother could be the queen of mean didn't stop her slinging

Bible citations with the best of them. "I have a good income and reasonable job security, at least for the moment. But I'm juggling multiple problems. Moving and making a fresh start might be the solution. I figured I'd start looking here rather than someplace unfamiliar."

"So tell me about these problems," her mother said. "Start from the beginning."

Roz did so, surprising herself with her own candor. She wished she were as cagey and guarded as Shawna, especially given her mother's penchant for barbed commentary. But once the tale came pouring out, she couldn't stop it. First, she spoke of the people she had laid off, and the vandalism to her car and house that followed. She talked about her best friend's departure from her church and from her life, as well as her growing discomfort with the atmosphere the pastor had created at Solid Rock. Mrs. Grimm escaped mention—her mother would not have understood the issues there—but Roz shared her concern for Mr. Schroeder, along with the harrowing events of the past twenty-four hours. She unburdened herself for a long time, and much to her surprise, her mother listened without interruption.

They had been sitting at the dining room table. When Roz finished her account, her mother gazed at her in silence for a few seconds. She stood and said, "Come with me."

"Where are we going? I've been driving all day!"

"You'll see. I'll drive. Maybe we can solve some of your problems."

They made their way to a newish Kia Sorento. Roz was silent as they drove up Canton Street, called Morris's Hill by most of the locals. At the top of the hill, her mom turned right and pointed out the pile of rubble that used to be the little store that gave the street its popular name.

Boarded-up windows had marked the face of Morris's since before Roz was born. Now the roof and walls had collapsed, leaving heaps of bricks to compete for space with the scrubby trees that were growing up through the floor.

From there, they zigzagged over to Delaware Avenue. "See that empty storefront? That was Diddio's Restaurant once upon a time. It's where I first had cheesecake with cherry topping instead of the weak strawberry sauce that all the other places drizzle on it. Fell in love with that dish. Haven't been able to find it anywhere since Diddio's closed back in the nineties. That building has been vacant since you were an infant. Even the gas station next door to it shut down years ago."

They made their way up to Brighton Avenue, the main street of Fairport's business district. "I remember how this all looked when I was a kid," her mother continued. "This street had everything. A furniture store, a shoe store, a bank, a five and dime called W.T. Grant. There wasn't an empty storefront anywhere. Now look at it! Most all these buildings are vacant, except for a couple of bars at the far end of the street. It's all so shabby now." She yanked the Kia into a sudden U-turn. There was no traffic to contend with, even though the time of day would have meant rush hour in most places.

"See that building on the left? It housed medical offices when you were young. But back in the day, it was the Penn Beaver

Hotel. Super upscale. My grandmother told me it was the most opulent hotel between Pittsburgh and Cleveland, a hundred miles away. Lots of famous people stayed at the Penn Beaver, including the Three Stooges when they were performing in the area. In those days, Fairport was a tourist destination, a major stop for the passenger trains that ran from the East Coast to Chicago. Fifty trains a day used to stop at the station here. Fifty trains a day! Hard to imagine that. Now it's none."

The tour continued like this for quite a while. They drove past the former community hospital turned nursing home, the former elementary school turned low-income housing, and the tiny little corner store that had stood whitewashed and abandoned for as long as Roz could remember. "That store doubled as the school bus stop for the entire neighborhood. We used to buy candy and stuff there every day after school. SweeTARTS, Pixy Stix, Nehi orange pop, or RC Cola. Spane's, that was the name of the store. I can still hear the screen door slamming on its big spring. That door hasn't opened in more than forty years.

"I've lived in this town my whole life. So did my mother and grandmother. Watching this town wither away is like keeping an endless vigil by the deathbed of a loved one. You alternate between praying for a miracle and wishing someone would pull the plug and have the funeral already. Your great-grandma was here in 1930 when Fairport reached its peak population. It's been losing people ever since, shrinking like an old tire with a slow leak for the last ninety years. Most of the other towns around here are faring no better. Take a gander at Beaver Falls, Midland,

Monaca, Freedom, and Ambridge. You'll see I'm right." Sounding more than a little irritated, she asked, "Do you understand why I'm showing you all of this?"

Roz said, "I guess because the area has been down on its luck for generations, and you think I should start over somewhere more promising."

Her mother grimaced. "Pshaw, I didn't need to play tour guide to tell you something anybody with one good eye could see. No, I hoped that my university-educated, corporate honcho daughter could discern the bigger picture."

She's always going to be like this, and I don't need it today. Roz inhaled deeply and let it out, trying to exhale her exasperation. "I'm tired, Mom. Just tell me what this bigger picture is that I'm supposed to be seeing."

"Well, let's start where you did, with the obvious: this place isn't what it used to be. But no place is what it used to be. People always find that surprising, like they expect to find something near perfect that stays that way. God doesn't change, but everyone and everything else does." They had pulled up to the house again, but her mother made no move to get out of the car. She wasn't finished instructing.

"Now if you accept that—and you'd have to be an extraslow learner not to—let's take it a step further: What can you do when you find yourself somewhere you're no longer happy to be? You've got three choices. Your first option is to escape. Get out. Look for greener pastures. More than half the people in this town have opted for that. The problem is that whatever place you run to will also change. Greener grass doesn't always stay green. Half the time, you bring your real troubles with you. And once you start running away, it becomes a habit. Ask your father about that."

Roz pursed her lips but let the remark pass without comment. She hated hearing her dad disparaged. Her mother's bottomless well of bitterness and criticism would have done in any man, eventually. His moving to Massachusetts had changed Roz's life for the better in more ways than one. Besides a change of scenery and a reprieve from her mother's withering commentary, the move to Boston Metro meant support, encouragement, and warm relations at home. But it didn't last. When Roz graduated from college, her dad retired to Florida with a live-in girlfriend about Roz's age. He and Roz didn't talk as often as they once had.

After a brief pause, her mother continued. "Your second option is to fix your problems instead of fleeing them. Doesn't matter whether we're talking about your job, your lost friendships, or your relationship with the neighbors. Put things back the way they were. Now most people will say they can't do that. They may even be right. But I admire those who try. I read where some man is planning to reopen the old Penn Beaver. It's going to have a restaurant and a billiards parlor and inexpensive room rates. Maybe Brighton Avenue will come back from the dead if this man can give enough people a reason to go there again. But I digress. The point is, if you don't like the way things are, option two is to change them."

She opened her door, and Roz thought they were done. But her mom added, "There is one more choice. If you don't leave, and you don't fix things, all you can do is moan about how bad things are. Wallow in sadness and self-pity for all that's lost. It was obvious you weren't enjoying my little municipal history lesson. Maybe you found it depressing. Well, mark my words, if you're not careful, you're going to end up feeling and sounding just like me. Not about this place, of course. You didn't live here long enough for this town to get into your heart.

"But I'll spell it out for you in case it's not clear yet: Solid Rock Church is your Fairport. It's a place with a glorious past and a tattered present. You linger there because you know it well. There is comfort in familiarity, even unpleasant familiarity. Plus, you hope the glory will return, but you know deep down it won't. You're trying to hold on to an echo. An afterimage. That's all memories are. They're not substantial enough to live in. Memories are wispy, unstable things, forever shifting, until they burn off like fog in the morning sun.

"Then what will you have to show for all the years you spent hoping? Life is too short for that. Leave that place. Or change it. But don't waste another minute complaining about what it has become."

Roz gasped when she saw tears spill down her mother's face. The woman had always been fierce, with anger as her emotional default. That was why Roz tried so hard to be pleasant to everyone. The last thing on earth she wanted was to end up sounding like her mother.

True to form, her mother got out of the car, closed the door harder than needed, and stalked toward her front porch without looking back. Roz stayed where she was, thinking. *There is comfort in familiarity, even unpleasant familiarity. Is that why I keep coming back here?* Despite her abrasive manner, Mom had been talking sense. The choices she laid out amounted to the old instincts of fight, flight, or freeze.

Fighting—changing or fixing things, as her mother put it—was out of the question. Fight the culture at her job? She wasn't privileged to help steer the corporate ship. Management title aside, she wasn't much more than another crew member lashed to an oar. Contest anything about the way Pastor Bowers was leading Solid Rock? And get away with it? Maybe when migratory swine soared overhead in V-formation on their way south for the winter. Change Brandon Heckler's evil ways? If her mother had gotten to meet the man, she would know how preposterous that idea was.

Flight was the only choice that made sense. But was it a realistic possibility? Could she follow through with quitting her job, selling her house, and cutting ties with church? Work and church were the binary stars around which her whole life orbited. Could her fear of Brandon Heckler propel her to escape velocity? Or would she forever be captive to their enormous gravitational pull? One thing was certain: she wouldn't get it all figured out while sitting in this car. Time to go back into the house and make some dinner arrangements.

As she stepped inside, she heard the harsh ringing of a phone. Not a cell phone, but her mother's landline. Or maybe it was VOIP by now, since so few people still had old-fashioned landlines these days. The phone was sitting on a little console table in the dining room. She heard her mother pick it up and say hello, followed by "One moment, please." She walked into the living room and said, "It's for you!" She sounded as surprised as Roz felt.

Roz picked up the receiver and said, "This is Rosalyn."

"Hello, neighbor! Or should I say former neighbor? I'm glad you took my advice and left town. That was a wise decision. I wanted to let you know about a brief conversation I had with that nice detective you sent over. I talked to him through the door for the few seconds it took to tell him I had no use for cops and no interest in speaking further. I told him to come back with a warrant or don't come back. He won't be returning. And neither should you. You'll be happier with family nearby. Safer too. By the way, that's a cute little house your mom has."

Roz slammed the receiver down.

"Who was that?" her mother asked.

"It was that horrible man I told you about."

"How in the world did he get my number? Who told him you were coming here?"

Roz wailed, "I don't know! I didn't tell anyone I was coming. But Mom, the man was in my house while I slept! He came and went without triggering the cameras. I don't know how he did any of that, never mind how he got this number or figured out I was here."

Her mother gave her a look of genuine pity. In other circumstances, Roz might have taken a few seconds to appreciate this rarity. "He's sending you a message that he can reach out and touch you anywhere, anytime. He knows you're running, but he wants you to look over your shoulder while you're running. You have the same three choices I mentioned before. Running won't make you feel safe, and venting about it can't help. From what you've told me, the police won't be much help either. You're going to have to save yourself. I don't envy you."

Roz barely registered her mother's words. In a quandary, she wandered back outside. Surely the man could not have followed her for six hundred miles. He couldn't be here watching her . . . could he? She looked up and down the street. No, he would stick out like a sore thumb in this little neighborhood full of old people. He couldn't be here. The only explanation that made sense was that Brandon had attached some type of tracker to her car. He could have done it when he broke into her house. *While I slept.* The mental image of his hands on any of her stuff was nauseating. She feared the memory of the home invasion would never fade. It gave her the shivers now. She had to stop freaking out long enough to figure this out.

She remembered some news story about car thieves using Apple Air Tags to track a car from, say, a mall parking lot to someone's home, where they could steal it later. The "buy here, pay here" type of used car lot used hidden GPS trackers to make sure they could repo a car from a customer who fell behind on payments. What stood out in her memory was the fact the devices were small enough to fit almost anywhere: under the car, inside a taillight, behind the glove box, or tucked up behind the pedals.

Early the next morning, she went out to look. She looked under the trunk lid and under the hood. Most of the stuff in there was unfamiliar. She could be looking right at the tracker and wouldn't know. There were no suspicious lumps or bumps inside the wheel wells or on the underside of the bumpers. If there was a tracker, she'd never find it like this. Perhaps a mechanic could locate it. But removing it would alert her stalker that it was gone. Much better to keep him thinking she was clueless—which she was.

On the evening of her third day back, she was pacing in her bedroom while her various problems chased each other in circles in her head. She hated bailing out on Mr. Schroeder in his time of need, but it wasn't safe for her to go home, and she couldn't help him from this distance. Days spent trying to draw her mother into something that felt like a normal conversation only added to her frustrations. While she brooded over these issues, a chime emanated from her purse. Incoming email. She fished out her phone and saw the email was from the church secretary at Solid Rock. Roz had been blind carbon copied, so the message must have gone out to the whole church directory. She read the contents:

I regret to inform the Solid Rock family that Brother Donald Caruthers passed away unexpectedly last night. We are all heartbroken by this news. Please keep his family in prayer. We will send an announcement concerning funeral arrangements as soon as details are available.

Pastor Bowers

Roz's hand flew to her mouth, and she squeezed her eyes shut. How much worse could this week get? When the initial shock wore off, she opened her eyes and reread the email, as if she might have misread it the first time. Donald Caruthers was the church's head usher, the deepest bass singing voice in the congregation, and loved by everyone there. The undisputed king of dad jokes, Roz thought him perhaps the nicest man she'd ever met. He was also the father of her old friend, Eddie Caruthers. To say that Eddie had suffered a rough patch over the past year was an understatement. And now this. None of Roz's friends knew where he had gone, but even Eddie would have to come back for his father's funeral. And Roz knew she needed to be there to offer support to him and his siblings. Solving her own problems would have to wait. She might leave Framingham for good one day soon, but for now she was returning home, come what may.

CHAPTER 13
FUNERAL FOR A FRIEND

Roz spent Wednesday researching the inventory of used car dealers within fifty miles of her mother's house. Although driven by the need to ditch her car and the hidden tracker she was sure was in it, the search wasn't all desperate necessity. There was an unexpected bright side. Riding in her mother's Kia proved she no longer required bench seats. She had suffered no discomfort in the bucket seats in that SUV. The Fatmobile would soon be a thing of the past.

That said, she didn't want an SUV or a crossover, as they were ubiquitous. She wanted something she wouldn't have trouble finding in a crowded parking lot. Something distinctive. Something special. One car that caught her attention when she first saw it online was a station wagon. It had everything her old Lincoln did not: a pleasing modern design aesthetic, all-wheel drive, and bucket seats that were both heated and air-conditioned.

The seats even had a massage function that would doubtless come in handy on the long drive home. It also had a handsome three-pointed star on the grille.

And so it was that Roz traded in her old car at a dealer to became the proud second owner of a Mercedes E400 wagon in Selenite Gray, with a two-tone beige-and-brown interior. That interior would take a little getting used to. But at least the car wasn't black on black, and it was a full two feet shorter than the old Lincoln, so she wouldn't have to hear any more Batmobile jokes. Best of all, Brandon would think she was still in Pennsylvania after she'd left the state. She'd be back home in Framingham before he had a clue.

Eleven hours after saying goodbye to her mother, an exhausted Roz pulled into her driveway. It was well after dark. She lowered her window and pulled a big stack of mail from the mailbox. She chided herself for not remembering to suspend mail delivery. Most of it was junk.

She slid the few bills into her purse and tossed the rest of the mail onto the seat beside her. Time to fish out the garage-door remote and sync it to the new car. Before she could begin, the unease that had been increasing the closer she got to home blossomed into acute fear. This bogeyman had broken in while she had been asleep in the house. The alarm system had proven to be no obstacle. What if he was there right now? He could be in a closet or lurking in the corner of any room. He could be lying on her bed right at this moment. That mental picture was too much to take.

In a panic, Roz opted to sleep elsewhere. She backed out of the driveway, but stopped long enough to put the junk mail back in her mailbox. If her evil neighbor wanted to verify that she was still away, the uncollected mail would suggest she was. That done, she hightailed it out of the neighborhood and made for a nearby Hampton Inn. She would sleep there until she figured out how to work up the nerve to enter her own home.

Brandon realized it had been a couple of days since he last confirmed the location of the GPS transmitter. He'd checked Roz's mailbox early that morning, and it was full of mail. Now a few keystrokes on his computer showed the fat lady's car was still in Pennsylvania, a few miles from Fairport.

Of course, she would have to come back at some point. She was going to have to come pack up her possessions, move out, and put the house up for sale. He had no problem with that, provided she stayed away from Uncle Al. Maybe he should pay her house another visit, leaving a note that spelled out the parameters of his tolerance. Might make her feel better about things to know he was not an unreasonable man. He would do it that very night.

Roz woke up in her hotel room, determined to get over her fear. Today was the last of her five days off from work. By Monday, she'd need to be back in some sort of routine. And she still needed to stop at home for something to wear to tonight's homegoing service for Donald Caruthers. Besides, she missed the comfort of her own bed. She wanted to reclaim her place, not run away to parts unknown. Roz remembered a book she had read by a sales trainer turned motivational speaker. The book was forgettable, but one idea from it had stuck with her. "Do the thing you fear most, and you conquer fear." So be it. This evening, she would go back home to stay.

At 5:30 she pulled into her driveway, got the mail from the box again, and synced the car's garage door buttons to her house. She pulled inside and parked, chastising herself at how frightened she'd let herself become the previous evening. *This isn't so bad. Everything is scarier at night.*

She walked into the living room and turned on the TV. She had no intention of watching anything, but hearing human voices was reassuring. A walk-through of all the rooms showed nothing out of place. Apart from the air being stale, everything was as it should have been. Good. Time to get ready. The service would start at 7:00 p.m.

At 6:45, she sat down in her customary spot on a back bench in Solid Rock's sanctuary. The huge sanctuary was almost full. Half the town must have known Donald Caruthers and had come out to pay their respects. The front row was for members of the immediate family. There was daughter Lorna and her husband, son Jason and his wife, and beside Jason, her friend and Donald's youngest son, Eddie. She hadn't laid eyes on him in a year. Joy at seeing him and sorrow because of the occasion made for an unsettling swirl of emotions. And while most of the family was as still and somber looking as you might expect, Eddie looked jumpy, as if he was expecting trouble. He kept turning to look toward the doors and scan the crowd.

As she waited for the service to start, Roz noticed the cascade of stage whispers and muttered comments that crisscrossed the sanctuary. People were talking about Eddie in shocked and disapproving tones. She couldn't catch it all, but what she heard was bad news. Word was that Eddie had been involved in more violence. This time he had shot someone. The incident had even made the local paper. Having been in Pennsylvania, this was the first Roz had caught wind of it. She tried to block the gossip out. Whatever Eddie had become involved in, whispering about him was no way to honor the memory of his dad.

The service itself was beautiful. Pastor Bowers reminded all assembled that the sorrow they all felt was not for Donald Caruthers, who was at this moment experiencing more love, comfort, and joy than any of them could imagine. No, the sorrow was for themselves, as all who knew Donald Caruthers were poorer for his absence. The preacher challenged all present to live such an exemplary life.

At the end, everyone lined up to give the members of the Caruthers family a handshake, a hug, and an expression of sympathy and support. Eddie still looked distracted, barely glancing at his well-wishers before casting his gaze around the room again.

It wasn't until she was standing right in front of him that Roz could see the pain in his eyes. She wondered what had given him the haunted expression. Roz had been to more church funerals than she could count. These services were almost always a celebration of a life of faith well lived, a fight well fought, a race finished with a victor's crown waiting on the other side. Sadness was part of it, of course, but the anguish she saw in Eddie's eyes was an order of magnitude greater than expected. Regret. Fear. The substance of the whispered tales must be an awful weight on him. She clasped his hand and said, "We all loved your dad. My deepest sympathies for your loss, but I'm here for you. Anything you need. We all are." He nodded and gave her a fleeting, half-hearted smile. Distracted, he scanned the sanctuary again. She wasn't positive he had even heard her.

Back at home, she sat in her favorite recliner. The burial would be tomorrow, but she didn't plan to go to the graveside service or to the enormous meal at the church that would follow it. She hoped Eddie would not disappear again after everything was done. She thought about him for a while. The clock chimed 10:00, and she rose to get a glass of water before going to bed. When she reached the fridge, she froze in her tracks. Affixed to the refrigerator door was a sheet of orange construction paper. The magnet that held it there was hers, but the paper was not. Nor were the peel-and-stick letters that covered it. Heart pounding, she picked it up and read:

Knew you'd have to return. As a goodwill gesture, I grant you one month to pack up your stuff and move out. The clock starts when you read this. You may come and go freely in the interim if you mind your own business. But if you play stupid games, you'll win stupid prizes. Telling the police about my visit would count as playing stupid games.

At the bottom of the page was a hand-printed addendum in black magic marker:

P.S. I thought you'd want to know that the milk in your fridge is spoiled. It's several days past the use-by date. Really, you ought to keep up with these things.

Roz wanted to scream. She wanted to run outside. She wanted to call the police, but knew it would accomplish nothing. With her luck, she'd get the same skeptical detective as before. This time, however, the initial spike of terror died quickly, as did the urge to flee. Those feelings retreated before an incoming wave of outrage and steely resolve. What she wanted more than anything was to show this jerk that he could not run her off. She would not sell her house and uproot her life. She was going to stay right here and sleep in her own bed tonight, and every night thereafter. Creeped out though she was, Roz climbed into bed with all the defiance she could muster.

But the house that had been her oasis seemed determined to keep her on edge. Its floorboards creaked and popped more than she remembered. The ticking of the kitchen clock was too loud. The central air whispered and sighed in the ductwork. And the moments of dead silence were even more unnerving than the random noises. It was a long time before she drifted off to sleep.

The night passed without incident, and Saturday was uneventful too, though Roz still found herself jumping at every little sound. Early on Sunday, the church secretary texted to ask whether she could spare a few minutes to meet with the pastor during Sunday School. She replied in the affirmative. To her surprise, she was ambivalent about the meeting. She figured Rev. Bowers must have come up with some insights regarding a calling, a purpose, a sense of what would give her life greater meaning. Not so long ago, that had been her most urgent problem. It would have excited her to receive the pastor's guidance. But Brandon Heckler had changed all that. Now that she had a dangerous enemy to deal with, she couldn't think of much else. But she couldn't let the tyranny of the urgent distract her from what was important in the long term. She promised herself she'd focus fully on whatever the pastor had to say.

When Roz, Rev. Bowers, and the pastor's wife were all seated in his office, he got right to the point. "Are you familiar with the Pastor's Aide Auxiliary?"

Roz answered, "I'm familiar with the name. I can probably call to mind who is in it. Don't know exactly what they do."

"They do crucial work. Crucial work," he repeated. His solemn tone underscored his words. "Let me give it some context." He opened a Bible on his desk. "I'm reading from Exodus 17:8: 'Now Amalek came and fought with Israel in Rephidim. And

Moses said to Joshua, Choose us some men and go out, fight with Amalek. Tomorrow I will stand on the top of the hill with the rod of God in my hand. So Joshua did as Moses said to him, and fought with Amalek. And Moses, Aaron, and Hur went up to the top of the hill. And so it was, when Moses held up his hand, that Israel prevailed; and when he let down his hand, Amalek prevailed. But Moses' hands became heavy; so they took a stone and put it under him, and he sat on it. And Aaron and Hur supported his hands, one on one side, and the other on the other side; and his hands were steady until the going down of the sun. So Joshua defeated Amalek and his people with the edge of the sword.'"

Bowers closed the book. "As it was with Israel in the wilderness, so it is with this church. To win the spiritual battles that we fight, there are many things I have to do. These things are difficult. Moses found it hard to hold that staff up in the air all day. Likewise, the burdens laid on me are taxing. Anything that makes the job a little easier for me helps the whole church to succeed. While no one physically props my arms up in the air, the work of the Pastor's Aide Auxiliary has the same effect in the spirit. They make sure there is plenty of cold water on the pulpit. And they supply me with hot tea after service, so that I don't preach myself hoarse. They take care of the dry cleaning of pulpit robes and baptismal robes. That's the easiest stuff."

He continued. "They commit to praying for me and Sister Bowers on a daily basis. And one of the most important roles of the PAA is to help the congregation live out the biblical instruction to recognize and honor the work of the ministry. The Apostle Paul wrote that the church was to 'recognize those who labor among you, and are over you in the Lord and admonish you, and to esteem them very highly in love for their work's sake.' Helping the congregation to do this can mean organizing the celebrations for things like our birthdays and wedding anniversaries, along with the church and pastoral anniversaries. The church always blesses us with some gift or another on these and other occasions, like Mother's Day and Father's Day. We can't be too involved in managing any of that, so the PAA does it on our behalf. Also, as you know, when we have fellowship dinners throughout the year, a handful of people testify something about the goodness of the Lord, their appreciation for the church, and their love and appreciation for their pastor and first lady." The preacher steepled his fingers and looked at Roz with a grave expression. "This is sensitive information, and I'm counting on your maturity and discretion. These testimonies don't fall together of their own accord. Someone has to choose which church members will speak, and maybe even coach them a little on how to make their testimony as effective as possible."

Here, the pastor's wife interjected. "For example, a testimony often lands better if the person delivering it cries. Not everyone has spellbinding rhetorical skills, but the tears show the remarks are from the heart." The preacher nodded his agreement.

All of this felt slimy and exploitative to Roz, and she hoped her face didn't betray her disgust. So someone recruited people to sing the pastor's praises, and coached them on how to tug at the heartstrings? Ugh.

Maybe the pastor sensed her mood. "I want you to know," he said, "that it is more than a little uncomfortable for us to sit through these public expressions of gratitude. Like anyone with humility, we'd rather labor in obscurity. It's all about Him, after all." He pointed heavenward in case there was any question about who *Him* was. "But like the scripture says, we 'Permit it to be so now, for thus it is fitting for us to fulfill all righteousness.'" Bowers gave Roz an earnest look that suggested his next utterance would be weighty. "Anyway, we feel you are the right person to head up the Pastor's Aide Auxiliary. Sister Smith is the current president, but we feel that it's time to make a change. Will you take on this task?"

Roz stammered a bit before regaining firm control of her tongue. "I appreciate you thinking of me. I think I need to pray about it and get back to you, if that's all right."

"That's a good instinct," said the pastor. "You should make all your important decisions only after prayer. But I want you to be assured that *we* have prayed about it. We would not have come to you unless we had. And we feel comfortable that this is in the will of God."

"I hear you on that," Roz said. "But with everything that's been going on in my life of late, not to mention the funeral this weekend, I'm tired and a little stressed. I don't want to take on a crucial responsibility without at least meditating on it for a bit. Can you give me this week to think about it and maybe ask some questions before I accept?"

The pastor smiled a magnanimous smile. "Of course we can do that. I appreciate your deliberate approach to things. It will serve you well in the position."

Roz made it all the way back through the sanctuary and outside before her composure broke and she let out a sardonic guffaw. She couldn't believe she had held out any hope for this meeting. She should have known it would be a joke.

Not that her surprise was total. Long experience had taught her that when church leaders said, "Only what you do for Christ will last," they almost always meant whatever you do within the four walls of the church building. They had a program to promote, names to shuffle around on an organizational chart, and their vision rarely went farther than that. Still, this time should have been different. She had sought his counsel about finding her calling. Her life's purpose. His response was to put her in charge of ice water and dry cleaning. Because who wouldn't find that fulfilling? She would also be in charge of hitting people up for gifts and arranging scripted testimonials complete with theatrical tears. That would feel emptier and more distasteful than anything in her life as a corporate minion ever had. Roz didn't need a week to decide. She had zero interest in heading up the PAA. She would never do it.

There was one insurmountable problem. When the pastor and his wife both asked you to do something, saying no was not an option. It was an unwritten law, as reliable as the law of gravity. That was one of the frustrating aspects of church life. Her mother's advice about job and church came back to her. *Leave them. Or fix them. But don't waste another minute complaining about what they've become.*

CHAPTER 14
SILLY LOVE SONGS

Each passing day brought Brandon's deadline another day closer. What would happen after a month? Roz found some welcome respite from that worry in an unlikely place: the office. There is comfort in familiarity, even unpleasant familiarity. The communal griping, the well-worn refrains about being overworked and underpaid, about clueless bosses and obscene corporate profits not shared with the folks whose labors made it happen—it was all comforting because it was a harmless ritual. It was a sing-along where everyone knew the words. These were people Roz had known for years, and they were grumpy but nonthreatening. The endless meetings, unrealistic deadlines, and petty disagreements at work provided a welcome distraction from the darker fears that plagued her at home.

At home, she set herself the task of making her house a harder target. She purchased a mail-order security system with motion detectors, door and window sensors, and inside cameras to complement her doorbell cameras. She put the supplied sign, the one that announced which alarm company the home was protected by, on a stake in the lawn near the front door. At a local hardware store, she bought reinforcing plates for her doorjambs. Home Depot sold her a solid-core door to replace the flimsy hollow door to her bedroom, and the store set her up with a handyman to install it. She augmented the new bedroom door with a portable brace she hoped would keep anyone from forcing their way in. Each improvement made her feel a little more secure, but there were still nights she retreated to a hotel to get a full night's sleep. She looked forward to church services and choir rehearsals, as they offered another reason to be out of the house.

Two Sundays after the funeral of Donald Caruthers, as Roz was settling herself on her bench for the start of morning service, Marvin Blackwell made a waddling beeline straight for her. She braced herself. "Starvin' Marvin Snackwell," as some members referred to him, was new to Solid Rock, having joined four months ago. She had nothing against Marvin, but he had been evincing a romantic interest in her for several weeks now. It was an interest she did not reciprocate. She suspected that Pastor Bowers had encouraged her portly suitor to set his sights on her. Matchmaking was an unofficial sport at Solid Rock, and nobody played the game with more intensity than the ministry. She remembered the look that passed between Rev. Bowers and his wife after they asked for her thoughts on dating. Maybe they had steered Marvin her way because of the two obvious things he had in common with her: melanin and a high body-mass index.

"Mornin', Sister! I wonder if you would be so kind as to help me resolve a Bible difficulty."

Roz made sure that none of the creeping dread she felt came out in either her facial expression or her tone of voice. "How can I help you?"

"Well, I was reading through the Book of Numbers and realized I don't have yours!"

In theory, there had to be cheesier lines out there, though Roz couldn't imagine one. "Oh, that's not a problem. After a while, you won't even notice." She hoped the sweet tone of her delivery took any sting out of her words. It must have.

Marvin loomed over her, closer than she would have liked. "Have you ever seen a suit like this? Do you know what this material is?" He proffered his sleeve.

Cheap was what it was. Ill-fitting was what it was. Roz felt bad for noticing, but since she made her living at the headquarters of a fashion retailer, noticing poor quality was unavoidable. It was an otherwise ordinary-looking suit, medium gray with dark pinstripes. The only distinguishing feature was its size. She knew she'd have to play along with whatever this ruse was, so she hazarded an answer. "Um . . . wool?"

"One might think so," he declared, his voice full of triumph, "But this here is boyfriend material!"

"Blessed are the merciful, for they shall obtain mercy." That quotation was all that kept Rosalyn from telling Marvin what

she thought of his banter. Instead, she managed a polite chuckle and gestured at the wall clock. Service was about to start. Marvin nodded his understanding. But before departing, he said, "Let me buy you dinner this evening and we can talk about it." Without waiting for a reply, he executed a rolling turn to starboard and navigated back to his seat.

Roz closed her eyes and pressed her fingertips to her temples. Maybe she should try to be grateful that someone was interested in her. *Fat chance.* Giving up, she opened her eyes in time to see Eddie Caruthers walking into the sanctuary. Talk about a rainbow after a rain. She grinned and gave him a little wave. He smiled back. She hoped they could talk soon and maybe even rekindle their friendship. She had what felt like a million questions for him.

The invocation and the song service flew by. Roz tuned out most of the morning message when she realized it was another angry harangue. After choosing a text from Luke 15 about the parable of the prodigal son, the pastor preached a fire and brimstone message whose principal aim had to be the humiliation of Eddie Caruthers. To preach a "private message" was a breach of the implied compact between leaders and followers. The preacher's job was to pray and study until he felt he'd received the message God wanted him to impart to the people. Using the pulpit to settle a personal beef was both a dereliction of duty and an abuse of power.

What a homecoming this was turning out to be for poor Eddie. Shouldn't there be a mandatory grace period after the death of a parent; a period of exemption from being raked over the coals in public? And if Eddie was the prodigal son, shouldn't the preacher be happy he had returned?

Roz tuned out the pastor's caustic commentary and began counting her blessings. She listed her salvation, her gainful employment, and her ongoing weight loss. All this, and she lived in the greatest, freest country on earth. After thinking of nine or ten more things she was thankful for, Roz sighed. Sometimes you had to bring your own sunshine, even to church.

The sermon ended. It was time for the altar call. Roz watched Eddie head for the exit instead of joining the crowd in the front. Much to her surprise, he sat down beside her when he reached her bench.

"Hey Roz," he said, keeping his voice lowered. "What's your favorite restaurant?"

Whatever she might have expected him to say, that wasn't it. "I don't know. I guess I'd say The Cheesecake Factory. Why?"

"Well, if you have no objections and no other plans, I'd like to take you there for dinner tonight."

She wondered whether she looked as surprised as she felt. "You want to take me out to dinner?" *Ugh, did that sound as dumb as I think it did?*

"Well, only if you're willing. I'm fresh out of social capital here. I don't want to get you in trouble with the powers that be. But I've got my life turned around now. I'm going to celebrate that, and I'd like it if you'd join me."

Roz smiled. "In that case, can you pick me up at seven?"

"It's a date. See you tonight."

As Eddie headed out the door, Roz realized she wasn't supposed to be eating tonight. She was fasting from dinner Saturday through lunch on Monday. Intermittent fasting was one tool she'd been using to attack her weight problem. And it was going to be the convenient excuse she'd planned to offer Marvin when he came to press his own invitation to dinner. Oh well. Plans change. And this was an important enough occasion to warrant breaking her fast. It wasn't every day the prodigal son came home, and somebody needed to give him a proper welcome. *And if I leave now, I won't even have to deal with Marvin.*

Roz changed out of the third outfit she had selected. Trying to decide what to wear was driving her crazy. *It's not a date.* Sure, Eddie's parting words had been "It's a date," but he doubtless meant it in the sense of an appointment, not a courtship ritual. He was an old friend who wanted to catch up on everything that had happened. He probably wanted to ask about Shawna's whereabouts and relationship status. Why would a guy like Eddie be interested in dating Roz? Still, she pondered which outfit was most flattering, in case he was.

The doorbell rang at 7:00 sharp. As they were walking toward his car, he noted, "You look great!" There was sincerity in his voice, and maybe a little surprise. She realized the slow transformation she'd made over the last eleven months must have seemed sudden to him. The most obvious change would be the fact that she no longer needed to lean on canes for the sake of her knees.

"Thank you. You can go ahead and say what you mean; I don't mind. I have, indeed, been losing weight. I'm down 110 pounds so far."

"Congratulations! That's awesome. How have you been doing it?"

"No magic involved. The biggest change I made was a change of heart. I decided I could go to my grave as the sad object of everyone's pity, or I could take it upon myself to become the person I wanted to be."

An odd look crossed Eddie's face for the briefest of instants. It was almost wistful, as if her comment reminded him of someone or something he missed. But he recovered himself, and his expression brightened again. "You're an inspiration. Tell me more."

"There's really not much to tell." That wasn't true. But Roz was pretty sure he wouldn't want to hear all the gory details. Her weight loss, impressive as it had been, was still a work in progress, and she'd had to make several adjustments to her strategy to keep her momentum going. "I started making small changes. For instance, I confined my snacking to nothing but cheese, baby carrots, nuts, that sort of thing. No candy, sweets, or chips. I replaced soda with mineral water or unsweetened tea. Then I started walking. At first, it was only from my door to the corner and back. Lord have mercy, that was hard! But I did it every day, rain or shine. One day, I managed to walk around the whole block. I walked early in the morning before most people were up. I didn't want to make a spectacle of myself, hobbling around. But it got a little easier every day. Now I walk a full mile at a time. Sometimes more. A year from now, I plan to run that mile."

Her voice was brimming with pride and determination. But the good feeling commingled with self-doubt. How was Eddie reacting to all of this? She stole a glance to see. He wasn't smirking or rolling his eyes. He didn't look bored. In fact, he looked interested. He had always been physically fit, so he couldn't relate to her struggles with weight and body image. Still, it looked like he understood on some level. Maybe whatever tribulations he had gone through made him more appreciative of hers.

"I'm happy for you, Roz. And I'm proud of you for your perseverance."

There was more she could have said, of course. She hadn't mentioned the time-restricted eating—she ate only between noon and 8:00 p.m., because eating triggered insulin production, and insulin triggered fat storage. Going sixteen hours each day with no caloric intake not only reduced fat storage, but it also helped stave off insulin resistance and the resultant diabetes. Nor had she mentioned the strength training three times per week. She believed that building and maintaining muscle was more important to long-term fat loss than was her aerobic exercise. Not to mention the importance of getting enough sleep every night. She had done so much research she could probably write a doctoral thesis on losing weight and keeping it off. But Eddie wouldn't want to hear a dissertation on managing hormones and circadian rhythms. His "I'm proud of you" was a pleasant note to end on.

At the restaurant, she ordered a small salad with no dressing, along with the petite grilled salmon. As they ate, she caught him up on all the news. "A lot happened while you were gone. Where should I start? Okay, you may have noticed the attendance was much smaller than before. We've had a bit of an exodus. Pastor preached a long string of angry messages after you left. Some families felt it was too much and stopped coming. The more people left, the angrier the preaching got. I'm hoping the vicious cycle ends soon, and not only because I like upbeat preaching. Church offerings are way down, and that puts pressure on the rest of us to give more and more."

Eddie nodded but said nothing. Inwardly, Roz kicked herself. She hadn't intended to start the evening with a complaint. Church tensions must have been weighing on her more than she thought. With a sigh, she took a different tack.

"You may also have noticed that you didn't see Shawna Bell."

Eddie smiled. "Yes, I briefly took note of that fact."

"She left about three months ago. She pined after you for quite a while, you know. Brought you up in conversation a lot. I think she felt bad about the way you two left things. At one point, she went to Pastor Bowers to ask what sort of outreach was being done to bring you back. He told her the ball was entirely in your court, and she wasn't at all happy about it. She gave him an earful about leaving the ninety-nine and going after the one lost sheep. He sat her down from the choir right after that."

Roz was scanning for some hint of Eddie's emotional reaction to this news, all the while trying not to look like that was what she was doing. Was he still smitten with the enigmatic Shawna? A lot could change in a year. Roz saw no trace of the wistfulness that had crossed his face earlier in the evening. Nor had his body language conveyed eagerness or hopeful anticipation at the mention of Shawna's name. On the one hand, Roz wanted Eddie to know that Shawna had stuck her neck out for him. He'd find that encouraging. Still, it wouldn't be a bad thing if this handsome young man had moved on enough to be emotionally available to . . . someone else.

Eddie replied, "Confronting Bowers took guts. I'm flattered to know she cared enough to do that. I feel bad about how it worked out for her."

"Well, it gets stranger," Roz continued. "Out of the blue, she started dating a minister from some Reformed Baptist church in Burlington. It was a whirlwind romance. They up and got married, and I don't think any of us have heard from her since." There. The big news was out, for better or for worse. No pun intended.

Eddie paused for a few seconds. "I'm not surprised to hear Shawna is gone. I kind of figured that was coming." He didn't say how he had foreseen that, and Roz didn't ask. "But I'm having a hard time picturing her as a Calvinist. I mean, that's quite a change in both style and substance."

"Yes, I imagine she had to walk back a lot of beliefs she spent her whole saved life affirming. But you know how it is when you feel you've met your soulmate."

"No, I can't say that I do. What exactly is a soulmate, anyway?"

Roz grinned. "Well, Aristotle said love is a single soul inhabiting two bodies."

"In that case, I'm inclined to agree with Plato, who said that love is a serious mental disease." He was smiling as he spoke, negating the otherwise depressing effect of Plato's sentiment.

Roz giggled. It wasn't every day that she conversed with someone who could keep up with her literary references. "'Love is of all passions the strongest, for it attacks simultaneously the head, the heart, and the senses.' That was Lao Tzu."

"Attacks, huh? Sounds like Pat Benatar was right when she sang 'Love Is a Battlefield.'"

"'Love Is Like Oxygen,'" Roz countered. "And I don't know who sang that."

"That was the band Sweet," Eddie explained. "It's like oxygen because 'Love Is in the Air.'"

A whole string of song titles used as dad jokes followed. None were all that humorous by themselves, but they were funny in that cumulative way terrible puns are. They kept the string going, naming every song they could think of with love in the title. Soon Eddie was singing "The Things We Do for Love" into a pretend microphone as Roz laughed until tears ran down her face.

She tried to reconcile her take on the man sitting across the table with the monster Pastor Bowers had portrayed him to be in his sermon. Eddie was funny and soft-spoken, a thoughtful and articulate man with muscular hands and gentle eyes. Yes, she had seen the damage he could do in a fight, but only because he had been defending her. As for the other things she'd heard, she knew she'd have to ask.

So they talked about everything: the events of a year ago, where he'd gone and why, and the deadly conflict that had shocked everyone they knew. Roz asked how he felt about having shot someone.

"Grateful to be alive. I'm not all shell-shocked and traumatized, if that's what you mean. I made my peace with the idea of self-defense when I was still a teenager. I've thought about situations that might require me to use lethal force. I've trained for them for years. That training saved two lives. I have no regrets about that."

They talked about Eddie's plans, wondering whether he could one day come back to Solid Rock, and whether he would even want to. Eddie said he didn't think the pastor would ever forgive him for his various transgressions.

"You need to break out the context spiders," Roz told him.

Eddie curled his lip. "Let's pretend, hypothetically of course, that I have no clue what that means. Could you explain it to me?"

"It's a little game I sometimes play with myself to keep my problems in perspective. When trouble comes, I imagine someone opening a cardboard box full of spiders and dumping them all over my bed. I'm talking about those big, muscular spiders that run like the wind. Hundreds of them scatter, and I just know they're under the sheets, inside the pillowcase, and in every nook and cranny of the room. Compared to that, none of my actual problems look so bad. So there you have it: context spiders."

"I think most people would settle for saying 'things could be worse,' without the *Arachnophobia* visuals." Eddie laughed, but his expression grew serious again. "Frankly, I think the spiders would be easier to deal with than the legal problems now hanging over my head. But in the meantime, I'm okay, Roz. I want you to know that your old friend Eddie is once again the same guy you used to know, no matter who else refuses to believe it."

"I believe it," Roz said. "And I'm very glad to hear it. Now, offer me dessert so I can practice saying no."

Sooner than Roz would have liked, it was time to go. She had wanted to mention some of her own difficulties, but she didn't want to dampen Eddie's spirits. Let him celebrate tonight before burdening him with tales of vengeful ex-coworkers and scary neighbors. She didn't want to be the damsel in distress again, seeing how saving her had caused Eddie so much trouble last time. She'd solve her problems some other way.

Eddie gave her his new phone number and email address. As they made their way to the exit, Roz glanced to her left to find she was looking directly into the eyes of Marvin Blackwell. Starvin' Marvin was eating alone, and the look he gave her could have withered a plant. *I didn't do anything to Marvin. I don't owe him an explanation, and I certainly don't owe him a date.* Her inner voice spoke with conviction, but she still felt her breath catch. It was unsettling to see such undisguised animus on the face of a fellow church member.

The damage to her mood was fleeting. By the next morning, Roz was her normal cheerful self, still basking in the warm glow of a friendship renewed. Her cell phone rang just as she arrived at work. The caller ID displayed the name of Pastor Bowers. Perhaps he had some better ideas to discuss regarding her desire to find her calling.

He got right to the point. "I know you had dinner with Eddie Caruthers yesterday. I'm calling to remind you he has been silenced. He's being kept outside the life of the congregation. I don't want you, or others who might have seen you, to think that it's okay to fellowship with him."

Others who might have seen me. We both know who that was. "It never occurred to me. All of that was a year ago. I've known Eddie for a dozen years and was just happy to see him come back to church."

"I know you were. You don't have a subversive bone in your body, so you're less inclined to see it in people who do. It's for your protection that I'm saying this. You're on the verge of stepping into an important role in the congregation. I think it's no coincidence that he showed up when he did. When God is opening a door for you, the enemy always tries to steer you toward a different one. I'd hate for you to get sidetracked from your potential at a time like this."

Roz said nothing, but her heart fell.

The pastor continued. "It would be better for all concerned if he found a new church home. If he comes back for another visit, I will inform him in person. In the meantime, trust your pastor. Protect yourself from Eddie's influence. Cut him off. You don't want to be at the bus station when your ship comes in." After a few platitudes that Roz only half heard, the preacher hung up.

Roz marveled at what she had just heard. She was a grown woman in her fourth decade of life. At work, she supervised a whole team of employees and oversaw a budget many times larger than Solid Rock's. And this man had just presumed to tell her she wasn't allowed to choose her own dinner companion. Her parents wouldn't try that. Her bosses wouldn't dare go there. Yet the preacher acted as though it was his natural right. She tried to imagine explaining this situation to a neighbor, a coworker, or her mother. Who would even believe it?

She reminded herself that obedience to spiritual authority was biblical. Pastors watched for the souls of the flock. That was their job. They had to give account to God for their job performance. But this preacher's motives didn't feel at all spiritual. He wasn't watching for her soul in this. Bowers was operating on the theory that the friend of my enemy is my enemy. This was about making her choose sides in a personal conflict that didn't involve her.

Yesterday, she had rejoiced to see her old friend return. Now she was supposed to ghost someone who had been kind to her, who had already lost so much by defending her.

She wanted to find a polite way to tell the preacher to take a hike. But if she did that, he was certain to retaliate. He'd relieve her of her choir duties, just as he had with Shawna. Other people in the congregation would be told to avoid her company. Roz was dealing with so many burdens: the lost friendship with Trina; the heavy workload and negative atmosphere at the office; the death of poor Mrs. Grimm; the disappearance of Shawna; the plight of Mr. Schroeder; and most of all, the threat that the scary, elder-abusing neighbor might come after her. Solid Rock Church, despite its problems, remained her strongest bulwark, her only real support system. She couldn't bear to lose that too.

At lunchtime, Roz dialed the phone. To her great relief, the call went to voicemail. She informed Eddie of what Pastor Bowers had said, including the part about him not being welcomed at church anymore. She paused and added, "For the record, I'm glad we got together. You're a great guy. In a better world, we'd be able to stay in touch. But you know how it is. Take care."

The realization of what she had done hit her the moment she hung up. *Who suspends a years-long friendship like that?* That's what she had asked herself when Shawna cut ties with her. How was this any different? Roz knew two things for certain. First, that the preacher had done Eddie wrong. And second, that she was now complicit in it. How had she let that happen? Tears of shame ran down her face. *You caved, girl. You totally caved.*

CHAPTER 15
DEVIL WITH A BLUE DRESS ON

Two weeks and three days after she'd last seen him, Roz strode up Mr. Schroeder's sidewalk. The van was gone, so the coast was clear. She rang the bell and waited a minute. No answer. She pulled her light sweater tighter around her shoulders. Now that the calendar was turning from September to October, the air held a hint of chill. She rang the bell again, and getting no response, put her key in the lock. As she swung the front door open, the homeowner poked his head into the sunroom and gave her a shushing gesture, index finger to lips. She stopped, confused. The evil nephew wasn't there, right? As if sensing her thoughts, the elderly neighbor smiled and nodded reassurance, but held up his index finger a second time. This time it was the gesture for "wait a minute."

He disappeared for thirty seconds, and Roz heard him rushing to various spots in the house. When he returned, he motioned her to follow him. As she entered the living room, he handed her a note written on an index card. His familiar spidery writing with oversized letters read: *He put in remote cameras. He watches and listens at random times. I've covered them now.* He pointed out different locations—a bookshelf here, a console table there—where Roz could see dish towels draped over something lumpy and camera-sized. She nodded her understanding.

He led her to the kitchen, where they sat down at the table. He handed her a stack of index cards and a pen, shrugging an apology. After a moment's thought, she wrote, careful to make her letters big enough. The note she handed him said: *Pharmacist says the pills are Ambien. Powerful sedative. Could we talk freely outside?*

Mr. Schroeder shook his head no and wrote: *Risky. He could drive up at any point and see.* As she digested that, he grinned, smacked his own forehead, and wrote: *Basement. No cameras.* He pointed toward the basement stairs, and they both trooped down. Now it was safe to talk.

Roz continued her story. "I didn't want to show the drugstore the actual pills. I figured if they were some kind of narcotic, I'd be breaking the law by having them. But the guy knew what they were in an instant, from looking at the pictures. Your nephew is up to no good, and those pills put you in all kinds of danger."

"I knew it! I felt so much better after I stopped taking them. He still tries to get me to take them, but I hold them between my cheek and gum rather than swallowing them. I throw them away once I'm out of his sight."

Roz could see that he looked less haggard than when she'd last seen him. And he didn't sound so out of it. This was great. "Now that you know what he's done, what are you going to do?"

"I don't know. Things have changed since we last talked. He went behind my back and got himself appointed as my legal guardian. He has control of everything now, including my finances. I'd like to appeal the court order, assuming that's even possible. And as you saw, he tries to watch my every move. He quit his part-time job so he can stay here most of the time. When he leaves, he activates those stupid remote cameras without rhyme or reason. I don't even have the code to the system."

"That's terrible!" Roz said. "And maybe criminal. Switching out your medicine sure was."

"Agreed. But I have no idea how to get my life back. We'd better get back upstairs. If he comes home now, we won't hear him coming until he's in the house. And there's no exit from the basement."

"You don't have to tell me twice," Roz said.

As they reached the main floor, they heard a disembodied voice speaking from the living room. "Uncle Al? Uncle Al! Why are the lenses on all the cameras blocked?"

"Because I deserve some privacy, that's why." As he spoke, he grabbed another index card from the dining room table and jotted a phone number on it. He handed it to Roz, holding his thumb and pinky finger to the side of his head while mouthing "Call me."

"Come on, man, you know we've talked about this. I have to look in on you for your own good. Now kindly uncover the cameras."

"I'm going to kindly unplug the cameras. So there!" As Roz watched from the archway between the kitchen and dining room, the old man went around the house unplugging cameras one at a time and cackling with glee.

To Roz's surprise, the voice continued to speak from the camera in the living room. "You're seriously annoying me now, Uncle. I guess you didn't know the system has battery backup. And now you and I are going to have a little talk." The cameras clicked off, the sound muffled under the towels. A vehicle door slammed. Seconds later came the sound of the house's front door opening.

In the dining room, the old man shot Roz a panicked look and pointed to a door halfway down the hall, motioning for her to go through it. She rushed into the hallway, getting out of the line of sight from the front rooms. No sooner had she done so than she heard the living room door open as Brandon came in from the sunroom, yelling. She was grateful for Mr. Schroeder's direction, as it was clear she wouldn't have made it out the back door without being seen.

Mr. Schroeder might have weak eyes, but he took a back seat to no one in terms of vocal power. He yelled back at Brandon with surprising volume. A distraction, Roz was sure, to cover any noise she might make. She stepped into the room he had pointed out and eased the door shut behind her, turning the knob to avoid any clicking of the latch. The sunlight shining through a single window illuminated the space she had entered. It revealed a small room littered with all kinds of clothes, books, magazines, a sewing table, and exercise equipment. She picked her way through the obstacle course, quiet as a cat on the prowl. She prayed the flooring wouldn't squeak, giving her away. Mr. Schroeder and Brandon were still jawing at each other, and from the sound of it, the older man had moved closer to the front door, keeping Brandon far away from her. Her friend was shielding her, protecting her just as he had done by pointing her to this room. After looking around for several seconds, Roz concealed herself behind a treadmill with a comforter draped over the handrails.

No sooner had she done this than the raised voices drew closer. They paused right outside the door. That was Roz's only way out. Brandon was warning his uncle about unspecified "consequences" should he ever choose to mess with the cameras again. On impulse, Roz pulled her phone from her jacket pocket, opened the camera app, and hit RECORD. Might come in handy for letting someone in officialdom know what kind of "guardian" Brandon was. She looked at her phone and felt a flood of relief that it was muted. Now would be an unfortunate time to receive an audible notification.

The voices outside the door moved farther down the hall toward Mr. Schroeder's bedroom. She heard Mr. Schroeder yell, "Hey! Don't you push me!"

Brandon replied, "Did I? You know, if you hadn't blocked cameras in here, you might have some evidence to back up your story. As it stands now, all you have is the ravings of a delusional old man who is under guardianship for good reason."

As they continued their quarrel, Roz realized that this was her best and perhaps the only chance to escape the house unnoticed. She rose from behind the exercise machine, padded quietly across the room, and cracked open the door. Looking to her right, she could see that the door to the primary bedroom was closed. She stepped into the hall, closed the door behind her without making a sound, and headed back the way she had come.

When she reached the dining room, she saw she wasn't the only visitor to the home. In the kitchen stood a smartly dressed older woman wearing a look that said she disapproved of what she was hearing. Roz's trained eye took in the woman's ensemble: navy blue skirt and jacket, silver satin blouse, understated jewelry, sensible black pumps. The woman looked well put together, every inch the professional type, perhaps a manager or director of some important agency like the local Council on Aging. Her face looked familiar, but from where? Roz had a mental image of Mr. Schroeder shuffling secret visitors all around the house. She wanted to ask this woman who she was and when she had come in, but knew neither of them could risk even a whisper. The woman's warning glance down the hall confirmed her agreement.

Time to go. Before Roz could turn toward the back door, the woman gestured forcefully at the kitchen table, pointing to the tabletop. The notes! Roz realized the index cards she and Mr. Schroeder had written on were still sitting in plain sight on the table. Wouldn't do to have Brandon find those. Without a word, Roz rushed over to the table, picked up the notes, and nodded her hasty thanks to the woman. After stepping outside, Roz turned to close the door behind her. She glanced toward the kitchen again, but the woman was already out of sight. Where could she have gone so quickly?

When Roz reached the wooded strip at the end of the yard, her heart thudded, and the back of her neck prickled. She knew that face, knew where she'd seen it. It looked out from picture frames all over the house. Despite having died five years ago, Mrs. Schroeder looked pretty good.

This could not be. Yet Roz knew she had not imagined the encounter. Which meant that Mr. Schroeder hadn't been imagining things either. She chastised herself for having doubted him. He had orchestrated her escape. By confronting Brandon near the front door, he'd bought her time to conceal herself. And by running for his bedroom with Brandon hot on his heels, he'd given her a path to a safe exit. These were not the actions of a befuddled old man. That was the epitome of quick thinking and bold action.

But if she and her elderly neighbor were both of sound mind, that could mean only one thing. And it wasn't something she wished to discuss with poor Mr. Schroeder, who had problems enough thanks to his abusive nephew. But there would be no avoiding it. She'd have to tell him what she had seen. And that she still didn't believe in ghosts.

CHAPTER 16

SPIRITS IN THE MATERIAL WORLD

The next afternoon, driving past the Schroeder house, Roz saw no van in the driveway. She continued on to her house and called from there. Mr. Schroeder picked up on the third ring.

"Hello?" His voice sounded firm.

"Hi, Mr. Schroeder, it's Roz. Are you free to talk?"

"I will be in a minute." Roz heard what sounded like footsteps on a staircase. Her neighbor spoke again. "I'm in the basement now. Go ahead."

Roz said, "I have a friend at church who is an attorney. He might tell you about possible legal avenues for getting that court order vacated. I don't know what the chances are, but he would."

"By all means. Give him this number. Tell him to text me instead of calling, and I'll call back whenever the coast is clear."

"Will do. Also, I wanted to say thank you for clearing me a path of escape yesterday."

"Yeah, we old folks aren't half as dumb as we look, you know. I don't think he ever suspected a thing."

"One more thing about yesterday . . ." Roz was still trying to figure out how to broach this next subject.

"Yes?"

"As I was leaving your house, I saw . . . I saw what appeared to be your wife standing in the kitchen."

Now it was her neighbor's turn to be silent for several long seconds. Speaking at lower volume, he said, "Forgive this next question, but it's important. What was she wearing?"

Roz thought it an odd question, but she described the outfit she had seen.

"Well, I'll be a monkey's uncle. When you said you saw her, I wasn't sure whether you were pulling my leg. I'm not sure why you would do that, but I had to know whether you were. You couldn't have known about the outfit unless you'd really seen her. It's not in any of the photos in the house. And it's not among the clothes in that room where you hid. It's the outfit she's worn every time I've seen her since her death. It's the outfit we buried her in."

The pastor clenched his jaw and squeezed his eyes shut. "Why can't people in this church ever just do what they're told?"

"Excuse me?" Roz tried to ensure that her tone didn't sound defiant, or anything else unflattering.

"I must admit, I'm disappointed. And you've put me in a bit of a quandary. I'm not in the habit of giving follow-up advice when my people have ignored my initial counsel. I think I was pretty clear in telling you to have nothing further to do with that neighbor of yours. The break-ins you've had, and now the spirit in his house . . . you wouldn't be dealing with any of this had you listened to me the first time."

Roz said, "The circumstances changed after I received your counsel. I was staying away. Hadn't been there for weeks. But the man reached out and pleaded with me for help. What kind of neighbor would I be if I ignored him?"

"And what kind of church member will you be if you get into the habit of disregarding your pastor? I know your heart was in the right place. Your intentions were good, as always. But you know what paves the road to hell. There are two kinds of church members. There are those who understand that my job is to plot the course. These people actually take some of the load off me by helping me drive. Contrast them with the people I call speed bumps."

His wife, heretofore silent, chimed in. "Yeah! Speed-bump saints!"

"They don't help drive," the pastor continued. "They lie there in the way like a speed bump and force the car and everyone in it to slow down. When you're trying to get somewhere in a hurry, the last thing you want to encounter is a series of speed bumps."

"Well, if that's how you see me, I'm sorry. But if the church won't help this man, who will? Who even can?"

The pastor leaned back in his chair and steepled his fingers. "All right, here's what needs to happen. Talk to Deacon Haynes about the man's legal situation. I don't know what your neighbor's financial condition is, but Deacon Haynes can explore that and charge whatever he thinks is fair. As for the evil spirit in his house, you'll need to level with this man, so he knows what he is dealing with. If he understands, and he wants it gone, I'll go there myself to deal with it."

Roz nodded, thanked the preacher for his time, and stood to leave. Bowers held up his hand. "Two more items. First, I think we shouldn't rush you into heading up the PAA. I want to see how all of this plays out before moving ahead with that. I want to see whether you're someone who can learn from her mistakes. Second, once this is over, I'll expect this Mr. Schroeder to be hungry to know more about the spiritual world and how he lived so long in apparent ignorance of it. He needs to understand that the war we wage is about souls, not random spiritual phenomena. Do your best to get him to come to church, or at least sign up for a home Bible study. At his age, your neighbor might not have much time to get right with God. If he is not receptive to that, my original direction stands. Walk away without guilt or misgivings. Shake the very dust off your feet if you must. There are nearly seventy thousand people in Framingham, and fewer than one hundred people attend this church. We're on a mission to improve that ratio, and we need all hands on deck helping. Agreed?"

"I understand," Roz said before heading back into the sanctuary. *Understanding is not the same as agreeing.*

"So, how do you feel each time you see her?"

The day after her meeting with Rev. Bowers, Roz had called Mr. Schroeder and persuaded him to meet her out in front of his house. She stayed on the sidewalk while they talked. No cameras, no microphones, and if Brandon came home, he could have no beef with her—she was on the sidewalk, and, therefore, not trespassing. If Mr. Schroeder spoke to her as she was walking past, who could fault her for that? She had her doubts that Brandon would see it the same way.

Her neighbor did his part to make it look like a chance meeting. He was wearing a garden apron and work gloves. There was a little pile of freshly pulled weeds at his feet, plucked from around the mailbox post. He considered Roz's question. "It's hard to say. I tried to explain it to Brandon. Guess we all know how well that went. Look, on the one hand, I'm glad that she's not a mere memory. She still has a connection to me here and now. That's powerful. Like love really is forever. By the same token, I worry she is stuck here. She never looks happy. She smiled so much in life, and I never see her smile now. People always want the dead to rest in peace. I wish I could feel like my Laura is at peace, but it doesn't seem that way. Instead of going wherever it is she's supposed to take her rest, she has lingered here for years. For her sake, I wish it wasn't so."

"Before your wife passed, had you ever believed in ghosts?"

"No, but before my wife passed, I'd never seen one with my own eyes."

Roz said, "I need to ask you an important question. Do you believe in the existence of angels?"

"Here you go, prying into my religious beliefs. Didn't we talk about that soon after we first met? I don't know how comfortable I am sharing this stuff."

"I remember that conversation. And I respect your desire for privacy. But I'm not asking you this out of idle curiosity. There may be a way to help you get what you want, to know your wife has moved on."

The old man looked thoughtful, but he did not speak for a moment. "Okay," he said at last. "I never bought into any of that otherworldly stuff. As an engineer, I believed in things you could measure, weigh, assay. My experience with Laura has shown me there is more out there than I thought. So I guess the answer to your question is I don't know. But at least I'm willing to admit that I don't know."

"Great. That puts you light years ahead of most people. So many folks assume that anything they haven't seen, weighed, measured, or whatever, can't exist. But to put it in terms of pure logic, absence of evidence is not evidence of absence. To say otherwise is just arrogance. So let's talk about spirits. What most people mean by the word *ghost* is the spirit of a departed person, right?"

When her neighbor nodded, Roz said, "Human spirits aren't the only spirits that exist. Angels are a company of spirit beings that God created to serve him. There are hundreds of mentions of angels in the Bible. And it also mentions they don't always look otherworldly. In fact, it says that many people have entertained angels unawares, which tells me they can look like ordinary people when they wish. I can't prove any of this to you, but for the moment, can you accept it may be true?"

"Fair enough. Since I don't know one way or the other, I'll accept that it may be true."

"Good," Roz continued. "Now let me add this wrinkle. Not all angels stayed true to their original mission to serve God. Some deserted their posts. They were rebels . . . mutineers, for lack of a better word. When people speak of devils or demons, they are talking about these renegade angels."

"I still think this all sounds like superstition."

Roz nodded. "So did ghosts not long ago, and now you're quite confident you've seen one."

"Okay, demons are another maybe. Where are we going with this?"

"If a demon wanted to trouble you, posing as the spirit of someone you loved might be an effective way to do it. You stress over the idea that your wife is not at rest. And a demon could keep his impersonation going for as long as you live."

Mr. Schroeder said, "I remember a few of the stories the nuns told me in my childhood. Demons are supposed to be at war with the good angels, at war with God himself, right?"

Roz nodded.

"And you're suggesting that what I have seen—what we have both seen—is not my wife, but one of these demons masquerading as Laura? And he or she is taking time out of the middle of this big cosmic war for no bigger goal than making me feel bad? Sounds like this devil has trouble prioritizing."

"The outcome of the war is a foregone conclusion. The devils know this. If they can bring a little pain or suffering to a human while awaiting the execution of their own sentence, they will." Roz put an extra measure of gentleness into her tone. "Besides, is the possibility of a demon spirit imitating your wife any more of a stretch than thinking your wife's spirit is popping in and out of your house wearing a neatly pressed copy of the outfit she had on when they closed the casket? You believe spirits exist. The only issue is discovering the true identity of the spirit you have seen. Appearances can be deceiving."

"Why tell me this? Even if you're right, it doesn't help me feel better. You want me to believe that Laura is gone, but some fallen angel is haunting my house. How's that idea supposed to bring peace to either Laura or me?"

"Well, we can cast out devils. Forbid them to return. If what we have seen is an imposter—and I think it is—casting it out means an end to the charade, and to the whole muddled mix of feelings you get with each sighting."

"Do all Christians believe as you do?"

"No, not at all. As with non-Christians, there are plenty of Christians who think that if they haven't seen or experienced something, nobody else has either. But there are millions who believe like me. Millions who know, based on scripture and personal experience."

Her neighbor looked at the ground, pushing a pebble with his toe. "I don't know what I'm supposed to say to all this."

"I'd recommend saying let's try getting rid of it. If we can prevent more of these appearances, you'll be happier. And if we can't stop them, you should be no worse off than you are now. So what have you got to lose?"

Mr. Schroeder stood there thinking for what must have been a full minute. At last he asked, "What do I have to do?"

Al Schroeder had persuaded his nephew to take his car to the shop for an oil change and coolant flush, an errand that would keep Brandon away from the house for a few hours. Two cars showed up half an hour after Brandon left. One belonged to Roz. The other, a black Cadillac Escalade, contained two men. Pastor Bowers climbed out of the passenger side of his own Cadillac, glanced at Roz's Mercedes wagon, and raised an eyebrow, though he made no comment. She introduced the pastor and his driver, Deacon Gonzales, to her neighbor. After all the handshakes were done, the foursome trooped inside. Roz noticed Mr. Schroeder had covered the cameras again. That would stop Brandon from seeing them, but not from listening in. Roz hoped his errand would keep him too busy for that.

Her neighbor must have followed her gaze and anticipated her concern. He said, "I bought us a little privacy. I didn't bother unplugging the cameras or taking out the batteries. Doing that would just send my nephew an alert and bring him home that much faster."

Bowers shrugged. "The Lord is my helper, and I will not fear what man shall do unto me. Roz has informed me of your situation. She says you've been getting visits from a spirit, one you have believed to be your wife?"

"That's right."

"Ah. I have dealt with such things for many years. This spirit is not what it appears to be. Devils are masters of disguise. The scriptures tell us in 2 Corinthians 11:14, 'and no marvel; for Satan himself is transformed into an angel of light.' That's the bad news. The good news is that the people of God have the power to resist the devil, and when we resist him, he will flee from us. We can rid your house of this deceiving spirit. Is that what you want?"

Looking a little uncomfortable, Schroeder said, "If that's what's here . . . then yes, I want it gone."

"Good," Bowers said. "Your home will feel clean again when the unclean spirit has left. Let me give you a little context from scripture, so that you may know we have the authority to deal with this spirit."

He pulled a New Testament from his jacket pocket and read from the Book of Luke, chapter ten:

And the seventy returned again with joy, saying, Lord, even the devils are subject unto us through thy name. And he said unto them,

I beheld Satan as lightning fall from heaven. Behold, I give unto you power to tread on serpents and scorpions, and over all the power of the enemy: and nothing shall by any means hurt you. Notwithstanding in this rejoice not, that the spirits are subject unto you; but rather rejoice, because your names are written in heaven.

"It's going to be good to rid your house of a devil," Bowers said. "You've done well to ask for our help. But the best thing you can do by far is make sure that you have a saving relationship with God. You want to know your name is written in heaven."

Mr. Schroeder looked at his shoes and said nothing.

Rev. Bowers called for prayer. They all formed a little circle. As they bowed their heads, the pastor asked God to extend grace to the homeowner and upon the house. Roz flinched but kept her eyes shut and continued praying when she heard the muffled click of the security camera shutters opening. She knew what that meant. Brandon was listening. Talk about bad timing. Fortunately, no angry voice issued from the speakers. Bowers finished his invocation with, "Lord God, we cast out every spirit that's not like your Spirit. We pray these and all blessings in the matchless name of our Lord Jesus Christ. Amen."

With the prayer finished, the minister took a vial of olive oil from his pocket, explaining that the consecrated anointing oil symbolized the power and presence of God. He dabbed some oil from the vial onto the tip of his finger and walked through the house, touching the top of each doorway and leaving a trace of oil there. As he walked, all three church members spoke to whatever demon spirits might be present, commanding them to leave the house and never return. They invoked the name of the Lord, the blood of Jesus, the authority of the word, and the power of the Spirit. This went on for several minutes until they had traversed every room in the house, including the basement.

When they concluded, the two churchmen wore satisfied expressions. Roz wished they could cast Brandon out while they were at it. Too bad life didn't work that way.

Pastor Bowers told Mr. Schroeder that Deacon Gonzales would be happy to teach him a free Bible study any time, that he might better understand the nature and destiny of spirits, his own most of all. Mr. Schroeder said he would consider the matter. The preacher and the deacon stayed to chat for just a minute or two before leaving.

Roz stood in the living room and prepared to take her own leave. As she shook her neighbor's hand in farewell, she looked over his shoulder into the dining room and froze. Not fifteen feet away stood the spitting image of Laura Schroeder, dressed exactly as before. She was staring at Roz and not looking happy. Seeing Roz's expression, Mr. Schroeder tried to follow her gaze. But by the time he turned, the dining room was empty.

"Was it her?" he asked.

"Sure looked that way."

PART THREE
THE BOOK OF ROZ

CHAPTER 17
SHOWDOWN

October

Roz felt defeated. Discouraged. And embarrassed. Mr. Schroeder must think her a fool. Slumped in her recliner, Roz considered the fiasco at the old man's house and tried to understand how it had happened. Her faith had been strong. She'd suffered no lack of prayer or fasting. She was aware of no unconfessed sin in her life and assumed the same was true of the pastor and deacon. All three of them had done everything they knew to do. So what could explain yesterday's abject failure? What was she going to tell her neighbor?

She got up and paced the room. A new thought intruded, another weight on her mind. She'd heard the cameras click on at Mr. Schroeder's place. Brandon had listened in on their gathering. He would not be happy. He had said he wouldn't bother her for a month, as long as she minded her own business. She hadn't. Nothing she could do about it now. Maybe he wouldn't do anything. After all, six weeks had gone by since he'd left that note. So she was already two weeks over the deadline. And come what may, she wasn't going anywhere. But despite her resolve, her sense of disquiet grew stronger by the minute.

She jumped when her phone rang at 9:30 p.m. The caller ID showed it was Pastor Bowers. She wondered what he could want. There couldn't be much to discuss since the prospect of heading up the Pastor's Aide Auxiliary had come to a merciful end. She took the call. "Good evening, Pastor Bow—"

He cut her off. "Is everything okay over there?"

"Yes, so far as I know. Why?"

"You've been weighing on my mind ever since we left your neighbor's house, and the feeling has become more urgent as the evening progressed. My wife and I have been praying for you, and I feel in my spirit that you are in real danger. I don't know what the specific threat is. But I don't give this warning lightly. Keep your eyes and ears open and your wits about you. We'll be praying here until I discern more, or until the danger passes. That's all for now, sister. Call us if you need us." He hung up the phone.

Brandon. This had to be about him. Roz knew she wouldn't be getting any sleep this night. If he broke in, she was going to be wide awake and ready. But ready to do what? If his intentions were to do something harsher than leaving a mocking note, what could she do about it? She could flee the house right now. All that would accomplish was to postpone the trouble to some other night of her enemy's choosing. And the running would never end. Her mother was right. If you ran once, it would become a habit. That was no way to live. Something had to be done.

In one motion, she stood to her feet, reached for her cell phone, and whispered her own prayer for help and safety even as she dialed.

To her great relief, the call didn't go to voicemail. Instead, the person she most wanted to talk to said, "Roz! This is an unexpected pleasure. What's up?"

"Oh, Eddie, I'm sorry to bother you. I need help, and I need it quick. My life might be in danger. There's a man who's been stalking me. He's broken into my house before, and I think he may come for me tonight. I know it's a lot to ask, but—"

"Say no more. I'll be at your front door in fifteen minutes."

It took him only ten. She heard him call her name as he rang the bell. Relieved, she threw open the door, saying, "Come in, come in!" Eddie was not alone. With him was a slender White woman who looked to be twenty-something years old. Stringy brown hair. Prominent ears.

"Roz, I'd like you to meet Melissa Devereaux. She was visiting me when you called, and if I understand your predicament, I think she can help. Melissa, this is my old friend Roz."

"Nice to meet you, Melissa."

"Call me Mel. Everyone does."

Eddie looked at Roz and said, "Tell me everything."

She did. From the first aborted handshake with Brandon Heckler on the day they'd met, to the unpleasant encounter on the sidewalk, to the abuse of Mr. Schroeder, and his plea for help. The first break-in. The apparent tracking of her old car, and the second break-in right after the homegoing service for Eddie's father. She talked about the mysterious fact that the intruder never showed up on the doorbell cameras, so she didn't know how he was getting in. She skipped the events of the previous day and concluded with the pastor's phone call to her that evening.

"So this all started long before we had dinner last month. Why didn't you tell me?"

"I considered it. I would have told you at some point. But you were burdened enough with your own troubles. It wouldn't have been right to load you down with mine. But now I feel I have no choice. You're the only person I know who can handle this level of threat."

"Agreed. Here's what I'm gathering: this guy tends to show up in the middle of the night. If you let Mel drive you back to my place, the two of you can hang out there while this plays out. We don't want my car sitting in the driveway advertising that you have a houseguest. If this guy shows up tonight, he'll get a surprise."

"Thanks, Eddie. You've been such a friend. I want you to know I'm sorry I gave in to the pressure to cut you off. You deserved better from me."

Eddie opened his mouth to speak, then changed his mind and closed it again. After a brief hesitation, he settled for "I understood the situation you were in. I've lived through the pastoral ultimatums, the fear that you can't afford to lose your church because there is nowhere else to go. I was disappointed to get your message, but we're good, Roz. No worries. Now I suggest we get this show on the road."

That sounded good to Roz, so she threw a couple of things into her duffel bag yet again and headed out to Eddie's car with Mel. As they drove away in silence, Roz felt the need to make some conversation. "So, where do you know Eddie from?"

"We've been dating off and on since July. I guess we're an item now. It took us a while to get some traction, but we've been through a lot together, and I think we might have a future."

"Oh, I see." Roz knew she should say something else—congratulations, maybe, or at least good luck. But she couldn't quite do it. Nor could she think of anything else to add. Her mind was racing, and she couldn't cut through the flow of thought to continue small talk with Mel. She couldn't believe that at a time like this, she could feel disappointed to learn that Eddie had a girlfriend. But she had long harbored a tiny, secret hope that he might become interested in her, now that Shawna was out of the picture. Should have known better. Of course, things might have been different if she hadn't frozen him out on the pastor's orders. She nipped that thought in the bud. She needed to be grateful her old friend had stepped up to fight for her a second time. *Yeah girl, just leave it at that.*

Brandon smiled as he approached the round reader's back door. It was 3:00 a.m. As before, the mylar space blanket he'd draped over himself prevented the doorbell camera's night vision from seeing his body. At most, it would see a few wisps of heat that escaped from the seams. Little greenish-white flashes on the video. Nothing to worry about. And the clear pane of glass he held in front of his face made sure his handsome visage wouldn't appear on video either. The walkie-talkie in his pocket was broadcasting at a frequency that would keep the entry sensors from talking to the alarm system's control unit when he opened the door. Nitrile gloves meant he'd leave no fingerprints. He'd be upon that meddlesome woman before she knew he was there.

Getting past the locks took only a few seconds. He eased the door shut behind him, put the pane of glass down on the counter, and crossed the kitchen. A hallway was coming up on the right. Her bedroom was down there. He reached into his pants pocket and withdrew a crumpled plastic bag. Uncrumpled, it would fit over her head.

The floor creaked once as he crept forward in the darkness. Such a faint sound would not have awakened her. Or maybe it had. Maybe she was lying there, eyes wide open, fearing, praying, hoping the out-of-place sound meant nothing. What a delicious thought. She deserved a little terror before the end. From what he'd heard through the camera, the fat fanatic and her friends were even nuttier than his uncle was. And she had defied him for the last time.

Brandon turned the corner, and something struck him hard in the face. No, not something. Someone. Not the woman. He knew at once he had suffered a broken nose. His eyes were tearing up and he could both feel and taste warm blood running into his mouth. The darkness in the hallway and his blurred vision made it impossible to see, but he threw a hard right at where he thought his attacker's head was. He missed. His opponent sidestepped the blow and pressed up to Brandon's right side, grabbing his arm near the elbow so he couldn't retract it. While Brandon was trying to disentangle his arm, he felt two punches to his lower-right torso. The pain took his breath away. He tried to twist out of the path of those blows, but caught another shot full in the face, followed an instant later by searing pain in his groin. All reflex now, his body curled forward and down, acting on instinct to shield that sensitive cluster of nerves from another strike. As he did, his opponent grabbed his head, twisted it, and drove it down into the knee that rose to smash into his ear.

Bang, bang, bang—the pain was coming from everywhere now as blow after rapid blow struck him. He couldn't see them coming, couldn't predict them, and couldn't react before the next agony erupted somewhere in his body. It was all happening too fast. This was sensory overload. He found himself face up on the floor, dizzy, gasping, overmatched, unable to defend himself from a fast-moving opponent who seemed to fight by feel, unhampered by the darkness. He was being picked apart.

He tried to yield, to yell, "Okay, stop, I give!" But between the pain, the breathlessness, and the blood in his mouth, he managed only an inarticulate gurgle. For a split second, an image of Peg head-down in the utility sink flashed through his mind. He had to find a way to make this stop, or he'd wind up dead like her. Maybe he could tap out. Would this guy even know what that meant? Suddenly there were fingers in his eyes, and all conscious thought evaporated. Panicked reflex made him reach up to pull the hands away. There was a sound like thick paper tearing. Fresh pain, this time from his right shoulder, unlike anything he'd ever felt. He heard a hoarse scream and realized the voice was his own. A door sprang open in his mind, a door into a dark hiding place where there was no sound and no pain.

Eddie turned the lights on and thought about monsters. Not monsters like the one splayed out unconscious in front of him. He was thinking about monsters like the one inside himself.

His long-time fight trainer, Mike, had always insisted one was there, languishing in a dark and disused corner of Eddie's psyche. Everybody had one, he said. Eddie's had been born in his childhood, conceived in the cauldron of fear and rage forged over years of being bullied at school. It had grown and fattened up on a diet of resentment for every injustice dished out by an authority figure in his life. He thought often of the high school teacher who had humiliated him by reading aloud and at great length from historic letters by Alabama's segregationist governor, George Wallace. Wallace filled his screeds with that most noxious of racial epithets. As the only Black person in the class, Eddie had held his peace through a torturous hour, doing his best to tune out the constant repetition of the n-word. But the teacher put him on the spot: "By the way, Eddie, does this bother you? Not that it would change anything if it did; I'd just like to know." Such staggering idiocy, along with Eddie's inability to do anything about it, made the monster bigger still. There was never a shortage of people willing to toss it a little more fodder. As it grew, Eddie assumed the only acceptable thing to do was to keep it locked away where no one could see it. Wasn't that what civilized people did?

Mike had helped him see it from a different perspective. He pointed out that peaceful nations preferred diplomacy to war, but still had armies for those times when diplomacy failed. Likewise, the beast within gave Eddie options for those times when civilized responses wouldn't do. Part of Eddie's training had been learning how to summon the monster at need. With the flick of a mental switch, he could bypass the shock, the paralysis, the denial with which the untrained reacted to sudden danger or assault. In place of those things, he could release something that knew no fear, no weakness, no scruples, and no mercy.

He remembered the first time it made a public appearance. His sparring partners had ganged up on him after a hard evening of training. The bell rang. Three of them attacked without warning. They punched and pummeled him before wrestling him to the floor. The trainer laughed and egged them on. If they were pulling their punches, it wasn't by much. These blows hurt. He was used to realistic training. He had even practiced some tactics for two-on-one situations. But three-on-one? That was hopeless. He decided the only option was to wait out the attack, turtle up, and survive until the bell announced the end of the round.

At least three minutes went by. There was no second bell. There was only Mike yelling at him, "Is that your strategy? Cover up and hope not to die? There are no rounds in a street fight, bro. No time limit. And no help. Nobody's going to save you but you. What are you going to do? Cry? Beg for mercy? Or are you going to man up and make it stop?"

Bruised, battered, bleeding from the nose, and gasping for air, Eddie didn't see how he was going to make it stop. The ridiculous injustice of it all was infuriating. His vision went red. He lost all sense of time and place. The next thing he knew, he was on his feet with fire in his veins and something akin to murder in his eyes. The two biggest guys in the gym were holding his arms and pulling him away from his three adversaries. They were trying to calm him down. "You did good," they were saying. "You did what you had to. It's over now." One of them handed him a rag to stop the nosebleed. The other steered him to a stool and pressed an ice pack to the side of his face.

The three sparring partners who had ganged up on him were taking off their grappling gloves and tending to their own fresh crop of cuts and bruises. Trainer Mike walked over to Eddie wearing a rare somber expression. "A bunch of us decided that this was your time. I told you long ago this night would come. A lot of guys fold when we throw this at them. They've locked the monster away and can't find the key to the cage. You needed to learn whether you could let yours out. Now you know. Out in the real world, when the odds are against you and losing is not an option, remember this night."

He'd kept the monster on standby for years. Tonight was only the second time it had appeared outside of the controlled chaos of the training gym. And this time differed from the first. It felt as though the beast within had expected the summons and let itself out. That was a bit unsettling.

So was the fact that it had stayed too long. His opponent had been face up on the floor, injured, dazed, no longer a threat. The two left hooks to the body early in the fight had put him down, though the effect had taken a while to kick in, as was typical of liver shots. That, coupled with all the other damage Roz's nightmare neighbor had absorbed, meant he was no longer dangerous, at least for the time being. Time to put the monster away. Instead, Eddie had taken the mounted position and faked an eye gouge to make the man bring his hands up to his face. The right arm had been the actual target. Eddie had trapped the arm in a joint lock, twisting the shoulder in its socket until the rotator cuff tore. The intruder screamed, and it took a hard elbow to the face to knock him out and restore quiet. Was the monster calling the shots now?

Eddie chided himself for harboring such thoughts. There was no reason to feel guilty. This jerk had invaded Roz's home under cover of night and headed for her room. He had earned every bit of tonight's pain. That was why Roz had called on the only friend she had who could dish it out. Her life was full of people who could supply sympathy, empathy, advice, and well wishes—everything except help. They would be fluttering their hands and running for the fainting couches if they could see what Eddie had done. None of them would comprehend the idea of violence as a force for good. They were talkers. Moralizers and theorizers. Eddie was a protector. The monster came with the territory. Squeamishness was a privilege of the protected.

The bad guy was coming to. Eddie took out a pocketknife and cut away most of the silver mylar the man had wrapped around himself. That done, he fished through the intruder's pockets. He knew he'd encounter no resistance. The downed man would not be quick to get up, as he had to clear his head, regain his equilibrium, and figure out how to get to his feet without further injuring his crippled right arm.

When Brandon's eyes opened and looked halfway focused, Eddie tossed the man's wallet onto his chest. "I took nothing from it," Eddie said. "All your cash is still there. But I took photos of your driver's license, so I know who you are. The invisibility suit was clever, but it's gone now. And I disabled the walkie-talkie. So the security cameras didn't see you come in, but they will see you leave. Now you've got more than your injuries to worry about. Still, I'm letting you go rather than holding you for the cops. But hear this: if you ever bother my friend again, you'd better hope and pray the cops find you before I do. We clear?"

The man nodded. Eddie kept watch as Brandon struggled to his feet, gritted his teeth, and wobbled his unsteady way to the back door. When he was gone, Eddie reached down to pat his right hip and his left calf. Both concealed firearms remained snug in their holsters, and he was glad for Roz's sake he hadn't had to use them.

Still, he had a bad feeling. There was nothing to suggest the intruder was ready to put this one in the loss column and move on. His acquiescence had looked grudging. Fury had smoldered beneath the surface of his dark gaze, strong enough to shine through the mixture of pain and fear there. This was not a man to let his humiliation go unavenged. He had monsters of his own. Since he did not know who Eddie was, he'd have to seek vengeance on someone else. That meant Roz, despite the warning he'd received, and Eddie couldn't always be around to run interference. He had to make Roz understand how much danger she'd be in when this guy recovered from his injuries. He'd do his best to prepare her. Whatever happened, this wasn't going to end well for somebody.

CHAPTER 18
SAVE YOURSELF

Roz needed to thank Rev. Bowers but was having trouble deciding what to say. Had it not been for the preacher's call to her, she wouldn't have called Eddie. The pastor's role in saving her life was as big as Eddie's. She wanted to tell the preacher the whole story but judged it too risky. He'd have a meltdown if he found out she'd involved Eddie. Such a confusing person, this preacher. Was he a good man who'd been having a lot of bad days? Or was he a bad man who still had some good left in him? Either way, she owed him a debt of gratitude. She decided to send an email that was light on details.

Pastor Bowers: Just a quick note to say thank you for your prayers, and for reaching out to me with a warning. I had been feeling a vague

*sense of danger myself. But whatever plans the enemy had for me, I
believe the danger is now past.*

> *God bless,*
> *Rosalyn Pitts*

This account was truth watered down and poured through
a fine filter. But she hadn't lied. She figured he would take "the
enemy" to mean the devil. If so, he would skim through this
spiritualized account and not give it another thought. That
settled it. She hit SEND and wished she had a less complicated
relationship with her church.

The next evening found Roz at Eddie's self-defense training
facility, housed in a barn in Framingham's Nobscot neighborhood.
He had invited her over to discuss several important things,
including some follow-up on the confrontation at her house.
She was eager to go. It would be something different to see and
do. And she wasn't in the mood to be alone.

The gym was impressive. Eddie showed Roz around and
explained the equipment. The space had a large central area with
a thick floor mat for training in grappling and groundwork. Four
heavy bags hung from beams around the perimeter. Between
each pair of heavy bags was a speed bag for boxers. A grappling
dummy lay near a corner. Roz reached out to tug at its hand and
founds its weight surprising. Eddie must have read her expression.
"That one's 170 pounds," he informed her.

"Impressive facility! How long have you been doing this?"

"I haven't started yet. This is what's next in my life. I'm getting it outfitted now, but I don't have a single student yet. I've been teaching classes at my trainer's place while he takes time off to deal with a medical problem. I'd been toying with building a dojo of my own. Filling in for him cemented it for me."

After Roz walked around and looked at everything, Eddie led them to some benches near the entrance. Mel came out of an inner office and sat close beside Eddie. The two women exchanged hellos.

"First things first," Eddie said. "I want to assure you that your criminal neighbor will be in no position to bother you for a while. I put a good whipping on him, including a couple of hard blows to the head that may have left him concussed. He also has a torn rotator cuff. Depending on how bad the tear is, it may require surgery and a long recovery period. In the meantime, the nightmare on Elm Street will have a hard time writing you any threatening notes. The bottom line is, your Dead Eyes is out of commission for a while. That's the good news."

"It feels so strange to think of someone's injuries as good news, but there's no denying that it's good news for me," Roz said. "What's the bad news?"

"I could see in his eyes that he's going to spend most of his recovery time plotting his revenge. He'll blame you for the beating I handed him. One day, he'll come back looking to even the score."

There weren't enough context spiders in the world to diminish the horror of that thought. She didn't want to live her life in fear. And she didn't want to flee her home. "What do you suggest I do?"

"Realize that you are your own first responder. If you're attacked, friends and neighbors won't be able to get there in time to help. When seconds count, the police are minutes away. You have to save yourself. And for that, you need an equalizer."

"And what sort of equalizer would I get?"

"I've given it some thought and brought you just the thing." Eddie reached under his bench and pulled out a long, thin, rectangular box.

Roz's breath caught in her throat. She didn't know for sure what a rifle case looked like, but she feared this might be one. From their conversation at The Cheesecake Factory, Roz thought Eddie was going to suggest carrying a gun like he did. She couldn't see herself owning a deadly weapon. No guns for her, even for the likes of her nightmare neighbor. Meanwhile, Eddie set the box on his lap, popped it open, and pulled out a gleaming metal object.

"A cane?" Roz sighed in both relief and disappointment. "I haven't needed one of those in months. You don't know how hard I've worked to make sure I'd never need one again."

"And I trust you'll never again need a cane for the purpose you used to. But don't let past emotional associations blind you to what this is. Look at it. Feel it." He handed it to her.

It was heavier than it looked. Roz ran her hand down its length and realized it was solid aluminum finished in black. A series of shallow cuts crisscrossed the shaft a few inches from both ends, giving the hand a firm grip on the otherwise smooth surface.

Eddie pointed out some details. "The crook is wider than most. Good for hooking an ankle to trip your opponent. Or hooking a neck, for when the stakes are at their highest. The tip of that crook is razor sharp and can do a lot of damage to soft tissue. Swinging the cane as a bludgeon is like hitting someone with a baseball bat. Here's the beauty of it: unlike most weapons, it's legal everywhere. You can take it into a post office or a courthouse or onto an airplane, and no one will look twice at it. What other weapon could you carry around that's already in your hand when you need it? Unlike pepper spray, you don't have to fish it out of your purse or worry about which way the wind is blowing. Defend yourself with a knife, and people will always look at you like it's unsavory. 'Oh, she carries a fighting knife. She's one of those people.' Brain someone with this, and people will feel only sympathy for you. 'Serves that mugger right for attacking a poor woman who used a cane.'"

Roz had to admit that sounded realistic.

Eddie took the cane back and stood. "While the use of a big stick as a weapon might be self-explanatory, there are techniques with this. Let me show you a little about using it to maximum advantage." He walked over to one of the heavy bags as Roz and Mel followed. "First, a rule of physics: A lever is a force multiplier. The longer the lever, the greater the force produced at the terminal end. That's why you can pry things open with a big crowbar that you can't pry open with a four-inch screwdriver.

"The energy delivered by the cane increases with distance from the end you're holding. When you swing this, you want the point of contact to be the far end of the shaft." Eddie showed her, taking a big swing and whacking the heavy bag with the last six inches of the shaft. Judging from the sound, the impact was considerable.

"The good news is most untrained opponents will help you do this. That's because they always try to back out of range, or at least lean away from the weapon. You can move forward faster than they can move backward, so you can keep yourself at the best striking distance. A trained fighter who sees a weapon like this will do the opposite—he'll rush toward you. He wants to close the distance before you can complete your swing. He knows that if you strike him with the upper end of the shaft, very near your hands, the blow is not much harder than an empty-handed punch. And once he gets well inside your swing, he can fight you for control of the weapon. That's not what you want. But most attackers won't know to close the distance, and we have ways to deal with those who do."

Eddie had Roz take some practice swings at the bag. Right-handed, left-handed, and two-handed—he showed her how to step into the swing, and how to turn her hips to add power. She was tentative at first, but was soon practicing with vigor.

"You never want to be guessing about the range," Eddie said. "You want to practice until you're so familiar with the distances that you know how close you have to be to connect with each type of swing."

After a few minutes of this practice, Eddie led her to a different punching bag. Instead of hanging from a beam, this one was a free-standing unit. And instead of a plain cylindrical bag, the top of this piece of equipment was a life-sized, rubbery cast image of a muscular man with an angry face. "Roz, this is Bully Bob. Bob, this is Roz."

Preparing to whack the image of a human being felt uncomfortable to Roz, like it was sketchy or improper.

Eddie must have sensed her ambivalence. "Don't worry, they built Bob for this. Remember, if you ever have to defend yourself, it will be against a flesh-and-blood human, not a leather bag."

Of course it will. Roz's grin was sheepish.

Eddie continued. "This cane is every bit as lethal as a knife, a gun, or a baseball bat. It can maim. It can kill. The only time the law justifies you hitting someone with this is when you're in imminent danger of him inflicting death or grave bodily harm on you. When it comes down to either him or you, apply enough force to make sure it's not you. Don't hesitate at that moment. I can promise your attacker won't."

Eddie showed her a sequence of three quick strikes. "The first strike should come as a surprise, since it is launched from a posture that doesn't look like a fighting stance. Observe." He stood holding the cane as any walker would, hand atop the crook, tip on the floor. Sliding his hand forward a few inches to the milled grip, he raised the tip in an upward arc, hitting Bully Bob's base in facsimile of a groin strike. "That's strike one."

Retracting the weapon, he grabbed both grips, and drove the tip like a spear into Bob. "That's strike two. The target can be the solar plexus or the face. The face is the more natural target. When your attacker sees the groin strike coming, he drops his hands and throws his hips back. It's a reflex. He doesn't think about it, and he can't help it. It's an automatic response to the threat, and it happens even if you miss the groin strike. These movements bring his face forward and down, leaving it wide open for the second strike."

Eddie showed her the last piece. "If you can, make this a two-handed strike. It's an almost overhead swing, coming in from about the 2:00 position on a clock face. He'll assume you're head-hunting and put his hands back up to grab the cane, or at least cover his head. At the last minute, you angle the chop toward the actual target—anywhere from the side of his knee to mid-thigh on the leg nearest you. Don't only use your arms. Put your whole body into it, like you're trying to hit a home run in softball. Get a good swing in and you can shatter his leg bone. He'll go down and stay down."

Eddie watched as Roz did a dozen repetitions of the combination on Bully Bob. He said, "This is basic stuff, but it's battle tested. It doesn't involve any silliness that looks good in a dojo but doesn't work on the street. It doesn't require a lot of finesse or fine muscle movement. If you practice these moves at home, proper body mechanics and all, they can save you. Practice them until you can do them fast, flowing from one strike to the next without thinking. You're welcome to come here and practice on the bags. But do it at home too. Learn how much room you have to swing in the rooms of your own house. I'll leave you to practice awhile and I'll come back in a few minutes." He returned to the bench where Mel still sat and took her by the hand. The couple disappeared into the office.

Roz turned her attention toward Bully Bob, concentrating on the task at hand. She heard the front door open and saw a man entering who filled the entire door frame. He waved in the general direction of Eddie's office and sat down on one of the benches. Dropping a gym bag on the floor, he pulled a pair of athletic shoes from it and took off his street shoes. The man changed his shoes in the manner most big men did, by laying one foot across the opposite knee rather than by keeping both feet on the floor and bending over from the waist. Aware that she'd been watching him for several seconds, Roz turned back to her work.

After a few minutes, she noticed the man was now standing off to one side, watching her. She felt self-conscious about her efforts. "Oh, I'm sorry. Were you waiting for this piece of equipment?"

"No, not at all," the man said. "Just observing. I like the way you move."

Roz looked askance at him.

"I mean, I've been watching your movements, and—"

Roz couldn't decide whether his clarification was alarming or funny. So she said nothing.

His face reddened. "No, no, that came out wrong. What I meant to say is your body mechanics are solid. You project decent power through the cane and still stay balanced on your feet. That's good."

"Well, thanks for that. I'm sorry, who are you? I could have sworn Eddie told me he had no students yet."

"Then you heard right. I'm not a student. I'll be helping him instruct from time to time. He and I trained together for years under another instructor before Eddie opened this place." He stepped forward and extended his hand. "Rogoff. Andrei Rogoff."

"Rosalyn Pitts. Call me Roz. Nice to meet you, Andrei Rogoff."

His huge, meaty hand swallowed hers. This guy was at least six foot four, maybe taller, and very strong looking. He wasn't "ripped and cut" the way professional bodybuilders were, but his enormous bulk had the look of lots of muscle and very little fat. Not handsome in the classic leading-man sense, but he had a wholesome vibe that Roz found endearing. And his size made Roz feel almost dainty by comparison. She rather liked the effect.

Roz got back to work on Bully Bob. Andrei excused himself before heading off to the other end of the gym. Maybe he could sense that she wasn't comfortable being watched. Or maybe he was embarrassed about making a hash of his "watching your movements" comments. If that was the case, she found his discomfiture kind of cute. She focused her attention on the drill and practiced until she felt winded. She packed it in just as Eddie returned.

"How do you feel about what I've shown you?"

"Grateful you took the time. And motivated to master this in case the dead-eyed nephew ever comes back. But I'm also a little weirded out by it all. I've never been a violent person."

"Don't think of it as being violent. Think of it as being free."

"What do you mean?"

Eddie said, "What's the primary difference between someone who is free and someone who is not? Think of a prison inmate who is subject to random searches of his cell, and even invasive body searches. He hates these things, but he can't refuse them. Or think of a slave in the antebellum South. Treated worse than livestock. Forced to work without pay, and subject to arbitrary and often brutal punishments for infractions. Liable to have a spouse or children sold away, families torn apart. The slave had no say in any of this, and no legal recourse.

"What the inmate and the slave have in common is the inability to set and enforce any boundaries. Free people set boundaries all the time. 'No trespassing. Don't speak to me like that. Don't touch me.'

"Most people respect your boundaries as soon as you articulate them," he continued. "But some won't. The home invader doesn't care that he shouldn't be in your house. The rapist doesn't care that you said no. If you can't bring yourself to be violent at need, you can't enforce your most important boundaries. If you can't enforce boundaries, you aren't free."

Roz let that soak in. No one had ever told her anything of the sort. And it sounded so self-evident. Setting boundaries was hard, because there was no map to help you negotiate the terrain that changed as you aged. Kindergartners had no boundaries they could enforce on anyone. Adults could order them around, move them out of their way, make them stand facing the corner as punishment, or send them to bed without supper. Little kids had no recourse. But kids grew. At some young age, you understood that you were past the point where an adult could dampen a handkerchief with her own saliva and scrub your face with it.

But as an adult, you could still lack the agency to enforce even the clearest of boundaries yourself. If your boss committed sexual harassment, employers insisted all you could do was tell HR. If robbers broke into your home, politicians advised you to call the police and hope they rode to the rescue in time. Governors and presidents had armed security, but those same politicians didn't trust civilians with the weapons of self-defense.

And church? What boundaries did a pastor have to respect? He played the role of surrogate parent to a congregation of people who would never feel mature enough to stand up to him or call out his unacceptable behavior.

At age thirty-one, Roz still lived within many of the strictures of her childhood. That was why she still couldn't bring herself to talk back to her mother, despite her mother's acid tongue. Eddie had laid it out nice and simple. "If you can't enforce boundaries, you aren't free."

She had one more thing on her mind. "Eddie, before I go, I'd like your opinion on something not related to fighting. You described this place as what's next in your life. How did you know? I would have assumed you'd come back to your family's business. You have so much history and expertise there. How did you know what you were meant to do next?"

Eddie considered the question for a few seconds. "I don't think of it as what I'm meant to do. It's what I choose to do next."

"Do you ever wonder whether you have a calling on your life? A specific purpose you're here for?"

Eddie smiled. "I used to. Now, not so much." Seeing Roz's face fall, he continued. "I know that there are people with specific callings. The Bible is full of them. Moses, Samuel, Jeremiah, John the Baptist, Saul of Tarsus. What I noticed about all of them is that God had no difficulty letting them know what their appointed task was. Moses got the burning bush. Samuel got a voice in the night calling his name. Zechariah got a visit from the angel Gabriel to tell him the news. Matthew was on the job when Jesus walked up to him and said, 'Follow me.' Saul had the Damascus Road experience. I believe all of that.

"What I don't believe is the idea that *everybody* has this one overarching purpose, one reason for being. I figured if there was something specific God was calling me to do, he'd make it clear. Maybe not in such dramatic fashion as with Moses or the Apostle Paul, but I wouldn't have to act like a detective trying to piece together the mystery of why I was born. The Lord knows where I live. And he's not shy."

Roz laughed. "You sound like Shawna. She also downplayed the idea that I have a calling and purpose I need to find. In fact, she told me my search for a calling came from a desire to be special, when by definition most people can't be special."

"I think," said Eddie, "you can be special with or without a special calling. Now there may be something your gifts and talents suit you for. Maybe more than one thing. But whatever it is, it's only a calling if God makes it one by commanding you to do that thing."

"If you're right, it takes some of the pressure off. For a long time, I've had the sense that I was wasting my potential at my current job. I want something more satisfying, more meaningful. I guess wanting the next phase of my career to involve a calling only complicates things."

"For most people, figuring out what to do with their lives is a matter of trial and error. The first job you select after high school or college need not be the thing you do for the rest of your life. Lots of people switch careers at some point. Some several times. And in the end, a job is a way to earn a living by getting paid to do something useful to others. I'm not sure it has to be much more than that."

"Pastor Bowers told me the satisfaction I'm looking for can't come from any secular career. He said only what's done for God can provide satisfaction. When I asked him for help to discern what God would have me do, he suggested I head up some make-work committee at church."

"No big surprise there. Most people in his position think your highest purpose and potential is to become a cog in their machine. It's an unavoidable conflict of interest for him. Like I said, I'm not convinced we all have a specific assignment. What we all have is opportunity and the power of choice.

Unless God tells you what to do, why not chart your own course? It's better than waiting around for an assignment that may never come."

"You think there is satisfaction to be had without a divine assignment? Do you think running this business teaching self-defense will feel meaningful enough to satisfy you in the long run?"

Eddie shrugged. "I don't know. It's the next chapter in The Book of Eddie. It may not be the last one. And I don't require the book to have cosmic significance. I want it to be a good read, so to speak. But that's all."

"That's an interesting way of looking at life. You know I love me a good book."

He walked her to the door, showing her how to hold the cane so she wouldn't look disabled and make herself a more attractive target for predators. "Walk head up, eyes up, erect posture. Look confident. Don't hobble, as if pretending you need the cane for mobility. Carry it the way people a long time ago carried walking sticks as a fashion accessory that could do double duty in a fight."

Roz promised Eddie that she'd practice the walk and the self-defense moves. She returned to her car and laid the cane across the back seat. Eddie was sweet to give it to her, but she had to admit it wasn't much of a fashion accessory. She hoped she would never need it.

Brandon was in a foul mood. First, because he was in a great deal of discomfort, despite the painkillers the hospital staff had pumped into him. Second, because he hated being poked, prodded, monitored, and harassed by the armies of doctors, nurses, and other hospital staff who paraded in and out of his room at all hours. Sometimes they came to poke and prod at his roommate in this semiprivate room, but that bothered Brandon too. Add the indignity of having to wear that baby-blue backless gown with the print pattern copied from some child's pajamas, and his mood wasn't about to improve while they kept him here.

Worst of all, it galled him to know the fat woman had set him up. She had not been home, even though her car was in the garage. Instead, some man had been waiting to jump him, and that unknown man was the reason for all he was suffering now. Brandon burned with the need to track him down and pay him back for all these injuries. The guy had threatened more violence if Brandon came after Roz. It was a threat the man had the skills to make good on. Plus, he'd implied he would not involve the police as long as Brandon kept his distance. But he might change his mind, despite what he'd said. He knew who Brandon was, but Brandon knew nothing about him. The twin threats of another beating and police involvement needed to be eliminated. Most of all, Brandon needed to deal with the meddling neighbor who had arranged the ambush. He needed to deal with her once and for all.

Using his left hand, he dialed the cell phone that sat on the tray in front of him.

A gruff voice answered on the third ring. "Warehouse."

"Yeah, hello, I'm trying to reach Vinnie."

"We got a couple of people named Vinnie. Vinnie who?"

"Vinnie in communications."

"And who's calling?"

"Brandon Heckler."

After several seconds of silence, Vinnie got on the line. "Bran the man! How can I help you?"

"I'm in the hospital in Framingham. There's a woman out here who is responsible for that. I'd like to send her a message."

CHAPTER 19
OVERKILL

Just before 7:00 in the morning, Roz rounded the corner from Pinewood onto Elm Street. She'd skipped this important part of her routine since coming back from Fairport, and she was determined to get back on track and walk her regular route. This was her second lap. She was moving a bit slower than she had been at the height of summer, but that was in part because she had less light. The shorter autumn days meant she was finishing this circuit a mere eight minutes after sunrise.

Autumn inspired mixed feelings. She loved the crisp air, the crunchy sound of leaves underfoot, and the absence of summer's oppressive humidity. But fall was full of surprises, not all of them good. Like when she looked out the window on a cloudless day and stepped outside to discover it was much cooler than it looked. Or when she ran an errand at 6:30 in the evening, only to be surprised that the sun had already set and it was nearly dark. And always in the back of her mind was the realization that winter was on its way. Winter, with its slippery sidewalks and temperatures that hurt her face. Spring spoke of promises and possibilities; summer heat induced a kind of stupor; and winter required perseverance. Roz was determined to enjoy fall while it lasted, whatever surprises it held.

She glanced at the house on the corner and noticed that Mrs. Grimm's old car was gone, the lawn was mowed, and the dead plants had been removed from the porch. Now there was a surprise. Was the county taking care of things? Or had someone already purchased the house? All Roz knew was that the place looked better, and it reminded her less of death and missed opportunities.

"Good morning, neighbor!"

Roz did a double take. The voice came from the yard next door. It was Mr. Schoeder.

"Hello!" Roz put her best, most melodic spin on the word, surprised that Mr. Schroeder was up and about and using Mrs. Grimm's trademark greeting.

Her neighbor suggested she stop by soon to chat. He had news to convey, but knew she had to get ready for work now. "And don't you worry about Brandon," he said. "His van will be here, but I promise you he won't. He won't be around for at least a week." That wasn't news to Roz, of course.

At noon Saturday, she rang the bell, and Mr. Schroeder answered the door without delay. He had ditched the rumpled clothing she had last seen him wearing for some dapper old-man duds. His eyes were clear, and there was even a little spring in his step. He looked very much as he had when they'd first met.

"Now's my chance," he said after they had exchanged hellos. "The lawyer has appealed the ruling that got Brandon appointed guardian. He thinks I have a good shot at winning. And thank my lucky stars, my nephew is unlikely to show up for the hearing. I hate to be so happy about his absence, given the reason for it, but I can't help it. Two guys mugged him the other night. They didn't get his money, but Brandon took quite a beating. His bruises have bruises. I ended up calling an ambulance to take him to the ER. The hospital says he suffered a concussion and might also have lacerations on his liver. His shoulder is torn up too. They admitted him for surgery, and he'll have to spend a little time in a rehab facility once he gets out of Framingham Union."

Roz sighed. "I have to admit I already knew about Brandon's injuries. He wasn't the victim of a pair of muggers. He broke into my house in the middle of the night, intent on harming me. But I had a friend who was house-sitting for me. It was that friend who gave Brandon his well-deserved injuries."

"Are you serious?" Mr. Schroeder's eyes widened. "He broke into your house?"

"Yes. He's done it twice before. I had no proof it was him the first two times. No one ever showed up on my doorbell cameras. But I knew it was him, and now I know how he did it. He was wearing a mylar sheet, a space blanket of some sort. I'm told those make a person invisible to night-vision cameras."

"Makes sense. He's a trained locksmith and a home security expert. He'd be able to defeat pretty much any home security system out there."

"Well, my friend tore the mylar off him. I've got a video of Brandon stumbling out of my home after the fight. He was there to hurt me or maybe even kill me because he felt my involvement with you was messing up his schemes."

"I'm sorry, Roz. I'm glad you had help when you needed it. I don't know what else to say. There are no words for this."

"Say that you'll do whatever you must to get this guy out of your house and life, and I'll be content."

"I am 100 percent on board with that," her neighbor said. After a brief pause, he added, "It seems almost nothing he's ever told me is true. So now I'm wondering what happened to his wife. Or if he even had one."

"What did he tell you?" Roz asked.

"That he was married, but his wife committed suicide earlier this year. He said grief overwhelmed him. But having been a grieving widower myself, I never thought he looked the part. For example, I asked him to show me a photo of her, since I'd never met her. He didn't have one. Not in his wallet, not on his phone, and not among the few possessions he bought with him. What kind of grieving widower doesn't keep one single, solitary picture of his wife? And he never brought her up in conversation after that one time."

"That does sound a bit strange," Roz said.

"It gets stranger. He told me he got depressed and lost his job when she died, which landed him in foreclosure. But I realized that couldn't be true."

"Why is that?"

"Too little time went by. I asked your lawyer friend about the foreclosure process in Massachusetts. He said it isn't fast. He explained it in minute detail, but I'll give you the short version. Your mortgage goes into default once its thirty days late. If that happens, the lender can start the foreclosure process, accelerating the mortgage and demanding the full payoff. You get at least ninety days after default to come up with the payoff. If you don't come up with it, then there's a court-ordered foreclosure auction, followed by formal eviction. All that takes time. At its fastest, it takes more than three months from the date of the default.

"Brandon said his wife died this spring. He said his grief cost him his job, which made him start missing mortgage payments. But even if he stopped paying in June, he'd have at least until November before he was forced out. So why did he show up here in July claiming he'd already lost his home?"

"Good question," Roz said. "What do you think it all means?"

Her neighbor sighed. "I'm not sure. Maybe he never had a wife. Maybe he made up the whole suicide and foreclosure story because he thought it would get him more sympathy than just saying he was underemployed and down on his luck. That might explain him having no photos of her, as well as the fact that the lawyer couldn't find any foreclosure records with Brandon's name on them. Would you know how to find out whether he was ever married?"

"No, not really. The lawyer probably could. Besides, I wouldn't want to spend any more time thinking about him than I had to. He's not the kind of research project I want to take up."

"Can't blame you there," her neighbor said.

Roz saw movement. At her sharp intake of breath, Mr. Schroeder turned to follow her gaze. Laura Schroeder was standing by the open door of Brandon's bedroom and pointing inside.

"Looks like that little exercise the other day was off the mark," the old man observed. "Do you want to say something, Laura?" He sounded hopeful, but the woman in blue said nothing. She continued gesturing toward Brandon's room.

Roz stood. Her hands trembled ever so slightly. Not that she shuddered because of devils. She had no fear of demons. There was security in knowing the scripture said, "greater is he that is in you, than he that is in the world." But she was no longer certain this was a demon at all.

Something about the lady in blue had been nagging her, tugging at the back of her mind. The first time she had seen the apparition, it had *helped* her. Devils thrived on chaos and conflict, but this one had prevented escalating conflict by pointing out the forgotten index cards Roz and her neighbor had written on. Brandon would have been furious to see those. A demon spirit should have wanted them discovered. Why hadn't this one?

The woman in blue looked as real and as solid as Roz herself did, though she made no sound. Even her clothing did not rustle. The situation felt uncanny, but not evil. She walked toward the spirit, who motioned for the two of them to follow her into the room.

When they entered, the woman in blue pointed toward the desk. The two flesh-and-blood people looked over the items on it. Mr. Schroeder picked up a little amber pill bottle from the back corner. Unable to read the print on the label, he handed it to Roz. It was a prescription made out to Brandon for Ambien. She opened the bottle and poured two pills into her hand. She thought back to her internet research and knew these were the statin pills her neighbor was supposed to have been taking all along. The evil nephew had swapped medicines with his uncle. Along with the fake label on the old man's bottle, this amounted to a smoking gun. Roz and Mr. Schroeder both turned back toward the spirit, as if seeking confirmation.

But the lady in blue had more to show them. She pointed toward the desk and held her hands as one might hold a sheet of paper while reading it. They turned back to the desk. Nothing on it looked important. Roz leafed through a couple of takeout menus from local restaurants. There were some envelopes that looked like bills. And there was a piece of copy paper with a playlist of popular music printed on it. Roz flipped it over and saw more songs handwritten on the back. She almost wished the spirit would talk, give them some kind of clue about what they were supposed to be looking for.

Mr. Schroeder must have been thinking the same thing. His voice tremulous, he asked, "What are you trying to show us, honey? Why won't you talk?"

The woman frowned. To Roz, the expression looked more like fierce concentration than it looked like anger. The apparition pointed at the piece of copy paper Roz held and gave an emphatic nod. Roz read Mr. Schroeder the song list. "Do these songs mean anything to you?" The old man shrugged. He looked miserable. They both turned back to the woman in blue, but she was gone.

Her neighbor looked like he might cry. Roz busied herself studying the sheet of paper they had looked at. The playlist on the handwritten side was shorter. There were four songs in total.

<table>
<tr><td>Mother's Little Helper</td><td>The Rolling Stones</td></tr>
<tr><td>Maxwell's Silver Hammer</td><td>The Beatles</td></tr>
<tr><td>Comfortably Numb</td><td>Pink Floyd</td></tr>
<tr><td>I Want It All</td><td>Queen</td></tr>
</table>

She knew three of the four songs. Two of them were about drugs. "Mother's Little Helper" depicted a woman who had become dependent on valium to get her through her banal days. "Comfortably Numb" was an analogy of sorts, comparing being drugged out to what it was like to give up on hopes and dreams. Two songs about drugs, and Brandon had weaponized a sedative against his uncle. That couldn't be a coincidence.

The other tune she recognized was a Beatles song about a serial killer who dispatches his victims by hitting them in the head with a hammer. To her knowledge, Brandon hadn't brought a hammer to her house, nor threatened his uncle with one. The song's inclusion on the list was a mystery . . . unless it described what happened to poor little Sarge. Roz didn't know the song

"I Want It All," but hadn't Brandon taken over his uncle's life and finances with the guardianship? This was all feeling creepy. But was it evidence? She envisioned trying to explain her suspicions to the same detective who had investigated the first break-in at her house. *Yeah, maybe not.*

She turned the paper over and scanned the printed list of songs and artists. She knew these songs but could discern no obvious pattern. "How did you say Brandon's wife died?"

"She jumped off a bridge. Or so Brandon said."

"A couple of these songs reference people dying. And there are four songs that talk about rivers or bridges. Where the River Flows, Dirty Water, Take Me to the River . . . and Ode to Billie Joe. That last one features a guy who jumped off a bridge and died."

Roz couldn't tell how the rest of the songs fit in, but she snapped photos of both sides of the sheet before putting it back where she had found it. Thanks to the exertions of Eddie, the lawyer, and the woman in blue, Brandon's plans were unraveling. Needing some alone time to think, Roz excused herself.

Back at home, Roz got to work on the problem of what to say to her neighbor about the apparition. In terms of pure logic, there could be only two possibilities: either it was a devil, or it was not. If it was a devil, they should have been able to cast it out—yet they had failed in the attempt. If it was not a devil, what else could it be? Not imagination. She and Mr. Schroeder couldn't have both imagined the same thing, right down to the clothes the lady wore. Maybe the woman was what Mr. Schroeder had believed her to be all along. Was that even possible?

Roz opened her laptop and pulled up a concordance on bible-gateway.com. She began by looking up the word *spirit*. Turned out there were 523 occurrences of that word in the King James Bible. The word *ghost* appeared 108 times. That was a more manageable list of verses, but it would still take a long time to read. It was soon apparent that the word *ghost* wasn't often used in the sense Roz was looking for, though she found it interesting that the scripture described several people's deaths by saying that they "gave up the ghost." Still, researching the issue this way would be a slow slog indeed. Maybe she could come at it from another angle.

Hebrews 9:27 said that it is appointed to men to die once, and afterward, the judgment. She knew many Christians who cited this verse as proof that ghosts could not exist. But Roz saw it as inconclusive, establishing a sequence of events without establishing a timeline. Judgment need not be an instant after death. In fact, Revelation 20:5 made it clear that for some, judgment came many years after the death of the body.

She found no Bible verses that endorsed the idea of haunted places. Neither did she find any that ruled out the possibility.

There was an intriguing story in 1 Samuel, chapter 28. It told the story of how a witch called up the ghost of the prophet Samuel on orders from Israel's backslidden King Saul. She jotted two quick thoughts in her notebook as she read.

- The narrator says this was Samuel's spirit for real. Not an illusion. Not a devil. If his ghost could walk among the living, might someone else's?

- I always figured death was a one-way trip. Like leaving a building through a fire exit. On the outside, the door closes flush with the wall and has no doorknob. People can't reenter.

No sooner had she written those words than a chill went through her. She remembered the strange sights on the endless staircase. She'd watched many people die there, watched their spirits exit the stairwell and fly into the void. At the end of this . . . experience, she'd glimpsed a spirit moving in the wrong direction, coming into the stairwell from the outside. She'd written the whole thing off as a psychological malfunction, a hallucination caused by stress and fatigue. Hypnagogia. But what if it wasn't? What if God had sent her a vision to prepare her for encountering the woman in blue?

With a click of her mouse, she switched from the King James Version to the New American Standard Bible for the additional clarity of modern English. Additional research found her focusing on Luke 16:19-31. The passage read:

[19] Now there was a rich man, and he habitually dressed in purple and fine linen, enjoying himself in splendor every day. [20] And a poor man named Lazarus was laid at his gate, covered with sores, [21] and longing to be fed from the scraps which fell from the rich man's table; not only that, the dogs also were coming and licking his sores. [22] Now it happened that the poor man died and was carried away by the angels to Abraham's arms; and the rich man also died and

was buried. 23 And in Hades he raised his eyes, being in torment, and saw Abraham far away and Lazarus in his arms. 24 And he cried out and said, "Father Abraham, have mercy on me and send Lazarus, so that he may dip the tip of his finger in water and cool off my tongue, for I am in agony in this flame." 25 But Abraham said, "Child, remember that during your life you received your good things, and likewise Lazarus bad things; but now he is being comforted here, and you are in agony. 26 And besides all this, between us and you a great chasm has been set, so that those who want to go over from here to you will not be able, nor will any people cross over from there to us." 27 And he said, "Then I request of you, father, that you send him to my father's house—28 for I have five brothers—in order that he may warn them, so that they will not come to this place of torment as well." 29 But Abraham said, "They have Moses and the Prophets; let them hear them." 30 But he said, "No, father Abraham, but if someone goes to them from the dead, they will repent!" 31 But he said to him, "If they do not listen to Moses and the Prophets, they will not be persuaded even if someone rises from the dead."

She'd heard several ministers preach from that passage. Still, the thoughts that came to her mind went beyond what she had heard across any pulpit. She jotted these down with a growing sense of excitement. It was as if she could feel discovery coming before it got there.

- The story presented Lazarus as a lame man. Someone had to lay him down at the rich man's gate to beg. His spirit would not be lame after the death of the body. That's why the now-dead rich man assumed Lazarus could be sent to him. Yet angels carried his spirit away. Maybe carrying people to paradise was part of the normal ministry of angels. If it was, the reason might be as simple as the fact that people wouldn't know where or how to find it on their own. They'd need an escort.

- Abraham did not say it was impossible for the dead to return to earth; only that it would be pointless. We know it wasn't impossible. Samuel did it.

- Hypothesis: People who "give up the ghost" need an escort to take their spirit from wherever their body died to their next abode in the afterlife. The redeemed get an angelic lift to paradise, as Lazarus did. The lost are supposed to get a demonic escort to drag them to hell. God's angels would do their jobs without fail. Maybe the fallen angels aren't so faithful in the execution of their duties. What would happen if an unsaved person died, but no escort came? That spirit would wander, lost in death's gray void, maybe choosing to return to the people and places it knew before. Such a spirit might be unaware of the torment that awaits in its terminal destination.

Could this be the explanation for Laura Schroeder? If it was, Roz knew she couldn't bring herself to spell it out for Mr.

Schroeder. In any case, she felt she needed more proof to be sure. That would have to wait for another day.

Excited as she was by her possible discovery, she wasn't looking forward to her next conversation with Mr. Schroeder. She'd have to try to explain how her church group could have gotten things so wrong. That hadn't been her first exposure to the world of spirits; she had seen devils cast out before. Though she didn't want it to be, Roz was thinking her new take on the story of Lazarus and the rich man might be the truth of the matter. On a sudden hunch, she grabbed her Bible and looked up a familiar verse in the New Testament's last book. She began reading at Revelation 20:12.

And I saw the dead, small and great, stand before God; and the books were opened: and another book was opened, which is the book of life: and the dead were judged out of those things which were written in the books, according to their works. And the sea gave up the dead which were in it; and death and hell delivered up the dead which were in them: and they were judged every man according to their works.

Her heart leaped. How had she never seen this? She'd read this passage an untold number of times but never seen the truth that was staring her in the face all along. The scene described the Great White Throne judgment, sometimes called the judgment of the wicked dead. And where did the Bible say those lost souls came from? Multiple places, not all of them associated with the afterlife. The sea was a physical place on earth, not some spirit realm. Yet some of the dead were there. And some were in hell, as would be expected. Still others, not in either place, were in unspecified locations within the realm of death. She saw the gray void in her mind's eye again, the nothingness beyond the exit doors in that metaphorical stairwell. The Bible didn't deny the possibility of ghosts; it confirmed it.

This conceptual breakthrough did not help with her most basic problem: How was she going to explain Laura Schroeder's presence to her husband?

On Sunday after church, she gave her neighbor a call to ask whether it was okay for her to stop by. He said he'd welcome the company. After a moment or two of chit-chat, she steeled herself and launched into her intended topic. She still had no firm idea of everything she needed to say. "I wanted to apologize for the way I handled things. I meant well, but I made the mistake of assuming I knew something I didn't. I'm talking about the situation with your wife."

The man arched one eyebrow. When he spoke, his voice was quiet. "My wife? You're calling her my wife, not some demon who imitates her?"

Before Roz could answer, the lady in blue was there, standing at the end of the dining room table nearest the kitchen. "Mrs. Schroeder, I was wrong about who and what you are. I jumped to a conclusion—not an unreasonable conclusion, but still an incorrect one. You have my sincere apology for that." The woman looked at Roz, her expression unreadable.

"Also, thank you for pointing out what Brandon was doing. We knew he was up to no good, but without your help, we never would have known how he switched the medications. That's twice you helped us, and I appreciate it.

"But now we have a favor to ask you. I think you're aware you've transitioned to another plane of existence. You're no longer part of all this," she said, taking in the room with her gesture. "There's someplace else you are supposed to be now. I'm confident you'll get there, though I don't know when. For now, please know that your visits here cause distress for your husband. He loved you in life, he cherishes your memory, but doesn't want to see you bound to this place, or to him, anymore. He'll be happier if he can believe you are at rest." *Talk about threading the needle.* Roz had cut things mighty fine, but she'd been honest without being brutal about it.

Mrs. Schroeder turned to look at her husband. He said, "It's true, Laura. I love you and miss you, but I need you to leave me with my memories now. Roz has been a real help to me, and I'm grateful for it. You can be sure that I am not without a friend. I'm in excellent hands." Tears glistened in the old man's eyes.

Laura Schroeder was becoming translucent. She'd always looked like actual flesh and blood before. Now she was indistinct, an impressionist painter's interpretation of the woman she had been. Roz remembered how the spirits in her vision of the stairwell had looked like a mixture of smoke and moonlight. Mrs. Schroeder was looking like that. Her expression softened, as if she were relieved of the effort it took to remain visible to the living. She leaned across the table and put a ghostly hand atop her former husband's. Her eyes, not much more than smudges now, looked sad. Still, she mustered a faint smile. Three more seconds, maybe four, and she was gone.

CHAPTER 20
CARS

It's hard to retain a sense of the extraordinary in the face of the mundane. Nothing like three days of putting out fires at the office to keep a person grounded. During hours of meetings and Zoom calls, Roz had to defend her departmental budget, deal with the fallout from people's impolitic emails, manage the unrealistic expectations of her superiors, and explain for what felt like the hundredth time why they couldn't edit the wording of a catalog that had already gone to the print shop. All while trying to encourage and motivate the always-disgruntled survivors of the summer layoffs. She knew today's office emergencies would be forgotten in two weeks, when new crises emerged to replace them.

Roz laughed to herself on her way to her car. Three days ago, she had been filled with wonder at both her Bible discoveries and the fact that she had spoken to a dead woman and persuaded her to move on. Today, the most exciting thing she could think of was getting a cup of coffee and resting her tired feet. And it was only Wednesday.

Evening rush-hour traffic was as bad as ever. A yellow traffic light on Speen Street turned red when she was halfway through the intersection. The SUV behind her went through too. The driver had to know he'd run the red light. With so many traffic cameras in use these days, it was a foolish chance to take.

Roz zigzagged her way toward home, trying to find something better than the day's aggravations to occupy her mind. Three traffic lights later, it happened again. She accelerated to make the yellow light, and the car behind her went through too. It appeared to be the same SUV that had been behind her on Speen Street. At least it was the same unusual color.

A quarter mile from home, Roz decided she didn't feel like cooking tonight. On the spur of the moment, she veered left onto Central Street instead of driving up Elm. She wanted to go to Stop & Shop and buy some prepared food. She'd need something with no carbs, no added sugar, and not too much salt. Believing the supermarket would have many options that fit the bill was a stretch. But making a mental list of acceptable choices at least got her mind off work. The drive to the store took fifteen minutes. She was in and out in another ten, despite struggling with the computer in the hated self-checkout lane. Why couldn't a regional powerhouse valued at over $60 billion afford to staff the cash registers? Back at her car, she put her food in the back seat footwell and her purse on the passenger seat. Driving toward the exit, she saw an orange-gold SUV in a parking space to her right. Under the parking lot lights, she could see the trademark oval and the word BRONCO on the grill. What she could not see was the driver. A male silhouette, most likely, but the window tint and the reflected light made it impossible to see the man's features. As she pulled into the exit line, it slid in behind her.

Was this a weird coincidence? Or was this guy following her? Was it even the same vehicle she'd seen earlier? She wasn't sure, but she was in no mood to take chances. She could call the police from her car. But what would she say? "I think I've seen the same car behind me three times?" That would hardly prompt law enforcement to drop whatever they were doing and ride to her rescue. She was going to have to lose this person herself. At the parking lot's exit onto Temple Street, she turned left instead of right, avoiding going back the way she had come. The Bronco also turned left, staying behind her.

Most of the traffic was turning left at the next intersection. Roz used no turn signal so as not to telegraph her move. She reached the corner and turned right. With no traffic in front of her for a few hundred yards, she floored it. The orange vehicle followed, laboring to keep up. A quarter of a mile down the road, Roz made a hard left onto Singletary Lane, tires squealing in protest. The narrow road ran straight, climbing a moderate grade. If she could get over the crest of the hill well ahead of him, she could lose herself in one of the neighborhoods that bordered the road.

She checked her mirror and saw the SUV near the bottom of the hill, charging hard to catch up. The road grew more winding, snaking along the edge of a residential neighborhood where a street sign read, "THICKLY SETTLED." Tree branches formed a canopy overhead, blocking out what little light remained in October's early dusk. Roz slowed a little. No point in risking any accidents. She'd turn at the first intersection she reached, hoping her pursuer would fail to notice. If the Bronco kept going straight, she could wait a minute before reversing direction and heading home.

Roz slowed for a right turn before realizing she'd spotted a long driveway rather than a narrow street. The dim light had tricked her eyes. If she went in there, her pursuer could pull in behind her and block her way out. She saw the street she was looking for about fifty yards ahead. But a glance in her mirror confirmed the SUV was gaining on her fast. At the rate he was going, he'd hit her when she braked for the turn. And her intention to turn was based on hiding. Now that he was right behind her, there was no point. She went straight, breathing hard, trying to formulate a Plan B and avoid hyperventilating. The distinctive headlights raced right up behind her. Roz screamed and braced for impact. At the last second, the other driver whipped his ride to the left as if to pass her. That could be a suicidal move on such a narrow road with short sightlines. If a car was coming the other way, there would be a horrific crash. She took her foot off the gas to let the maniac get by. When the Ford's front end was a little past her rear bumper, he swerved right and banged into her car.

The impact was loud and jarring. Roz shrieked again. Her wagon spun out 180 degrees, crossed the road going backward, and slid off the pavement. There was no true berm on this road, and the soft ground fell away at a steep angle. When the car came to a stop, she was parallel to the road, but canted steeply to the right and sinking into a muddy slope. The passenger side was so far below the driver's side that she feared the wagon might roll over. Hitting the gas demonstrated that she could spin her wheels in the soft dirt but couldn't go anywhere. Trapped!

She reached for her purse, but it wasn't there. All the careening around had flung it into the passenger footwell, spilling all the contents. Her phone was somewhere in that mess. She couldn't see it. Couldn't be sure it hadn't broken on impact. First priority was getting out of the car before it rolled over. She tried and failed to open the driver's door, not being strong enough to open it upward against the force of gravity. It might be possible to get out the other side, but she feared crawling over the center console to the passenger seat would unbalance the car further.

Someone pulled the driver's door open for her. Roz looked up—way up—at a heavyset man standing uphill from her. "Did you see what happened? Some guy chased me, hit me on purpose, and ran me off the road! He was driving an orange SUV. Did you see it?"

"I did see it," he said. "I'm the guy who was driving it, Rosalyn."

Hearing her name come from this stranger's lips was a shock. A cold feeling crept up her back. How did he know her? What was going on here? The man bent and offered her his gloved hand to help her out of the car. She declined, hand up, palm out.

"Suit yourself," he said. "We need to talk, and this looks like an ideal place. I'm here to give you a message. And this is it: actions have consequences. You listening? The sender of that message asked me to beat some information out of you. Lucky for you, it takes a lot to make me hit a woman. So I'll make you a deal. Give me the name of your houseguest who went all John Wick on my client a while back. Full name, address, phone number, pics if you have them, the whole works. Do that right now, and I'll leave you to deal with your car troubles unmolested." He spoke in a lighthearted, casual tone, as if he was discussing the weather or inquiring about weekend plans.

Roz was incredulous. "I know your client is Brandon Heckler. Did you know he broke into my house at 3:00 a.m. intending to harm me? That's where and why he got beat up. And now he's acting like somebody wronged him?"

"Lady, none of that stuff is my concern. What, where, when, or why he did something makes no difference. I don't want to hurt you. But I will if I have to. I won't leave my client thinking you didn't get the message. Give up your bodyguard, or I'm going to reconsider my commitment to chivalry, you understand?"

"No." Roz surprised herself by saying it. It was such a simple word, so strong and resolute. Not that she felt strong or resolute. Her knees were knocking. She felt a twist in the pit of her stomach, like she might throw up any minute. The tiny syllable she had uttered could prove life-altering, or even life-ending. But an idea was fighting its way clear of the jumble of her emotions and physical reactions. It had to do with boundaries and freedom and being able to live with herself for however long her life might be.

The man's voice lost all of its pretend lightheartedness. "No? No, you don't understand what I'm telling you, or no, you don't have sense enough to avoid ticking me off?"

Roz swallowed hard and closed her eyes. This wasn't the first man to tell her to throw Eddie away. Rev. Bowers had done it, and she had complied, to her shame. She wouldn't do that again. She wouldn't sell out someone who had shown her so much kindness. Looking up, Roz locked eyes with this newest enemy. "You scare me. But you can't control me. The answer is no." She averted her eyes and resigned herself to whatever was going to happen next. Like the man said, actions had consequences.

From up on the road came the sound of a car door slamming. Footsteps approached the edge of the embankment. She and the SUV driver both turned to look, though Roz couldn't see because the man's body blocked her view. A smoky contralto voice asked, "Is everyone all right here? Do you need me to call for help?"

Roz knew that voice. "Julianna? It's me, Roz. So glad to hear a friendly voice! You came along at the perfect time. This man ran me off the road on purpose. And now he's threatening to hurt me."

"Is that true?" Julianna stepped closer. "If you attack this woman, you'll have to deal with me."

The man favored Julianna with a dismissive smirk. He lifted his shirt to reveal the butt of a gun shoved into his waistband.

"I'm not worried about you, whoever and whatever you are. I can make quick work of you."

"I've earned the Distinguished Pistol Shot Badge in the Marine Corps. If you think you're the faster draw or the better shot, go for it. Otherwise, I suggest you leave now."

The man stared at Julianna for several long seconds. He made no move to draw his weapon. Instead he turned back to Roz, speaking with the same casual tone he'd adopted when they first met. "You got a steel spine, lady. I'll give you that. You also got lucky today. Enjoy today. As for tomorrow, who knows?" He gave Roz a jaunty two-finger salute before turning away and climbing back up the embankment. His path angled well away from Julianna, who kept one hand shoved into a purse while watching the retreating figure's progress.

Roz waited until the sound of his footsteps faded before addressing Julianna. "Thanks for that. You may have saved my life. Given our history, I didn't know whether you were going to stick up for me or cheer him on. He was only the latest close call I've had with dangerous people. And to think a few months ago, my biggest problem was former coworkers vandalizing my stuff."

Julianna considered that. "When it rains, it pours, huh? Well, I'm not admitting to anything, but I think I can promise you there's no more petty vandalism coming your way from former colleagues. You and I may never be friends, but we don't have to be enemies. Sounds like you've had a bad enough time of things. Want me to call the police for you?"

"Please and thank you. What brings you here, anyway? As I recall, you live some distance from here."

"I'm headed home from an early dinner at John Stone's Inn in Ashland. I've always wanted to go there. It's supposed to be one of the most haunted places in all of New England. Not that I expect you to believe in such things."

"You might be surprised," Roz said. Then almost as an afterthought, she asked, "Did you really win marksmanship medals? Would you have had a shootout with that guy?"

"Yes, to the first question. As for the second, I'm glad he didn't accept my challenge. I almost always have a pistol on me. But now I realize it's sitting in the center console of my car."

Roz didn't know what to say to that. Her ex-colleague reached the Framingham police and handed the phone to Roz. Roz provided the best description she could of the man and his SUV, and ended by explaining she would need a tow truck to get her car back up onto the road.

When they arrived and Roz and her car were back on solid ground, she retrieved her phone and the items strewn from her purse. She breathed a sigh of relief. Not a bad outcome, considering what could have happened. It was going to be a while before she got home, and she doubted she'd sleep much that night.

"Well? Please tell me you've got good news."

Visiting hours were almost over, but Brandon was happy to see Vinnie walk in. The leg-breaker shook his head. "No news, other than the woman has guts. And loyalty. She wouldn't provide the information on your sparring partner, even when I made it clear it would be in her best interest. To be honest, I'm not feeling this one anymore." He tossed an envelope onto Brandon's bed. "It's all there. Minus expenses, of course. I'm out." With those words, he turned and left as quickly as he had come in.

Brandon picked up the envelope and clenched his teeth in frustration. He didn't want a refund. He wanted the job done. *It's like people say. If you want something done right, you have to do it yourself.*

CHAPTER 21
FIGHT THE GOOD FIGHT

The dishwasher was humming in the kitchen. Roz was humming in her recliner, listening and half singing along as her stereo served up some tasty gospel music. "Jesus Be a Fence All Around Me" was a favorite choir selection from back in the day. Fred Hammond's rendition of this 1959 Sam Cooke tune bore little resemblance to the original. Hammond had reimagined the chord progression, ramped up the tempo, and turned a slow crooner into something you could shout and dance to. This Sunday evening Roz was too tired to do either, but she was enjoying the performance from the comfort of her chair.

On an occasional table halfway across the room, her phone rang. The music was too loud for her to hear the ringtone, but she could see the screen light up. Whoever it was would have to wait. She was enjoying this song too much to interrupt it.

She reached out and grabbed her cane from where it stood in the corner. Eddie's gift was a thoughtful one, and her skills with it had notably improved. But she wondered how long the cane would remain useful. At the rate she was losing weight and getting fit, it wouldn't be a believable stage prop for much longer. She'd have to figure out something to carry in its stead. But that was a puzzle for another day. For tonight, it made an adequate percussion instrument. She shifted it from hand to hand, tapping it on the floor in time to the quarter-note triplets that helped give the bridge such a catchy rhythm.

As Roz conducted from her chair, preparing to lead the band back to the top of the chorus, her front door crashed open and bounced off the doorstop with a bang. Roz looked to the doorway and saw Brandon Heckler charge into her home. Shocked, she surged to her feet and called, "Jesus!" in accidental unison with the recording.

Brandon's right arm was in a sling. In his left hand he held a large military-style knife. His expression was one of pure animal rage. He wore a bandana that hid the lower half of his face from the security camera at the front door. Not much effort put into sneaking or hiding this time.

Roz acted according to her training. Eyes on his chest to find his body's centerline, she snapped the tip of the cane up. Brandon saw or sensed the groin strike coming and tried to turn his hips away and raise a knee to block it. Even so, the reflexive compulsion to block the target with his one mobile hand proved impossible to resist. Roz's strike missed by a scant few inches, but she withdrew the cane as fast as she had deployed it and rammed it straight toward his face. With one arm in a sling and the other hand too low to protect his head, all Brandon could do was turn his face away to avoid taking the shot in the eye. He took the blow high on his right cheek. The tip of the cane made a scraping cut and blood flowed.

Roz was no stick-fighting expert. She knew only one sequence. But she had practiced it hundreds of times on Bully Bob and visualized it hundreds of times more. Without conscious thought, she flowed into the third move of that sequence, putting all of her weight and power into a two-handed swing. The cane whooshed through its downward arc like an ax in the hands of a lumberjack. Roz's eyes were focused on the knife, which might be why she forgot to execute the feint. Instead of changing the trajectory of her swing to strike his leg, she kept the cane on its original course. As a wobbly Brandon turned back toward her, the cane caught him a glancing blow atop the right side of his head. He did not cry out. The only sounds were the crack of the weapon on his cranium, and the heavy thud of his body hitting the floor. He lay on his back, stiff, crabbed up, as if frozen in the middle of doing some bizarre, herky-jerky dance.

Roz ran to lower the volume on the triumphant strains of the song and reached for her phone to call 9-1-1.

Emergency personnel arrived. In ten minutes, EMTs had loaded Brandon into an ambulance and rushed him away. *I guess that means he's alive.* Roz was not sure how to feel about that. With the ambulance gone, a police officer began securing the residence and putting up yellow crime scene tape, while another peppered her with questions. He wanted her to explain the encounter, step by step.

Roz kept her answers short. "The man broke in and attacked me. He had a knife, which you can see on the floor there. I was in fear for my life and defended myself with my cane. There will be time for statements later, but for now, I'm stressed out. I need time to compose myself, get checked for any injuries, and consult with my attorney."

That was something else to thank Eddie for. He'd explained to her that a physical fight is only half the battle. The legal fight came next, and it began the second she dialed 9-1-1. If the police decided she'd done something wrong, anything she said would be used against her—never for her.

The officer looked surprised at her determination to say no more, but he nodded his understanding and didn't press further. He ushered her to the porch so she wouldn't interfere with the investigation in the house. A few minutes later, a detective arrived. Roz recognized him as the one who had investigated the first break-in. He went into the house and came back out a minute later.

"The officer tells me you declined to make a statement."

"That's correct."

"If the man lives, I'm sure he'll have his own version of things to tell us. Don't you want to get your side of things on the record before he gets his?"

"Like I told the officer, I'll cooperate when I've sought medical care and talked with a lawyer. Besides, I was plenty talkative last time you were here, and you all but accused me of making up stories in a pathetic bid for attention. You can see my broken front door. You can see the knife he brought here. This time, there will be video evidence. Those things can speak for me until I feel ready to talk." Her tone made it clear the matter was not up for debate.

Roz stepped off the porch. The night air was making her cold. There were two police cars in her driveway, people going in and out of her broken front door, and a little clump of bystanders eyeing the proceedings from across the street.

From outside the line of tape, a voice asked, "Roz? Are you all right?"

She knew that voice. "I think so, Mr. Schroeder. I'm going to have a doctor tell me for sure." Roz felt her adrenaline wearing off, and sudden exhaustion setting in. She appreciated her neighbor's concern but was in no mood to talk right now.

"I got here as fast as I could. Brandon returned to my house from rehab this evening. He flew into a rage and stormed out when I told him I'd taken my life back. I figured he'd come here. I tried to call you, but got no answer. And the walk over here . . . I'm almost blind in the dark, I guess. Anyway, I know you did what you had to do. He's family to me, but he is an evil man. I saw them carry him out. If he doesn't make it, I believe the blame is all his. I wanted you to know that."

"Thank you. That means a lot."

"I know you have things to do, so I'll be going home. But take this." He reached for her hand and put a small wad of cash into it. "You're going to need to buy a new door in the morning. It's the least I can do."

"Again, thank you." Roz wanted to say something wise, or meaningful, or even something friendly but innocuous. She was too tired, and no words came to mind.

"We'll talk again," Mr. Schroeder said. "Maybe in a week or two you could come over and get reacquainted with some of my books."

"I'd like that." After saying farewell to her neighbor and to the detective, who promised to station a car outside her home to monitor her front door until morning, Roz got into her rental car for the precautionary trip to the ER. She unfolded the currency she'd received. Five one-hundred-dollar bills. Hard to believe that Mr. Schroeder and that monster were kin.

CHAPTER 22
ALL WE LIKE SHEEP

Pastor Gregory Clement Bowers was on a roll. Roz listened as the fire and brimstone rained down hotter and heavier than usual. Tonight was midweek Bible study, a service that rarely had visitors. The pastor had taken to using that service for what he called his come-to-Jesus meetings; those times when he felt the need to deliver a rhetorical beat-down he wouldn't want visitors to hear. His chosen text was Isaiah 53:6. "All we like sheep have gone astray; we have turned every one to his own way; and the Lord has laid on Him the iniquity of us all."

Preaching to a half-empty sanctuary, Bowers focused on the second clause of his text, about everyone turning to his own way. "The church isn't Burger King," he intoned. "Remember their old marketing slogan? Well, in God's house, you don't get to have it your way." He catalogued and condemned a laundry list of wrongs he felt all boiled down to people trying to have it their way: the people who seemed to show up for church only when they felt like it; the people whose financial support fell short of expectations; the people who voiced criticisms of God's program and God's chosen leaders. It was as if he'd combined all his diatribes from the last six months into one toxic stew.

"I'm not surprised by any of this," he said, striding back and forth on the platform. "We're living in the last days, and iniquity is waxing worse and worse. People will sit on the receiving end of the miraculous and not utter so much as a thank you. About a week ago, I visited the home of a man who lives here in town who needed deliverance. He had a demon in his house. This demon was tormenting the poor man by impersonating his dead wife. It had been going on for years. I went there, and a few of the saints went with me. Deacon Gonzales and Sister Pitts can both bear witness. We went to this man's house and went to war in the Spirit. We cast the devil out in the name of the Lord. After we were done, I offered the man a Bible study. He said he'd think about it. Did I get a heartfelt thank you for cleansing his house? No! Has he set foot inside this church at least once to give God some praise? No! That's the way of the world today. It's bad enough that the people out there act like that. But to make matters worse, that blasé worldly mindset has crept in here. Somebody who was there that day should already have testified about what God has done, rather than holding your peace and acting like there's nothing to get excited about. Am I right, Deacon Gonzales?"

"Yes sir, you're right," said the dutiful deacon, looking chastened.

"Am I right, Sister Pitts?"

Roz was silent.

"I can't hear you, sister. You've got the biggest voice in the entire congregation. You bless us with it on the regular. This man is your neighbor, your project. The church extended itself to help him at your request. This is no time to get quiet, is it?"

Roz sighed. "The reason I haven't testified is that we failed. Within a minute or two of your departure, the spirit was back."

The pastor looked thunderstruck. "Your neighbor told you this?"

"He didn't need to. I saw it with my own eyes."

The preacher had a deer-in-the-headlights look. There was a strained silence throughout the sanctuary. One could almost hear the mental gears turning as people worked things out. Bowers regained his voice, saying, "You saw this and neglected to inform me? Why didn't you call me at once?"

Roz knew that everyone in the building feared this man to one degree or another. But she had persuaded a ghost, defied a leg-breaker, and subdued a homicidal maniac. She would no longer live in fear of this preacher's anger.

"No disrespect, Pastor, but I could ask you a similar question. Why not check with me or my neighbor to see how things worked out instead of making a premature declaration of victory? If you had, you would have avoided rebuking people in public for failing to testify about something that never happened."

Roz hadn't yelled. She hadn't even sounded angry; she was more disheartened than anything else. The pastor's face reddened, not with apparent embarrassment, but with obvious rage. "That was way out of order. If you had an issue with me, the acceptable thing to do would have been to see me in private, not bring your complaint before the whole church." About half the congregation seemed to murmur its agreement with this. Roz heard a smattering of amens.

"You said that without irony," she replied. "After singling out Deacon Gonzales and me from the pulpit and charging us with ingratitude and having a worldly mindset. You brought that complaint in front of the whole church. I tried to remain silent, but you insisted I answer this unfounded charge so everyone could hear it—you wanted my answer to be public right up until you heard it spoken. You were eager to embarrass me, but now you are angry that my answer embarrassed you. I'm not the first person in this congregation you've rebuked for giving an honest answer to a question you asked. It's a pattern with you, and it wounds people. It shouldn't be that way. We should all expect the Golden Rule to be observed here. Even by you."

The other half of the congregation nodded and murmured agreement with Roz. There were more amens, louder this time. Battle lines were being drawn.

Someone else spoke up. "Don't do the devil's work, Sister. God hates the sowing of discord among brethren."

The speaker was Marvin Blackwell. Maybe he was still mad about seeing her dining with Eddie at The Cheesecake Factory.

She responded with a level tone, surprised at her own sense of calm. "Speaking the truth in love is never the devil's work."

The veins in the pastor's neck were bulging. He slammed his fist on the podium and yelled, "Order! Order! I still have the floor. No more side conversations. No one should be talking but me."

He launched into a rambling tirade, decrying disloyalty, insubordination, wolves in sheep's clothing, and tares among the wheat. "It's shocking what some church members do," he said. "I can't explain it or account for it. Maybe it comes from a place of bitterness—bitterness over lost opportunities. Being dissatisfied with their lot in life."

Roz didn't hear him. She withdrew into herself, lost in her own thoughts. She hadn't asked for any of this. He had forced her hand. Now she was on the outs with the pastor, and it didn't look fixable. Maybe she'd get the boot. No wonder Shawna had opted to preempt any drama by running away when no one was looking. Poor careful, cagey, cryptic Shawna. She'd spent her whole saved life trying to protect herself from stuff like this. She'd gone in search of a church that didn't turn everyone into the walking wounded. Did such a place exist? There ought to be a Hippocratic oath for ministers: first, do no harm.

Once upon a time, Roz had craved acceptance more than anything else. It wasn't much to ask for. She'd nursed that trivial ambition since elementary school, where she'd been nothing more than the fat girl, scorned and ridiculed by almost everyone. And none of those mean kids had rejected Roz harder than her own mother had. This church had been the first place where she'd felt as if she belonged. The acceptance she had enjoyed up to this point was already a thing of the past. That knowledge hurt.

But she didn't regret today's actions. If bullying, gaslighting, and public humiliation were the price of acceptance here, she'd do without it. That was now nonnegotiable. Besides, she reminded herself, the special people who lined her bookshelves never enjoyed universal acceptance. Not William Wilberforce, and not Martin Luther King Jr. Not Hank Aaron or Muhammad Ali or Elon Musk or Billie Jean King. Mr. Rogers and Mother Teresa might have been exceptions to the rule—but maybe not. Regardless, exceptional trumped accepted.

And Roz *had* done something exceptional here. Without planning to, she'd struck a minor blow for justice in a setting that was tyrannical by tradition. She'd articulated a personal boundary to a man who always got away with disregarding boundaries. Few people here would have stood up for themselves the way she had. Maybe it wasn't much in the grand scheme of things. Still, it was encouraging. She almost smiled. Bringing her own sunshine was so much better than sitting under someone else's rain cloud.

The sound of many voices yanked her attention away from her ruminations. The service had stopped, though she was sure there had been no benediction. Whatever had happened, things had escalated. Pastor Bowers was standing on the far side of the platform, having a heated discussion with a deacon. The assistant pastor was trying to interpose himself between them. Two members of the church board were striding down the center aisle toward the platform. Another member of the ministerial staff positioned himself at the top of the platform steps as if to defend this high ground from the advancing board members. The assembled congregants had stood and broken into several small groups, each facing off with another and speaking with raised voices accompanied by emphatic gestures.

Roz heard her mother's voice in her head. *You alternate between praying for a miracle and wishing someone would pull the plug and have the funeral already.* Was the scene unfolding here the seeds of restoration or the death throes of Solid Rock? Either would be preferable to the status quo. Roz stood and walked to the exit without looking back. She had tears in her eyes, but not for herself.

Shawna had blocked Roz's number after their last conversation. But according to her LinkedIn profile, she still worked at the same place. Using the dial-by-name directory, Roz called Shawna's extension at work. While the out-of-office message played, Roz wondered how long a message the system would let her record. When it was time to leave her message, she packed as much in as she could.

"Hello, Shawna, it's Roz. Don't worry, I'm not going to become a stalker. I'll call you here just this one time.

"I've learned a lot these last few months. More than I can tell you in a short message. So let me focus on two things: First, you were right about me. I want to do something special. And I have. It started right down the street, just like you said. I'd love to tell you the story sometime.

"Second, I've been thinking about all the people I know, and how we're all more alike than different. But one of the key differences between us is how we each deal with conflict or opposition. I always yielded to it. Offered no resistance. I guess my childhood shaped me that way." As she said these words, her mother's face flashed through her mind.

"When Rev. Bowers encounters opposition, he resents it. Tries to bully and belittle the opposition until it goes away. Our friend Eddie attacks it head on when he feels he has to. And you, dear sister, either avoid it or flee from it. I'm not saying that one size fits all, or one approach is always right. But I've learned that I can't fold all the time.

"Great achievements happen in the face of opposition, not in the absence of it. Even if that achievement is only the care and nurturing of a long friendship. We won't always agree on everything, Shawna, but I hope you'll agree that true friendship can persevere through occasional conflict.

"Oh, and by the way, Eddie has—" A loud electronic beep cut her off. She'd found out how much recording time the system would give her.

In a converted barn in Nobscot, Bully Bob was taking a beating of surpassing ferocity. Filling in for Eddie, Andrei Rogoff walked over to observe the exertions of Bob's assailant.

"I hope it wasn't something I said."

Roz grinned a sheepish grin. "No, I'm extra motivated today."

"What's got you so fired up?"

"Sheep." Roz swung the cane in a wicked two-handed chop to Bob's head.

"All this brutality because you don't like lamb chops? I don't understand."

Roz stopped to catch her breath for a few seconds before explaining. "Something my pastor said in service the other day got me thinking. He preached from a Bible verse that says, 'All we like sheep have gone astray.'"

Andrei nodded. "Isaiah 53. One of the most gripping chapters in the Bible. Teaches on substitutionary atonement."

Roz gawped at him, but managed to stop when she caught herself doing it.

"What, you think fighting is the only thing in my life?"

"Well, your work as a fight trainer is all I know about you. But you're right. It wasn't reasonable of me to be surprised that you know the passage. Sorry."

"No worries. You were about to explain how a Messianic prophecy moved you to the attempted murder of the training dummy."

Roz considered how to respond for a few seconds. "Two things," she said. "First, the pastor wasn't talking about messianic prophecies or substitutionary atonement. He commandeered the phrase 'we have turned every one to his own way' to berate people about whatever he was in the mood to fuss about."

"I'm told it's a common problem. For many preachers, context is everything until it doesn't support their point. Then they discard it."

"You're not a new churchgoer, that's for sure. But I'm digressing. I said there were two things. Have you ever watched those nature shows about lions in the Serengeti, or wolves hunting bison, or wild dogs chasing antelope?"

"Of course. But I don't think I'm following your line of thought here."

"It will make sense in a minute. When you watch those shows, you see that the prey animals way outnumber the predators. It's five lionesses trying to catch a wildebeest out of a herd one thousand strong. If the wildebeest would ever turn as a group and charge the lions, they could gore them and trample them to death. But they never do. When the lions catch one, you know what the rest of the herd is thinking: I'm glad it wasn't me."

Andrei looked interested, but still unsure where this was going. Even Roz was a bit frustrated, because she'd never thought this through well enough to explain her thinking to someone else.

"What I am trying to say is we are the sheep of His pasture, right? And sheep are another herd animal that acts like the wildebeest and the gazelles. It's our undoing in church. If a pastor abuses someone, the entire flock sees it. But the individual sheep put their heads down and think 'I'm glad it wasn't me.'

"In the last twelve or fourteen months, my church has lost around half its members. Some got discouraged and left. Some left under duress. But we all saw the way the pastor was manhandling people. We saw him stand in the pulpit and single folks out for savage comments more times than I can count. He had temper tantrums in meetings. He gaslighted people who tried to bring these things to his attention. If we had stood up as a group, we could have put a stop to it. But sheep don't do that. They watch one of their fellows get eviscerated, and they go right back to grazing. 'I'm glad it wasn't me.' I don't think the sheep analogies in scripture are intended to make us behave like that."

Having vented, Roz found herself out of steam, and more than a little embarrassed at having dumped so much on a guy she didn't know well; a guy whose personal interest in her began and ended with teaching her how to wield a stick in self-defense. She was about to apologize for her tirade and change the subject when Andrei chimed in.

"It's unfortunate, but I think most humans are hardwired with the herd instinct. You see it with little kids on the playground. It's the same dynamic around the high school bully. Nasty boss at work? Same thing. Every sheep for himself. All the genocidal dictators in history killed the millions they did because the people did not rise up in unison and stop them. You've observed it in your church. I guess that's one reason none of us can justify hating anybody. On some level, we are all more alike than we are different. We're all kindred spirits."

This dude's a thinker. Considering how Roz had always tried to make her life a refutation of stereotypes, she felt guilty for being surprised that this mountain of a fighting man was so articulate. In fact, he checked a lot of boxes. He was decent looking, had a sense of humor, knew his way around a Bible, and had the size, strength, and skills to keep a girl feeling safe anywhere. Roz gripped her cane and hoped she didn't look as sweaty and unattractive as she felt.

CHAPTER 23

INTO THE GREAT
WIDE OPEN

Roz slowed her good-as-new Mercedes wagon as she approached her driveway. After several weeks in a rental, she was relieved to have it back. It had a new left rear quarter panel, along with several steering and suspension components. A careful paint job completed the illusion that nothing had ever happened. The car looked and drove like she remembered, and Roz was in a buoyant mood.

So she took it in stride when she received a text message from the church secretary informing her of a closed door, members-only meeting at Solid Rock in a week. She did not know what to expect. Maybe the pastor was about to resign in frustration. Or maybe he would dig his heels in, disfellowship her and half the remaining members, and carry on with business as usual. The best outcome would be if he used the meeting to

331

apologize for past transgressions, promise to do better about modeling kindness, and lead everyone in a couple of rounds of Kumbaya. Roz could not see that happening, not even with her most rose-colored glasses.

It was Saturday morning. The sun was shining, and the air was cool. Still pleasant, though the rustling of dry November leaves warned that shorter, much colder days were not far off. Still, it was hard to be anything but happy on a day like today. She reached her neighbor's driveway as one of those blue-and-white junk removal trucks with the familiar phone number painted on the side was pulling out. She walked up to the front door and rang the bell.

Mr. Schroeder greeted her with obvious surprise and delight. It had taken Roz longer than intended to make this visit. Brandon's attack on her had been three weeks ago. She was eager to see how her neighbor was doing.

They sat in the living room. Roz heard a jingling sound, and a low-slung little dog with a bell on his collar padded in. "You got a new puppy?"

"Indeed! This is Orzo. He's a Pembroke Welsh Corgi."

"And he's got a tail!" Roz managed not to squeal with delight. "I never liked the practice of tail docking. They look so much better the way God intended." She petted the little pooch and said, "You named him after . . . pasta?"

"Well, orzo is a short-cut pasta shaped like a grain of rice, so I think the name fits. Also, I'm told that a simple, two-syllable name ending in a vowel is easy for the dog to pick out of human speech. I like it."

"So do I." Roz fussed over the dog for another minute before looking up. "I noticed that the security cameras are gone. I bet they were on that truck I saw pulling out of the driveway."

"You better believe it. Along with a lot of other things. Come look."

Roz followed him to the back room in which she had once hidden from Brandon. When she had secreted herself in there, the room was full of stuff belonging to Laura Schroeder. Now it was empty. No treadmill, no piles of clothes, no stacks of magazines.

"It needs some furniture. I'm still not sure what use I'm going to put the room to. But I realized if I was going to let go of the past, I had to discard all that stuff."

Roz beamed approval, and they went back to the living room.

"I'm sure you are wondering about Laura. She hasn't appeared since that day we both saw her fade. I'm amazed. Not about the fact that she hasn't come back, mind you. I'm amazed that you had the mental flexibility to try a different approach when your first one failed. No offense intended. But you and your friends seemed sure she was a devil. I think most people in your shoes would have doubled down on that theory. What made you change your mind?"

"Short answer? I let the Bible speak for itself rather than rely on the consensus from expert commentators. When I considered what the scripture said, I realized my thinking had been too narrow." She shrugged. "No big deal on my part. Learning and growing is a lifelong pursuit."

"Au contraire. I think it was a colossal deal. I'm impressed. Maybe when you get back to reading aloud, you can read me some highlights from that book of yours. If you're willing to be open to changing the way you think, I guess I can be open too."

"It would be my pleasure," Roz said. They talked about a variety of innocuous things before Roz broached the topic that most concerned her. "So after they took your nephew to the hospital, did he recover? He's not—"

"Dead? No, he survived. But he won't be bothering you again. Here, let me show you something."

They stood again and Mr. Schroeder led the way to the room Brandon had occupied. When the old man opened the door, Roz stopped in her tracks. A hospital bed dominated the interior, with metal side rails, electric controls, the works. And laid out on this bed was Brandon Heckler, though he looked nothing like his old self. His body was still twisted, as if he'd never moved after the moment he fell on Roz's floor. His mouth was stretched in a permanent grimace, and his eyes were unseeing, rolled up into their sockets. As if it were a pendulum, his head lolled back and forth with near mechanical steadiness.

Roz was horrified by what she saw of the consequences of her actions. She had made Brandon what he was now. Not that she felt guilty. She'd been given no choice but to defend herself. If she hadn't dropped him, he'd have killed her without a second thought. Brandon was more monster than man. But even monstrous people were still people, and she hated to see any human being in such a state.

"Does he ever stop?" she asked in a half whisper.

"No. The brain damage is profound. I don't think he's aware of much. He still has a swallow reflex, so I can keep him fed and hydrated. His doctors say he'll never be more than what you see now. They think he'll never leave that bed. They were going to put him in a nursing home to live out whatever remaining days he has."

"And you became his caretaker, after all he did to you? My turn to be impressed. Maybe moved is a better word. I don't know many people who would have showed him so much compassion."

"It's not all me. A visiting nurse stops in twice a day to help with the heavy lifting. It would be too much for me alone. Like I said, he's family, and that carries certain obligations. That doesn't let him off the hook for his crimes. If he ever wakes up, becomes halfway coherent, the police will want to talk to him about what he did at your house. I will turn him over to them without a moment's hesitation. If he never wakes up . . . well, I guess he could outlive me. I have money set aside to fund his care in a nursing home for however long he lives. I'll never understand why he did so much evil. But actions have consequences. I guess he never got that memo."

The next year, a Saturday in May

It had been a beautiful wedding. A small one, to be sure, with only a dozen guests in attendance. The chairs in the function hall formed a single block, without the traditional left/right split with ushers to ask whether arriving guests were friends of the bride or of the groom. As far as Roz could tell, no family of the bride was present.

Not that Melissa Devereaux, now Melissa Caruthers, seemed to mind. She looked radiant, with a smile that made the onlookers happy for her. She smiled so much her cheeks were bound to hurt later. Roz hadn't been sure what to think of Mel when they'd first met, especially as she had once day-dreamed about the possibility of dating Eddie herself—but it was not to be. Watching the bride and groom together made it easy to see how much they were in love. They seemed made for each other.

With the vows exchanged and the newlyweds congratulated, everyone trooped to the next room where a buffet awaited. Roz took a seat, thankful she no longer needed to worry about the size and strength of chairs. She'd lost over 160 pounds since the start of her weight loss journey. She still carried a little extra weight, but as she stood five foot nine inches tall in stocking feet, she knew she wore it well.

"Pardon me, is this seat taken?" It was Andrei Rogoff asking to sit next to her.

"It is now," Roz said. "Please, sit." She let her eyes take in his custom suit. Whoever tailored it had done a great job. A guy his size couldn't buy off-the-rack even at stores that specialized in big men. Accustomed to seeing him in workout gear on the occasions he subbed for Eddie at the gym, she decided he cleaned up well.

"Do you know where the happy couple is going on their honeymoon?" Roz asked.

"Everywhere! They've planned a six-week-long road trip. They're going to loop around the eastern half of the country on back roads, seeing as much as they can in the time they have. I think Eddie said they would pass through seventeen states in forty-five days."

"Wow, that sounds like the Eddie I know. He was always in love with cars and driving."

"Being in a car and driving with the girl he loves has got to be his idea of heaven," her newest friend agreed. "So what's new and exciting? Have you been up to anything interesting?"

Roz dove into the topic with enthusiasm. "Well, I have an elderly neighbor with poor eyesight. I've been reading his books to him for a while. He's always telling me I have a magnificent voice. So I'm starting my own YouTube channel. It's called Rosalyn's Reading Room. I read excerpts from my favorite books and poems and offer commentary and reviews. Even song lyrics might be part of the mix."

"That sounds like a lot of fun."

"I think so. I hope so! For me, it's a journey of self-discovery. For so many years, all of my time went either to my job or to my church. Now I'm making room in my life for other things. The end goal with the reading is to get training as a voice actor so I can hire myself out as talent to read audiobooks. My YouTube channel should prove whether there's an audience for my voice, and the revenue from it should help pay for the voice actor training. And I'm just getting started. There are so many things I want to try."

"That's awesome. What triggered the change in your thinking? You know, going from being focused on work and church to making room for a lot of different things?"

"It was something Eddie said months ago. He described his gym as the next chapter in The Book of Eddie. I had forgotten about the comment until one evening I was studying Revelation. There's a verse in chapter 20 that talks about books being opened, and the dead being judged out of those things that were written in the books. That's when Eddie's words came back to me. I'd always heard that the books referred to in that verse are the books of the Bible. But I realized that couldn't be right."

"Why can't it be right?"

"Because it would be like introducing evidence at trial that never existed during the life of a defendant. Cain never had a Bible. Neither did anyone on earth who lived during the thousands of years before the Bible was complete. Would God charge millions of people with violating laws from the distant future?"

"Now that you put it that way . . . no. Of course not." Andrei looked as if he was starting to connect the dots as understanding dawned. "Judgment is according to knowledge. In Romans, it says that only those who sinned under the law would be judged by the law. Those who didn't have the law would be judged according to conscience."

"Exactly! So if those books at the Last Judgment aren't Bible books, what are they?"

Andrei's smile was mischievous. I'm guessing you've already figured that out."

"I think I have. There's a clue in Psalm 56. 'Put my tears into Your bottle—'"

"'Are they not in Your book?'" Andrei finished the verse for her.

"Since the Bible doesn't memorialize all the psalmist's tears, we know that can't be the book he means. I think he was talking about heaven's record of his life. I think there's a written record of everyone's life."

"Sounds like heaven is chock full of books."

"I hope so," Roz laughed. "With eternity in front of me, I'll finally have time to read everything I want to." She paused a few seconds to imagine such a future. "But in all seriousness, I realized what Eddie was talking about. So now my life is about uploading good material for The Book of Roz. It's about creating a life story interesting enough to want to read. Even if I don't turn out to have a special calling."

Rosalyn and Andrei didn't mingle. They sat at the table as if they'd taken root there. They talked with almost no one else all evening. Roz wanted to talk to him about what had become of Solid Rock Church, but she judged it to be a conversation for another day.

After the food was gone, the bride and groom got ready to depart. Andrei said, "Looks like we'll have to continue our conversation some other time. Maybe you'd be free to have dinner next weekend?"

"I would." She smiled. No point in playing hard to get.

The guests followed the bride and groom out to the parking lot. Andrei offered Roz his arm as they walked, and she took it without hesitation. They stood and watched as the newlyweds roared off in Eddie's car. A sign in the rear window said, "Eddie & Melissa's Excellent Adventure." As Roz was waving goodbye, she surprised herself by bursting into tears. The unexpected geyser of emotion was embarrassing. She fished in her purse for a tissue but couldn't locate one.

"Here you go, allow me." Andrei withdrew a handkerchief from his pocket and offered it to her.

"Oh, that's all right. You keep it. I'm sure I have a tissue in here somewhere."

"I insist. It's a spare. An extra. My mother always warned me to bring two handkerchiefs to a wedding. She told me someone always cried."

ABOUT THE AUTHOR

John F. Harrison wrote the Solid Rock Survivor series about tough issues and thorny questions Christians often face but rarely discuss. Besides being a writer, John has been a minister, a musician, and a business owner. He is still happily involved with three of those, and greatly misses his music. His greatest ambition is to get up eight times after falling down seven. He chronicles the tribulations and triumphs of deeply flawed people because he knows no other kind. Though a firm believer in hope, he doesn't own a single pair of rose-colored glasses.

Find him online at www.jharrisonwrites.com.

9 780999 805682 1